Five Nights at Freddy's

THE FOURTH CLOSET

by
SCOTT CAWTHON
KIRA BREED-WRISLEY

Scholastic Inc.
New York

Photo of TV static: © Klikk/Dreamstime

All rights reserved. Published by Scholastic Inc., *Publishers since 1920.* SCHOLASTIC and associated logos are trademarks and/or registered trademarks of Scholastic Inc.

The publisher does not have any control over and does not assume any responsibility for author or third-party websites or their content.

This book is a work of fiction. Names, characters, places, and incidents are either the product of the author's imagination or are used fictitiously, and any resemblance to actual persons, living or dead, business establishments, events, or locales is entirely coincidental.

Library of Congress Cataloging-in-Publication Data available

ISBN 978-1-338-13932-7

10 9 8 7 6 5 4 3 2 1   18 19 20 21 22

Printed in U.S.A.   40

First printing 2018

Book design by Rick DeMonico

CHAPTER ONE

harlie!" John clambered through the rubble toward the place where she'd been, choking on the dust of the explosion. The ruins shifted beneath his feet, and he stumbled over a block of concrete and caught himself just before falling, scraping his hands raw as he grabbed frantically at the broken surface. He reached it, the place where she'd been—he could feel her presence beneath him. He took hold of an immense block of concrete and hefted it with all his strength. He managed to tilt it from the pile and overturn it, where it fell with a thud, rattling the ground he stood on. Over his head, a steel beam creaked, wavering precariously.

"Charlie!" John cried her name again as he shoved another block of concrete away. "Charlie, I'm coming!" He was gasping for breath, moving the remains of the house with desperate, adrenaline-fueled strength, but the adrenaline was running thin. He set his jaw and pressed on. His palms slipped as he tried to lift the next block, and when he looked he realized, dazedly, that his hands left streaks of blood wherever they touched. He wiped his palms on his jeans and tried again. This time the broken concrete moved, and he balanced it on his thighs and took it three steps away, then dropped it on a pile of debris. It crashed down onto the rubble and shattered rock and glass beneath it, starting an avalanche of its own, and then, beneath the sounds of wreckage, he heard her whisper: ". . . John . . ."

"Charlie . . ." His heart stopped beating as he whispered back to her, and again the rubble moved under his feet. This time he fell, landing hard on his back, knocking the wind out of him. He struggled to inhale, his lungs useless, then haltingly he began to breathe. He sat up, light-headed, and saw what the collapse had revealed: He was in the little, hidden room in Charlie's childhood house. Before him was a plain, smooth metal wall. At the center was a door.

It was only an outline, without hinges or a handle, but he knew what it was because Charlie had known, when she stopped running in the midst of their escape, and pressed her cheek against the surface, calling to someone, or something, inside.

". . . John . . ." she whispered his name again, and the sound seemed to come from everywhere at once, bouncing off the walls of the room. John got to his feet and put his hands on the door; it was cool to the touch. He pressed his cheek to it, just as Charlie had, and it grew colder, like it was draining the warmth from his skin. John pulled back and rubbed the cold spot on his face, still watching the door as the shiny metal began to dull before his eyes. Its color paled *and then the door itself began to thin, its solidity vanishing until it looked like frosted glass, and John saw there was a shadow behind the glass, the figure of a person. The figure stepped closer, the door clarifying until he could almost see through it. He moved closer, mirroring the figure on the other side. It had a face, sleek and polished, its eyes like a statue's, sculpted, but unseeing. John peered through the door between them, his breath clouding the near-transparent barrier, then suddenly the eyes snapped open.*

The figure stood placidly before him, the eyes fixed on nothing. They were clouded, and unmoving—dead. Someone laughed, a frantic, mirthless sound that echoed in the small, sealed room, and John looked wildly around for the source. The laughter rose in pitch, growing louder and louder. John covered his ears with his hands as the piercing noise became unbearable. "CHARLIE!" he cried again.

John jerked awake, his heart racing: the laughter went on, following him out of the dream. Disoriented, his eyes darted around the room, then lit on the TV, where a clown's painted face filled the screen, caught in a convulsive fit of laughter. John sat up, rubbing his cheek where his watch had been pressing into it. He checked the time, then breathed a sigh of relief—he had just enough time to get to work. He sat back, taking a moment to catch his breath. On the TV screen, a local news anchor was holding a mic up for a man dressed as a circus clown, complete with a painted face, a red nose, and a rainbow-colored wig. Around his neck was a collar that looked like it belonged in a Renaissance painting, and he was wearing a full yellow clown suit, with red pompoms for buttons.

"So, tell me," the anchor said brightly. "Did you already have this costume, or did you make it especially for the grand opening?"

John switched the TV off, and headed for the shower.

He'd been at it all day, but the noise was still unbearable: a rattling, clanging din punctuated by shouts and the inter-mittent, earthshaking clatter of jackhammers. John closed his eyes, trying to blot it out: the vibrations resounded in his chest, filling him up, and amid the noise the sound of des-perate laughter suddenly rang in his ears. The figure from his dream came to him again, just out of sight, and he felt as though, if he just turned his head the right way, he could see the face behind the door . . .

"John!"

John turned: Luis was standing a foot away, giving him a puzzled stare. "I called your name three times," he said. John shrugged, gesturing at the chaos around them.

"Hey, some of the guys are going out after this; you com-ing?" Luis asked. John hesitated. "Come on, it'll be good for you—all you do is work and sleep." He laughed good-naturedly and slapped John on the shoulder.

"Right, good for me." John smiled back, then looked at the ground as the expression faded. "I just have so much going on right now." He tried to sound convincing.

"Right, lot's going on. Just let me know if you change your mind." He clapped John on the shoulder again and headed back to the forklift. John watched him stride away. It hadn't been the first time John had turned them down; not the second time or the third; and it occurred to him that eventually they would stop trying. That there'd be a moment when they would all just give up. Maybe that would be for the best.

"John!" another voice called.

Now what?

It was the foreman, shouting at him from the door of his standalone office, a trailer that had been brought onsite for the duration of the construction and sat precariously on a dirt ledge.

John trudged across the construction zone, ducking through a vinyl sheet in the trailer's doorway. Moments later he was standing across a folding table from the foreman, the plastic wood-textured paneling barely holding to the walls surrounding him.

"I've got a couple guys out there telling me you're distracted."

"I'm just focused on my job, that's all," John said, forcing a smile and trying to prevent his frustration from leaking out. Oliver smiled, unconvincingly.

"Focused," Oliver mimicked. John dropped the smile, startled. Oliver sighed. "Look, I gave you a chance because your cousin said you're a hard worker. I overlooked the fact that you walked off your last job and never came back. You know I took a risk on you?"

John swallowed. "Yes, sir, I know."

"Stop with the 'sir.' Just listen to me."

"Look, I do what I'm told. I don't understand the problem."

"Your reactions are slow; you look like you're daydreaming out there. You're not a team player."

"What?"

"This is an active construction zone. If you're in la-la land, or you're not thinking about the safety of the other men out there, someone's going to get hurt, or killed. I'm not saying you have to share secrets and braid one another's hair; I'm saying you have to be on the team. They have to trust that you're not going to let them down when it counts." John gave an understanding nod. "This is a good job, John. I think these are good guys out there, too. Work isn't easy to come by these days, and I need you to get your head in the game. Because next time I see it in the clouds . . . well, just don't put me in that position. Understand?"

"Yeah, I understand," John said numbly. He didn't move, standing on the shag brown carpet that came with the portable office as though waiting to be dismissed from detention.

"Okay. Get out." John went. The dressing-down had taken up the last few minutes of his workday; he helped Sergei put away some of the equipment, then headed to his car with a muttered good-bye.

"Hey!" Sergei called after him. John stopped. "Last call!"

"I . . ." John broke off, spotting Oliver out of the corner of his eye. "Maybe next time," he said.

Sergei pressed. "Come on, it's my excuse to avoid that new kid's place—my daughter's been begging to go there all week. Lucy's taking her, but robots creep me out."

John paused, and the world grew silent around him. "What place?" John said.

"So, you coming?" Sergei asked again.

John took a few steps backward, as if he'd come too close to a ledge. "Maybe another time," John said, and walked decidedly to his car. It was old and brownish-red, something that might have been cool in high school. Now it was just a reminder that he was still a kid who hadn't moved on, a mark of status that had become a mark of shame within the space of a year. He sat heavily, a plume of dust shooting out the sides of the car seat as he dropped onto it. His hands were shaking. "Get a grip." He closed his eyes, and clutched the wheel, steadying himself. "This is life now, and you can do it," he whispered, then opened his eyes and sighed. "Sounds like something lame my dad would have said." He turned the key.

The drive home should have been ten minutes; but the route he took was closer to half an hour, as it avoided driving through town. If he didn't drive through town, there was no risk of running into people he didn't want to talk to. More importantly, he didn't risk running into the people he did want to talk to. *Be a team player.* He couldn't muster real resentment toward Oliver. John wasn't a team player, not anymore. For almost six months, he had been coming and going from home to work like a train on a track, stopping to buy food now and then, but not much else. He spoke only when necessary; avoided eye contact. He was startled when people spoke to him, whether they were coworkers saying hello, or strangers asking the time. He made conversation, but he was getting better at speaking while walking away. He was always polite, while also making it clear he had somewhere to be—made obvious, when necessary, by suddenly turning in the opposite direction. Sometimes he felt like he was fading away, and it was jarring, and disappointing, to be reminded that he could still be seen.

He pulled into the lot of his apartment complex, a two-story building not really meant for long-term tenants. There was a light in the window of the manager's office: he had tried for a month to track the open hours, then given up, concluding that there was no pattern.

He grabbed an envelope from the glove compartment and headed toward the door. He knocked, and there was no response, though inside he could hear sounds of movement. He knocked again, and this time the door opened partially: an old woman with the skin of a lifelong smoker peered out at him. "Hey, Delia." John smiled; she didn't smile back. "Rent check." John handed an envelope to her. "I know it's late. I came by yesterday, but no one was here."

"Was it during business hours?" Delia peered into the envelope carefully as though suspicious of what might be inside.

"The lights were off, so . . ."

"Then it wasn't during business hours." Delia bared her teeth, but it wasn't really a smile. "I saw you hung up a plant," she said abruptly.

"Oh yeah." John peered over his shoulder toward his apartment, as though he might be able to see it from where they stood. "It's nice to take care of something, right?" John tried to smile again but quickly gave up, engulfed in a vacuum of judgment that allowed for no levity. "That's allowed, right? To have a plant?"

"Yes, you can have a plant." Delia took a step back inside and looked poised to close the door. "People don't usually settle in here, that's all. Usually there is a house, then a wife, and then the plant."

"Right." John looked down at his shoes. "It's just been a rough"—he began, but the door closed with a firm *thunk*—"year."

John considered the door for a minute, then headed to the ground-floor apartment at the front of the complex, now his for another month. It was a single-bedroom unit with a full bath and half a kitchen. He kept the blinds up while he was away, to show that he had nothing: the area was prone to burglaries, and it seemed like a safe bet to telegraph the fact that there was nothing to steal here.

Once inside, John locked the door behind him and carefully slid the chain into place. His apartment was cool and dark, and quiet. He sighed and rubbed his temples; the headache was still there, but he was growing accustomed to that.

The place was sparsely furnished—it had come that way—and the only personal touch he had added to the living room was to stack four cardboard boxes full of books against the wall below the window. He glanced at them with a disappointed familiarity. He went to the bedroom and sat down on his bed, the springs creaking stiffly beneath him. He didn't bother turning on the light; there was enough daylight still leaking through the small dingy window above his bed.

John looked toward his dresser, where a familiar face looked back at him: a toy rabbit's head, its body nowhere to be found.

"What did you do today?" John said, meeting the plush rabbit's eyes as if it might show a spark of recognition. Theodore just stared back blankly, his eyes dark and lifeless. "You look terrible; worse than me." John stood and approached the rabbit's head; he couldn't ignore the smell of mothballs and dirty fabric. John's smile faded, and he grabbed the head by the ears and held it in the air. *Time to throw you away.* He considered it almost every day. He clenched his jaw, then set it back on the dresser carefully and turned away, not wanting to look at it further.

He closed his eyes, not expecting sleep to come, but hoping. He hadn't slept well the night before, or the night before that. He had come to dread sleep; he put it off as long as he could, walking miles of road until late at night, returning home and trying to read, or just staring at the wall. The familiarity was frustrating. He grabbed his pillow and went back to the living room. He lay down on the couch, swinging his legs over the arm so he could fit. The silence in the little apartment was beginning to ring in his ears, and he grabbed the remote off the floor and turned on the TV. The screen was black and white, and the reception was terrible: he could scarcely make out faces through the static, but the chatter of what sounded like a talk show was rapid and cheerful. He turned the volume low and settled back, staring at the ceiling and half listening to the television voices until slowly, he drifted into sleep.

Her arm was limp, the only part of her he could see dangling from the twisted metal suit. Blood ran in red rivers down her skin, pooling on the ground. Charlie was all alone. He could hear her voice again if he tried: "Don't let go! John!" She called my name. And then that thing—He shuddered, hearing again the sound of the animatronic suit snapping and crunching. He stared at Charlie's lifeless arm as if the world around them had disappeared, and as the noise echoed in his head, his mind conjured up thoughts unbidden: The crunching sounds were her bones. The tearing was everything else.

John opened his eyes with a start. A few feet away, a studio audience laughed, and he looked at the TV, its static and chatter bringing him back to waking life.

John sat up, rolling his neck to work out kinks: the couch was too small, and his back was cramped. His head ached, and he was exhausted but restless, the shot of adrenaline still working its way through his system. He went out, locking the door forcefully behind him, and breathed in the night air.

He started down the road, heading toward town and whatever might still be open. The lights on the road were far apart, and there was no sidewalk, just a shallow dirt shoulder. Few cars passed him, but when they did, they loomed up from around corners or cresting hills, blinding him with headlights and rushing by with a force that sometimes threatened to knock him back. He had begun to notice himself edging ever closer to the road as he walked, playing a halfhearted game of chicken. When he found himself too far out, he would always take deliberate steps back to the shoulder, and it was always with a secret, sinking disappointment in himself that he would do so.

As he approached town, lights pierced the darkness once again, and he shielded his eyes and took a step back from the road. This one slowed as it passed, then came to a sudden stop. John turned and walked a few steps toward it as the driver's window rolled down.

"John?" someone called. The car went into reverse and haphazardly pulled onto the shoulder; John jumped out of its path. A woman stepped out and took a few quick steps toward him, as if she might try to hug him, but he stayed planted where he was, his arms stiff at his sides, and she stopped a few feet away. "John, it's me!" Jessica said with a smile that quickly faded. "What are you doing out here?" she asked. She was wearing short sleeves, and she rubbed her arms against the night air, glancing back and forth along the near-deserted road.

"Well, I could ask you the same thing," he answered as though she had accused him of something. Jessica pointed over John's shoulder. "Gas." She smiled brightly at him, and he couldn't help but mirror her a little. He had almost forgotten this ability of hers, to turn on cheerful goodwill like a faucet, splashing it all over everyone. "How have you been?" she asked cautiously.

"Fine. Working, mostly." He gestured down at the dusty work clothes he hadn't bothered to change out of. "What's new with you?" he asked, suddenly aware of the absurdity of the conversation as cars passed nearby. "I really have to be going. Have a good night." He turned and began to walk away without giving her a chance to speak.

"I miss seeing you around," Jessica called. "And so does she."

John paused, digging at the dirt with one foot.

"Listen." Jessica took a few quick steps to catch up to him. "Carlton's going to be in town for a couple of weeks; it's spring break. We're all getting together." She waited expectantly, but he didn't respond.

"He's dying to show off his new cosmopolitan persona," Jessica added brightly. "When I talked to him on the phone last week, he was faking a Brooklyn accent to see if I'd notice." She forced a giggle. John smiled fleetingly.

"Who else is going to be there?" he asked, looking directly at her for the first time since she got out of the car. Jessica's eyes narrowed.

"John, you have to talk to her sometime."

"Why is that?" he said brusquely, and started walking again.

"John, wait!" Behind him, John heard her break into a run. She caught up quickly, slowing to jog beside him, matching his pace. "I can do this all day," she warned, but John didn't answer.

"You have to talk to her," Jessica repeated. He gave her a sharp look.

"Charlie's dead," he said harshly, the words rasping in his throat. It had been a long time since he spoke the words aloud. Jessica stopped in her tracks; he kept going.

"John, at least talk to *me*."

He didn't answer.

"You're *hurting* her," she added. He stopped walking. "Don't you understand what you're doing to her? After what she went through? It's insane, John. I don't know what that night did to you, but I know what it did to Charlie. And you know what? I don't think anything hurt as badly as having you refuse to speak to her. To say she's *dead*."

"I saw her die." John stared out into the city lights.

"No, you didn't," Jessica said, then hesitated. "Look, I'm worried about you."

"I'm just lost." John turned to her. "And after what I've been through, after what *we've* been through, that's not an unreasonable reaction." He waited a moment for her to respond, then looked away.

"I get it. I really do. I thought she was dead, too." John opened his mouth to speak, but she pressed on. "I *thought* she was dead until she turned up, *alive*." Jessica pulled at John's shoulder until he met her eyes again. "I've seen her," Jessica said, her voice breaking. "I've talked to her. It *is* her. And this . . ." She let go of his shoulder and waved her hand over him as though casting a spell. "*This* thing that you're doing, that's what's killing her."

"It's not her," John whispered.

"Okay," Jessica snapped, and turned on her heel. She walked back to the car and after a few moments, pulled back out into the road, then made a screeching U-turn. John stayed where he was. Jessica roared past him, then stopped abruptly, her breaks squealing, then backed up to where he stood. "We're meeting at Clay's house on Saturday," she said tiredly. "Please." He looked at her; she wasn't crying, but her eyes were shiny, her face red. He nodded.

"Maybe."

"Good enough for me. I'll see you there!" Jessica said, then she drove off without another word, the engine roaring in the quiet of the night.

"I said maybe," John muttered into the darkness.

CHAPTER TWO

The pencil squeaked against the paper as the man at the desk carefully filled out the form in front of him. He paused suddenly, a wave of dizziness overtaking him. The letters on the page were fuzzy, and he adjusted his reading glasses, his head swimming. The glasses made no difference, and he took them off and rubbed his eyes. Then, just as suddenly as it had come, the sensation was gone: the room righted itself, and the words on the page were perfectly clear. He scratched his beard, still disconcerted, then began to steadily write again. A ring sounded and the front door opened.

"Yes, sir?" he barked without looking up.

"I wanted to have a look around the yard." A woman's voice echoed softly.

"Oh, pardon me, ma'am." The man looked up and smiled momentarily, then went back to his form, writing as he talked. "Scrap is fifty cents a pound. It might be more if you find a specific part, but we can see when you come back in. Just go have a look around; you have to bring your own tools, but we can help you load it up when you're ready to leave."

"I'm looking for something specific." The woman peered down at him, observing his name tag. "Bob," she added belatedly.

"Well, I don't know what to tell you." He set his pencil down, then reclined and crossed his arms behind his head. "It's a dump." He laughed. "We try to at least separate the junk cars from the tin cans, but what you see is what you get."

"Bob, you received several truckloads of scrap metal on this date, and from this location." The woman set a piece of paper down on top of the form Bob had been working on. Bob picked it up and adjusted his reading glasses, then looked up at her over them.

"Well, as I said; it's a dump," he said slowly, growing more concerned as the moments passed. "I might be able to point you in the right direction; I mean, we don't catalog the stuff."

The woman walked around the side of the desk, stepping up beside Bob's chair, and he straightened nervously in his seat. "I hear you boys had some trouble here last night," she said casually.

"No trouble." Bob furrowed his brow. "Some kids snuck in; it happens."

"That's not what I heard." The woman studied a picture on the wall. "Your daughters?" She asked lightly.

"Yes, two and five."

"They are beautiful." She paused. "Do you treat them well?" Bob was taken aback.

"Of course, I do," he said, trying to hide his indignation. There was a long pause; the woman tilted her head, still looking at the picture.

"I heard you called the police because you thought someone was trapped in the scrap heaps out there," she said. Bob didn't answer. "I heard"—the woman continued, leaning in closer to the picture—"that you thought you heard screaming, and sounds of distress and panic. Something was trapped; a child was trapped, you thought. Maybe several."

"Look, we run a clean business and we have a good reputation."

"I'm not disputing your reputation. Quite the opposite. I think what you did was honorable, running to the rescue in the middle of the night, cutting your legs on jagged scraps of metal as you ran blindly through the yard."

"How do you . . ." Bob's voice trembled, and he stopped talking. He moved his legs under the desk, hoping to hide the bandages that bulged out visibly under both pant legs.

"What did you find?" the woman asked.

He didn't answer.

"What was there?" she pressed. "When you got on your hands and knees and crawled through the beams and the wire? What was there?"

"Nothing," he whispered. "Nothing was there."

"And the police? They found nothing?"

"No, nothing. There wasn't anything. I went out again today just to be . . ." He spread his hands on the desk in front of him, collecting his nerves. "We run a good business," he said firmly. "I don't feel comfortable talking about this. If I'm in some kind of trouble, then I think—"

"You're not in any trouble, Bob, as long as you can do me one little favor."

"What's that?"

"Simple." The woman leaned over Bob, bracing herself on the arms of his chair, so close her face almost touched his. "Take me there."

John pulled into the parking lot at the construction site and immediately saw Oliver standing in front of the gate of the chain-link fence. His arms were crossed, and he was chewing on something, his face grim. When it became clear that he wasn't going to move out of the way, John slowed to a stop and got out.

"What's going on?" he asked. Oliver continued to chew on whatever was in his mouth.

"I have to let you go," he said at last. "You're late, again."

"I'm not late," John protested, then glanced at his watch. "I mean, not by much," he amended. "Come on, Oliver. It won't happen again, I'm sorry."

"Me too," Oliver said. "Good luck, John."

"Oliver!" John called. Oliver let himself in through the gate and glanced back one more time before walking away. John leaned against his car for a moment. Several coworkers were staring at him, suddenly turning away as John noticed them. John got in his car and headed back the way he had come.

When he returned to his apartment, John sat down on the edge of his bed and buried his face in his hands. "Now what?" he wondered aloud, and glanced around the room. His eyes lit on his only decoration. "You still look terrible," he said to Theodore's disembodied head. "And you're still in worse shape than me." The notion of attending the party that night suddenly returned to him. The thought of it set off a nervous fluttering in his stomach, but he wasn't sure what it was— anxiety, or excitement. *I thought she was dead, too,* Jessica had said the night before. *I've seen her. I've talked to her. It is her.*

John closed his eyes. *What if it is her?* He saw it again, the moment he always saw: the shuddering suit, Charlie trapped inside as it crunched and jerked—and then her hand, and the blood. *She couldn't have survived that*. But another image came to mind, unbidden—Dave, who became Springtrap: he had survived what happened to Charlie. He had worn the yellow rabbit suit like it was a second skin, and had paid for it twice: the scars that covered his torso like a shirt of gruesome lace told the story of one narrow escape, and the second . . . Charlie had killed him when she tripped the spring locks, or so they all believed. No one could have survived what they saw. And yet, he had returned. For an instant, John pictured Charlie, scarred and broken, yet, miraculously, alive. "But that doesn't sound like the person Jessica saw," John spoke clearly to Theodore. "Someone broken and scarred; that's not who Jessica was describing." He shook his head. "That's not the person I saw at the diner."

The next day—she looked like she'd just stepped out of a fairy tale. John caught himself and shook his head, trying to focus on the present. He really didn't know what had happened to Charlie. He felt himself edging toward the glimmer of hope. *Maybe I was wrong. Maybe she's all right*. It was what he'd wished for—what anyone wishes for in the throes of grief: *Let it not have happened. Let everything be all right*. The precarious ledge became solid ground, and John felt a weight lifted, his neck and shoulders relaxing from a cramped position he had not been aware of. The fatigue from so many months of misspent sleep caught up to him all at once.

He looked at Theodore; he was clutching the rabbit's head so tightly that his knuckles had gone white. He slowly released the toy, propping it up on the pillow.

"I'm not going," he said. "I was never really considering it, I just wanted Jessica to leave me alone." He held his breath for a moment, then let out a deep sigh. "Right?" He said, his tone becoming more agitated. "What would I even say to these people?" Theodore stared at him blankly.

"Damn." John sighed.

The fluttering in John's stomach grew worse the closer he came to Clay's house. He checked the dashboard clock—it was only six. *Maybe no one will be there yet*, he thought, but as he made his way down the winding road toward their house, cars lined both sides of the street for half a block. John wedged his car between a pickup truck and a rusted sedan almost as beat-up as his own, then got out and headed toward the house.

All the windows of the three-story house were illuminated, standing out against the trees like a beacon. John hung back, staying out of the light. He could hear music from inside, and laughter; the sound of it made him balk. He forced himself to walk the rest of the way to the door, but stopped again when he reached it: Going inside felt like an enormous decision, something that would change everything. Then again, so did walking away.

He raised his hand to ring the bell, then hesitated; before he could decide, the door swung open in front of him. John blinked at the sudden light and found himself face-to-face with Clay Burke, who looked as startled as he was.

"John!" Clay reached out and gripped John with both arms, pulled him in and gave him a hug, then quickly pushed him back to where he started and firmly patted his shoulders. "Right, come in!" Clay stepped back to clear the way, and John followed him in, looking around the room cautiously. The last time he was here, the whole house had been a wreck, strewn with signs of a man falling to pieces. Now, the piles of laundry and evidence files were gone; the couches and the floor were clean, and Clay himself was beaming with a genuine smile. He caught John's eye, and his grin faded.

"A lot has changed." He smiled as though reading John's mind.

"Is Betty—" John broke off too late. He shook his head. "Sorry, I didn't mean to—"

"No, she's still gone," Clay said evenly. "I wish she'd come back; maybe she will someday, but life goes on," he added with a brief smile. John nodded, uncertain what to say.

"John!" Marla waved from the stairs, and immediately came bounding down with her usual eagerness, wrapping him in a hug before he could so much as say hello. Jessica appeared, coming in from the kitchen.

"Hey, John," Jessica said more calmly, but with a glowing smile.

"I'm so glad to see you again, it's been a long time," Marla said, releasing him at last.

"Yeah," he said. "Too long." He tried to think of something else to say, and Marla and Jessica exchanged a glance. Jessica opened her mouth, about to speak, but was interrupted as Carlton ran excitedly down the staircase.

"Carlton!" John called with his first genuine smile of the evening. Carlton raised his hand in an answering wave, and came to join the group.

"Hey," he said.

"Hey," John echoed as Carlton tousled John's hair.

"What, are you my granddad now?" John made a half-hearted effort to straighten his hair while searching the crowd with his eyes.

"I'm surprised you came." Marla slapped him across the shoulder.

"I mean of course you were going to come!" Carlton corrected. "I just know you've been busy! Too many girlfriends, am I right?"

"How's New York?" John asked, fishing for something to talk about as he straightened his clothes.

"Great! College, city—learning—friends. I was in a play about a horse. It's great." He bobbed his head in a rapid nod. "Marla's in school, too."

"In Ohio," Marla jumped in. "I'm premed."

"That's great." John grinned.

"Yeah, it's been a lot of hard work but it's worth it," she said cheerfully, and John began to relax, falling back into the familiar pattern of their friendships. Marla was still Marla; Carlton was still inscrutable.

"Is Lamar around?" Carlton asked, looking from face to face. Marla shook her head.

"I called him when . . . a few months ago," she said. "He's on track to graduate early."

"But he's not coming?" Carlton persisted. Marla smiled slightly.

"He said, 'I'm never, ever, ever setting foot in that town again, not ever, never for as long as I live, and you shouldn't, either.' But he said we're all welcome to visit him."

"In New Jersey?" Carlton made a skeptical face, then turned his attention to Jessica. "Jessica, what's up with you these days, anyway? I heard you've got the dorm room to yourself now."

John stiffened, suddenly aware of what Carlton was really asking; the lights seemed blinding, the noise louder. Jessica glanced at John, but he didn't acknowledge her.

"Yeah," she said, turning back to the others. "I don't know what happened, but I came home one day right after . . . about six months ago, and, she was packing what she could carry. She left me and John to clean up the rest. If we hadn't happened to walk in, I don't think she was even going to tell me she was leaving."

"Did she say where she was going?" Marla asked, her brow furrowing. Jessica shook her head.

"She hugged me and said she'd miss me, but all she'd say was she had to leave. She wouldn't tell me where."

"Well, we can always ask her," Carlton said. John looked at him, startled.

"You've seen her?"

Carlton shook his head. "Not yet, my plane just got in today, but she'll be here tonight. Jessica says she looks good."

"Right," John said. They all looked at him as if they could see what he was thinking: *She looks good, but she doesn't look like Charlie.*

"John, come help me in the kitchen!" Clay called, and John broke away from the group relieved, but also fully aware he couldn't possibly provide any help in the kitchen.

"What's up?" he asked. Clay leaned back against the sink and looked him up and down. "Need me to open the ketchup bottle?" John asked, growing nervous. "High shelf?"

Clay sighed. "I just want to make sure you're all right out there."

"What do you mean?"

"I thought you might be nervous; I know it's been a while since you and Charlie talked."

"It's been a while since you and I have talked, too," John said, unable to keep the edge out of his voice.

"Well, that's different, and you know it," Clay said drily. "I thought you might need a pep talk."

"A pep talk?" John retorted.

Clay shrugged. "Well, do you?" Clay stared at him firmly, but with kindness in his eyes, and John's nerves calmed.

"Jessica told you?" he asked, and Clay tilted his head to the side.

"Some. Probably not all. Here." Clay opened the refrigerator door he had been leaning against and handed John a soda. "Try to relax, you're here with friends. Those people out there love you." Clay smiled.

"I know," John said, setting the can on the countertop next to him. He eyed it for a second but did not pick it up, feeling like if he drank it, he would be giving in, accepting everything he was told. It would be like taking whatever pill everyone else had already swallowed.

John eyed the back door.

"Don't even think about it," Clay said abruptly. John didn't try to pretend it wasn't what he was thinking. Clay sighed. "I know how hard this must be for you."

"Do you?" John responded sharply, but Clay's expression didn't change.

"Stay and talk to her. I think you owe that to her, and to yourself."

John's eyes were still fixed on the door.

"All of this heartache that you're putting yourself through; that can't be what you want." Clay leaned to the side, interrupting John's gaze.

"You're right," John said. He stood up straight and met Clay's eyes. "This isn't what I want." He went to the back door and pushed it open, rushing down the concrete steps as though Clay might pursue him, then walking around the side of the house toward his car, his heart pounding. He felt a little light-headed, and completely unsure he was making the right decision.

"John!" someone called from behind him. The familiar voice sent a jolt through him, and he stopped, closing his eyes for a second.

He heard her heels tapping on the stone walk, the sound vanishing as she crossed the grass to him. He opened his eyes and turned toward the voice; she was standing a few feet from him.

"Thanks for stopping," Charlie said. Her face was anxious, her arms wrapped tightly across her body like she was cold, despite the mild weather.

"I was just going to get my jacket," John said, trying to sound casual in the midst of an obvious lie. He looked her up and down, and she didn't move, like she knew what he was doing, and why. *It's not her.* She looked like some stunning cousin of Charlie's, maybe, but not her. Not the round-faced, frizzy-haired, awkward girl he had known almost all his life. She was taller, thinner, her hair longer, darker. Her face was uncannily different, though he could not have explained how. Her posture, even as she stood hugging herself in anxiety, was somehow elegant. As he looked at her, the first shock of recognition gave way to an acute revulsion; he took an involuntary step back. *How can anyone think that's her?* he thought. *How can anyone think that's* my *Charlie?*

She bit her lip. "John, say something," she said, pleading in her voice. He shrugged, holding both hands up in resignation.

"I don't know what to say," he admitted.

She nodded. She uncrossed her arms as if she had just realized she was holding them that way, and began to pick at her nails instead. "I'm so happy to see you," she said, sounding like she was about to cry. John softened, but tamped the feeling down.

"Me too," he said in a monotone.

"I missed you," she began, searching his face for something. John had no idea what he might look like, but he felt like stone. "I, uh, I had to get away for a while," she went on uncertainly. "That night, John, I thought I was going to die."

"I thought you did," he said, trying to swallow the lump rising in his throat.

She hesitated.

"You don't think I'm me?" she asked softly at last.

He looked down at his feet for a moment, unable to say the words to her face.

"Jessica told me. It's okay, John," she said. "I just want you to know that it's okay." Her eyes were bright with tears. His heart lurched, and in an instant, the world came into a different focus.

He gazed at the woman huddled in front of him trying to suppress her sobs. The stark differences he saw in her were suddenly things that seemed so easily explained. Her shoes had heels, so she was taller. She was wearing a form-fitting dress, instead of her usual jeans and T-shirt, so she appeared thinner. She was wearing elegant clothing, and her gestures were confident, sophisticated, but it was all no more than if Jessica had given her the makeover she was always threatening. No more than if Charlie had just grown up.

We've all had to grow up.

John thought of the way he drove home from work—or, had until this morning—the way he avoided ever driving past her house, or the site of Freddy Fazbear's. Maybe Charlie had things she wanted to avoid. Maybe she just wanted to be different.

Maybe she wanted to change, like you did. When you think of that moment, what it did to you—what must it have done to her? What kind of nightmares do you have, Charlie? He was seized by a sudden, visceral desire to ask her, and for the first time he allowed himself to meet her eyes. His stomach jolted as he did, his heart racing. Tentatively, she smiled at him, and he smiled back, unconsciously mirroring her, but something frigid twitched inside him. *Those aren't her eyes.*

John shifted his gaze, a calm coming over him; Charlie looked momentarily confused. "Charlie," John said carefully. "Do you remember the last thing I said to you, before you—were trapped in the suit?" She held his gaze for a moment, then shook her head.

"I'm sorry, John," she said. "I don't remember a lot about that night, whole pieces are just—missing. I remember being in the suit—I passed out, I think for hours."

"So, you don't remember?" he repeated gravely. It seemed impossible that she could have forgotten. *Maybe she didn't hear me.*

"Were you hurt?" he asked brusquely.

She nodded silently, her eyes filling again with tears, and she hugged herself; this time she didn't look cold, she looked like she was in pain. Maybe she was. John took a step closer to her, wanting suddenly, desperately, to promise her that everything would be all right. But then her eyes met his again, and he stopped, stepped back. She extended a hand, but he didn't take it, and again she crossed her arms over her body.

"John, would you meet me tomorrow?" she asked steadily.

"Why?" he said before he could stop himself, but she did not react.

"I just want to talk. Give me a chance." Her voice rose shakily, and he nodded.

"Sure. Yeah, I'll meet you tomorrow." He paused. "That same place, okay?" he added carefully, waiting to see how she would reply.

"The Italian place? Our first date?" she said easily and gave a gentle smile; her tears seemed to have stopped. "Around six?"

John let out a deep breath. "Yeah." He met her gaze again and did not look away, letting himself take rest in her eyes for the first time that night. She looked back at him, motionless, like she was afraid she might scare him away. John nodded, then turned and left without another word. He walked quickly back to his car, struggling to keep his pace even. He felt like he had done something wonderful, and also like he had made a horrible mistake. He felt strange, riding an adrenaline rush, and as he drove through the dark he pictured her face again.

Those weren't her eyes.

Charlie watched him go, rooted to the spot as if it were the only place she'd ever stood. *He doesn't believe me.* Jessica had not wanted to tell her about John's strange yet adamant conviction, but his refusal to speak to her now, his unwillingness even to acknowledge her presence that day in the diner was too bizarre to be dismissed. *How can he think I'm not me?*

The taillights of John's car vanished around a bend. Charlie stared into the dark where he had been, not wanting to return to the bright, noisy house. Carlton would tell her a joke; Jessica and Marla would comfort her the way they had in the diner that day, when she had come to show them that somehow, impossibly, she had survived. The walk from her car—really Aunt Jen's borrowed car—toward the diner had felt like miles that day, her stomach fluttering anxiously even though she knew, of course, that they would be happy to see her. How could they not be? Every step was stiff, uncertain; every time she moved it hurt, her body sore all over from the day before, though there were no marks on her to show it. Even breathing was strained and unfamiliar, and she had a persistent feeling that if she forgot to do it, she would stop, die of asphyxiation right there on the pavement, unless she was reminded, *take a breath.* She could see them through the window as she made her way to the front of the diner, her heart racing, and then they saw her and it was everything she had dared to hope: Marla and Jessica ran to the door, jostling over who would hug her first, crying at the sight of her living face. She let herself be wrapped in the warmth of their relief, but before they even let her go, she was looking for John.

When she saw him, his back to the door, she almost called out his name, but something stopped her. He said something she could not hear, and she watched, incredulous, as he failed to come to her, clenching a spoon in his hand like a weapon. "John!" she called at last. But he did not turn around. Marla and Jessica ushered her out of the restaurant, making reassuring sounds that must have been words, and Charlie strained to see him through the window: he had not moved. *How can he pretend I'm not here?*

A shock of pain hit her suddenly, yanking her back to the present, and Charlie hugged herself tightly, though it didn't really help: it was everywhere, sharp and hot. She clenched her jaw, unwilling to make a sound. Sometimes it eased to an ache she could push to the back of her awareness; sometimes it vanished for days at a time, but always it came back.

Were you hurt? John had asked, the first—the only—sign he'd given that he might still care, and she had been unable to reply. *Yes,* she could have said. *Yes, I was and I still am. Sometimes I think I'll die of it, and what I feel now is just an echo of what it used to be. It feels like all my bones are broken; it feels like my guts are twisted and torn; it feels like my head has cracked open, and things are leaking out, and it happens again and again.* She clenched her teeth, taking deliberate breaths, until it began slowly to recede.

"Charlie? Are you okay?" Jessica said quietly, appearing beside her on the sidewalk outside Clay's house. Charlie nodded.

"I didn't hear you come over," she said hoarsely.

"He doesn't mean to hurt you. He's just—"

"Traumatized," Charlie snapped. "I know." Jessica sighed, and Charlie shook her head. "Sorry, I didn't mean to be rude."

"I know," Jessica said. Charlie sighed, closing her eyes. *He's not the one who died—and it did feel like dying.* She could only remember that crucial night in fragments: her thoughts were all scraps and whispers, hazy and muddled, everything circling slowly around a central point: the single unmistakable snapping sound of the spring locks. Charlie shivered, and felt Jessica's hand touch her shoulder. She opened her eyes, looking helplessly at her friend.

"I think he just needs time," Jessica said gently.

"How much time can he need?" Charlie asked, and the words sounded like stone.

CHAPTER THREE

t's ready." A soft voice rang out in the dark.

"I'll tell you when it's ready," said the man slumped in the corner, studying a monitor intently. "Raise it a few more degrees," he whispered.

"You've said before that might be too much," she said from the opposite corner, leaning over a table. The light shimmered off her contours as she carefully examined what lay before her.

"Do it," the slumped man said. The woman touched a dial, then recoiled suddenly.

"What is it?" he demanded. He didn't take his eyes off the monitor. "Raise it two more degrees," he ordered, his voice rising. For a moment, the room was silent. Finally, the man turned toward the table. "Is there a problem?"

"I think it's . . . ." The woman trailed off.

"What?"

"Moving," she finished.

"Of course it is. Of course, *they* are."

"It looks like it's . . . in pain?" she whispered. The man smiled.

"Yes."

A bright light flashed on abruptly as a sudden noise resounded from the center of the room. Red, green, and blue lights flashed in sequence and a cheerful voice erupted from the speakers embedded in the walls, filling the room with song.

Every light shone down on him: the sleek white-and-purple bear. His joints clicked with every pivot; his eyes jolted back and forth randomly. He stood about six feet high; his rosy cheeks like two balls of bright cotton candy, and he wielded a microphone with a head like a shimmering disco ball.

"Shut that thing off!" the slouched man shouted, getting to his feet with obvious difficulty. He moved slowly toward the center of the room, leaning heavily on his cane. "Get back, I'll do it myself!" he screamed as the woman retreated to the table in the corner. The man pried a white plastic plate off the chest of the singing bear, and reached inside the cavity, extending his arm all the way into the opening and pulling at whatever he could find. As he disconnected the wires inside, first the eyes stopped turning, then the eyelids stopped clapping shut, then the mouth stopped singing and the head stopped turning. Finally, with one last jostle, the eyelids clamped shut and the head dropped to the side lifelessly. The man stepped back, and the heavy plate of the bear's chest cavity swung shut with a clang, as the animatronic bear filled with the sounds of servos and wheels, broken and disconnected, unable to move or function. Spurts of air burst from between the seams of his body casing as the air hoses misfired.

The sound came to a stop, the echoes from it lingering for a moment before dying away. The man turned his attention back to the table and lurched to it. He looked down, studying the writhing figure that lay there for a moment. The table's surface was glowing orange, and the hot metal hissed. He took a syringe from the woman's hand and thrust it into the squirming thing forcefully. He drew the plunger up, holding the needle steady as the syringe filled with molten substance, then finally pulled away with a jolt. He staggered back toward the bear.

"Now, let us put you to greater purpose," he said to the glowing syringe. The man again pried open the heavy chest plate of the standing, broken bear, then carefully inserted the syringe he held directly into the chest cavity and began to press the plunger down. The cavity snapped shut, too heavy for the frail man to hold open, and he fell backward clutching his arm. The syringe clattered to the ground, still nearly full. The woman rushed to kneel by his side, feeling his arm for breaks. "I'm fine," he grumbled, and glanced up at the still motionless bear. "It needs to be heated more." The hissing sound continued as the figure turned on the table, pushing off plumes of steam as it rolled on the hot surface.

"We can't heat it more," the woman said. "You'll destroy them."

The man looked up at her with a warm smile, then jerked his eyes back to the bear: he was now looking down at them, his eyes open wide and tracking their subtlest movements. "Their lives will now have a greater purpose," the man said contentedly. "They will become *more*, just like you did." He looked up at the woman kneeling over him, and she looked back, her glossy painted cheeks gleaming in the light.

John let himself into his apartment and locked the deadbolt behind him, sliding the chain into place for the first time since he moved in. He went to the window and fiddled with the blinds, then stopped, pushing back the impulse to close them and seal himself away completely from the outside world. On the other side of the glass, the parking lot was still and silent, cast in the eerie light of a single streetlamp and the blue neon sign of a nearby car dealership. There was an unfamiliar whirring sound coming from somewhere, and John watched the parking lot for a moment, not sure what he was expecting to see. The sound was gone soon after anyway, and he went into the bathroom to splash water on his face. When he came back into his bedroom, he froze: it was the sound again, this time louder—it was in the room with him.

John held his breath, straining to listen. It was a quiet noise, the sound of something moving, but it was too regular, too mechanical to be a mouse. He flipped on the light: the noise continued, and he slowly turned, trying to hear where it was coming from, and found himself looking at Theodore.

"Is that you?" he asked. He stepped closer and picked up the disembodied rabbit's head. He held it to his ear, listening to the strange sound emanating from inside the stuffed creature. There was a sudden click, and the sound stopped. John waited, but the toy was silent. He put Theodore back down on the dresser and waited for a moment to see if the sound would begin again.

"I'm not crazy." John said to the rabbit. "And I won't let you, or anyone else, convince me that I am." He went to his bed, reaching under the mattress with a suspicious glance at the toy rabbit, suddenly feeling watched. He took out the notebook he had hidden there, and sat back on the bed, looking at its black-and-white cover. It was a plain composition notebook, the kind with a little place on the front for your name and class subject. John had left that blank, and now he traced the empty lines with his finger, not really wanting to open the book that had sat, untouched, beneath his mattress for nearly three months now.

At last he sighed and opened to the first page.

"I'm not crazy," he spoke to the rabbit again. "I know what I saw."

Charlie. He filled up the first page with nothing but facts and statistics, of which he knew embarrassingly few, he realized. He'd known Charlie's father, but not her mother. Her brother was still a mystery. He didn't even know if she'd been born in New Harmony, or if there was some other town before Fredbear's, the diner they had discovered that first time they all returned to Freddy's. He had painstakingly written out their shared history: childhood in Hurricane, then the tragedy at Freddy's, then her father's suicide. She had moved in with her aunt Jen after that. As he wrote that down, John realized that he had never known where Charlie and Jen lived. Close enough to Hurricane that she had driven rather than flown there for the dedication of Michael's memorial scholarship, nearly two years ago, but it seemed odd that she had never even mentioned the name of the town where she now—and then—lived.

He flipped through the pages; they grew less and less sparse as he had continued, the details filling in more and more as he called them over and over to mind. He had scribbled whole scenes of memory: like the time he put gum in her hair, thinking it would be funny. Charlie had stared at him with an impish look on her face as their first-grade teacher cut it out of her hair with little blue-handled safety scissors. Charlie had managed to retrieve that clump of hairy gum from the trash when no one was looking, and took it outside with her during recess. As soon as they were out the door, Charlie grinned at John. "I want to give you your gum back," she said, and the afternoon became a game of chase, as they careened around the schoolyard, Charlie determined to shove the hair-encrusted piece of chewing gum back into John's mouth. She had not succeeded: They were caught, and both given time-out. John smiled as he read the scribbled version of the story. It had seemed important to start with their childhood, to ground himself in the Charlie-that-was, and the John-that-was, as well. Now he sighed, and flipped ahead.

In the later pages, he had tried to capture everything about her: the way she moved, the way she spoke. It was hard; the more time passed the more the memories would be *John's memory of Charlie* and not *Charlie*, and so he had written down as much as he could, as fast as he could, starting three days after that night. There was the way she walked, self-assured until she realized someone was looking at her; there were the non sequiturs she tended to toss out every time she got nervous around people, which was often. There was the way she sometimes seemed to sink into herself, as if there were another reality going on inside her head, and she had stepped momentarily outside this one and into somewhere he could never follow. He sighed. *How do you check for that?*

He flipped the notebook over: he had started a different set of thoughts from the back.

What happened to Charlie?

If the woman at Carlton's party, the woman who had appeared so suddenly at the diner, was not Charlie, then who was she? The most obvious answer, of course, would be her twin. Charlie had always referred to a boy, but Sammy could easily be short for Samantha, and the memory Charlie had confided in him, of Sammy being taken from the closet, was a kidnapping, not a murder. What if Charlie's twin was still alive? What if she had been not only kidnapped by Springtrap, William Afton at the time, but raised by him? What if she had been shaped and molded by a psychopath for seventeen years, primed with all the knowledge Springtrap could glean from Charlie's life, and now she had been sent to take Charlie's place? *But why? What would be the point of that?* Afton's fixation on Charlie was disturbing, but he didn't seem capable of anything so elaborate—or of caring for a human child long enough to brainwash her.

He had written out a dozen other possible theories, but when he read them over now, none really felt right: They either fell apart upon scrutiny, or, like the imagined Samantha, they made no real sense. And in all cases, he could not match them to the Charlie he had met earlier that night. Her sorrow and her bemusement had seemed so real; picturing her face now raised a dull ache in his chest. John closed the book, trying to imagine for a moment the situation reversed: Charlie, *his* Charlie, turning from him, insisting that he was not himself—that he, the real John, was dead. *I'd fall apart.* He would feel the way Charlie had looked tonight, pleading, hugging herself as if it was all she could do to hold herself in one piece. He lay back on the bed, holding the book to his chest, where it sat, heavier than its weight. He closed his eyes, clutching the book like a child's toy, and as he drifted to sleep he heard the sound from Theodore's head again: the whirring, and then the click.

The next day, John woke up late and filled with a rootless dread. He glanced at the clock, realized in a panic that he was late for work, and almost simultaneously recalled that there was no more work, a reality that would have consequences soon enough, but not today. All he had to do today was meet Charlie. The dread swelled again at the thought of it, and he sighed.

Late that afternoon, as he dug through his dresser for a presentable shirt, someone knocked at the door. John glanced at Theodore.

"Who?" John whispered. The rabbit didn't answer. John went to the door; through the front window he saw Clay Burke standing outside staring at the door, apparently politely ignoring the fact that he could see right into John's apartment if he wanted to. John sighed and slid the chain off the latch, then opened the door wide.

"Clay, hey. Come in." Clay hesitated on the threshold, glancing at the interior that was too sparse to be a mess. John shrugged. "Before you judge, remember that I've seen your place look worse than this," he said, and Clay smiled.

"Yes, you have," he said at last, and came inside.

The noise from Theodore's head started again, but John chose to ignore it.

"What is that?" Clay asked after a few seconds. John waited to answer, knowing the sound would stop soon, and after a moment it did, with the same click as before.

"It's the rabbit head." John smiled.

"Right, of course." Clay looked toward the dresser, then back at John as though nothing was out of the ordinary. Considering what they'd been through in the past, it really wasn't. "So, what can I do for you?" John asked before something stranger could happen. Clay rocked on his heels momentarily.

"I wanted to see how you were doing," he said lightly.

"Really? Didn't we have that talk yesterday?" John said drily. He stood again and grabbed a clean shirt from his dresser and went into the bathroom to change.

"Yeah well, you know, you can never be too sure," Clay said, raising his voice to be heard. John turned on the faucet. "John, what do you know about Charlie's aunt Jen?"

John turned the faucet off abruptly, jarred out of his petulant mood. "Clay, what did you say?"

"I said what do you know about Charlie's aunt?"

John changed his shirt quickly and came back out into the bedroom. "Aunt Jen? I never met her." Clay gave him a sharp look.

"You never saw her?"

"I didn't say that," John said. "Why are you asking me this now?" Clay hesitated.

"Charlie became very eager to see you again when I mentioned that you had seen Jen that night," he said, seeming to choose his words with care.

"Why would Charlie care if I saw Jen or not? For that matter, why do you?" John reached past Clay to grab a belt hanging off the foot of the bed, and began to slip it through the loops of his jeans.

"It just made me realize that there is a lot we don't know about that night," Clay said. "I think your conversation with Charlie tonight can help fill in those gaps, if you ask the right questions."

"You want me to interrogate her?" John laughed without humor. Clay sighed, frustration leaking through his habitual calm.

"That's not what I'm asking, John. All I'm saying is, if Charlie's aunt was there that night, then I'd like to ask her a question or two." John stared at Clay, who just looked back at him placidly, waiting. John grabbed a pair of socks and sat down on the bed.

"Why are you suddenly coming to me, anyway?" he asked. "No one's believed anything I've said so far."

"It's what we found at the compound," Clay answered, more easily than John had expected. He straightened.

"The compound—you mean Charlie's dad's house?" Clay gave him a level look.

"I think we both know it was more than just a house," he said. John shrugged and said nothing, waiting for him to go on. "Some of the things we found in the wreckage were . . . they didn't mean much to anyone else, but what I saw— some of the things I saw down there were pretty scary, even though most of it was buried under concrete and metal."

"'Scary'? Was that the conclusion of your entire team, or just you?" John said, not bothering to keep the sarcasm out of his voice. Clay didn't seem to hear him, his eyes fixed on a point between them. "Clay?" John said, alarmed. "What did you find? What do you mean, 'scary'?"

Clay blinked. "I wouldn't be sure how else to describe it," he said. John shook his head. "I will say this," Clay said harshly. "I'm not ready to close the book on the Dave/ William Afton/whatever else he was calling himself—"

"Springtrap," John said quietly.

"I'm not ready to close the book on that case," Clay finished.

"What does that mean? You think he's still alive?"

"I just think we can't make any assumptions," Clay said. John shrugged again. He was out of patience—out of interest, almost. He was sick of intrigue: Clay withholding information, trying to protect them—as if keeping secrets had kept any of them safe, ever.

"What do you want me to ask her?" John said plainly.

"Just get her to talk to you. It's been wonderful having her here again, don't misunderstand, but it seems like she's holding something back. It's like she's—"

"Not herself?" John said with an edge of mocking.

"That's not what I was going to say. But I think she might know something she hasn't told us yet—maybe something that she hasn't felt comfortable sharing."

"And she might feel comfortable sharing it with me?"

"Maybe."

"That feels morally ambiguous," John said wearily. From the dresser, the whirring noise started again. "See? Theodore agrees with me," he said, gesturing toward the rabbit.

"Does it always do that?" Clay reached for the rabbit's head, but before he could touch it, Theodore's jaw snapped open and the head jerked in place. John startled, and Clay took a quick step back; they both watched, transfixed, as the sound went on, though the head did not move again. The sound it was making became a distorted murmur, louder and softer, at times almost mimicking words, though John could not even begin to make them out. After a few minutes, the head fell silent again.

"I've never seen it do that before," John said. Clay was bent over the dresser, his nose almost touching Theodore's, as if he could see inside.

"I need to go soon," John said shortly. "I don't want to be late, right? For this new open and honest relationship that I'm starting with her." He made brief, accusing eye contact with Clay and went briskly to the door. "Don't you need to lock it?" Clay asked as John brushed past him.

"It doesn't matter."

It was still light out when John got to St. George, and when he looked at the dashboard clock, John saw that he was over an hour early. He parked in the restaurant lot anyway and got out, glad for the opportunity to walk around and burn some nervous energy. He had avoided St. George, the town where Charlie and Jessica had been in college—*Jessica probably still is in college*, he thought with a pang of guilt. *I should know basic stuff like this.*

He walked past a few storefronts, heading semiconsciously for the movie theater he had been to with Charlie the last time he was here. *Maybe we can go see a movie. After the dinner-and-interrogation.* John stopped short on the sidewalk: The theater was gone. Instead, two gigantic clown faces grinned at him from the windows of a gleaming new restaurant. The faces were almost as large as the wide front door, painted on either side, and above them was a sign, in red and yellow neon letters: CIRCUS BABY'S PIZZA. The neon lights were on, glowing uselessly in the daylight. John stood motionless, feeling like his sneakers had fused to the parking lot. A group of kids rushed past him on their way in, and a teenager bumped into John, breaking him out of his daze.

"Just keep walking, John," he muttered to himself, turning to move away, but he stopped again after only a few steps. "Just keep walking," he repeated in a sterner tone, and turned to face the restaurant defiantly. He approached the front door and pushed it. It opened into an empty vestibule, a waiting area, where smaller versions of the clowns out front smiled crazily from the walls, and a second door read WEL-COME! in painted cursive letters. There was a familiar smell in the air: some particular combination of rubber, sweat, and cooking pizza.

John opened the second door, and noise exploded. He blinked in the florescent lights, bewildered: Children were everywhere, screaming and laughing, and running across the floor, and the jingles and blips of arcade games sounded discordantly from around the room. There were play struc-tures, something like a jungle gym to his left, and a large ball pit to his right, where two small girls were throwing brightly colored balls at a third girl, who was shouting something he could not make out.

There were tables set up in the center of the room, where he noticed five or six adults talking to one another. Occasionally they'd look over their shoulders at the chaos surrounding them, at the stage in back of the room, its red curtain closed. A chill went down his spine, and he looked around again with a terrible déjà vu at the playing children and complacent parents.

He started toward the stage, twice stopping just in time to avoid tripping over a game of tag. The curtains were brand-new, the red velvet plush and gleaming in the light, and trimmed with golden ropes and tassels. John slowed his pace as he got closer, the pit of his stomach tensing with an old, familiar dread. The stage floor was about level with his waist, and he stopped beside it and glanced around, then carefully grasped the thick curtain and began to pull it back.

"Excuse me, sir," a man's voice came from behind him, and John straightened like he'd touched a hot stove.

"Sorry," he said, turning to see a man wearing a yellow polo shirt and a tense expression.

"Are you here with your children, sir?" he asked, raising his eyebrows. The shirt read CIRCUS BABY'S PIZZA, and he was wearing a name tag that read STEVE.

"No, I . . ." John paused. "Yes. Several children. Birthday party, you know. Cousins, so many cousins, what can you do?"

Steve was still looking at him with raised eyebrows.

"I have to go meet someone . . . somewhere else," John said. Steve gestured to the door.

CHAPTER FOUR

No!" Jessica cried in dismay as she wrangled her keys from the pocket of her fashionably too-tight jeans. An apple tumbled out of the paper grocery bag she was struggling to balance on her hip and rolled away down the hallway. It came to rest on the welcome mat of her worst neighbor, a middle-aged man who seemed capable of detecting the tiniest noise, then promptly complaining about it. In fact, since she moved in to the apartment six months ago, leaving behind the dorm room she and Charlie had shared, he had come to her door three times to complain about her radio. Twice it had not even been on. Mostly, he just glared at her whenever they passed in the hall. Jessica didn't really mind the hostility; it was a little like being back home in New York. She left the apple where it was.

Having managed to get the door open, Jessica dropped the bags on the kitchen counter and looked around the room with a quiet satisfaction. The apartment wasn't very fancy, but it was *hers*. When she first moved in, she had gone on a cleaning rampage, scouring out the baked-in dirt that must have been lining the baseboards since the building went up some fifty years ago. It had taken almost two weeks of nothing but scrubbing between classes and homework, and she went to bed every night with sore arms, as though she'd done nothing but weight training. But now the apartment was clean enough for Jessica—albeit just barely—which was no small bar to clear.

She began taking things out of the grocery bags, lining everything up on the counter before putting each item away. "Peanut butter, bread, milk, bananas . . ." she muttered to herself, then fell silent.

Something is wrong. She looked around the room carefully, but there was no one there and everything seemed to be where she'd last left it. She returned to the grocery bags.

As she closed the refrigerator door the hair at the back of her neck prickled. Jessica whirled around as though expecting to catch a burglar in the act, her heart jolting with adrenaline, but the room was still. Just to be sure, she went to check the door: it was locked, as expected. She stood in silence for a moment, listening to the distant sounds of her apartment complex—the hum of an air-conditioning unit outside, a leaf blower across the street—but nothing seemed out of the ordinary. She stepped carefully back to the counter and finished putting away the groceries, then headed to her bedroom. She turned the corner to the hallway and screamed: a figure stood in the dark, blocking the way.

"Jessica?" said a familiar voice, and Jessica reached hastily for the light switch, tensed to run. The light flickered on slowly: it was Charlie.

"Did I scare you?" Charlie said uncertainly. "Sorry. The door was unlocked—I should have waited outside," she added, looking down at her shoes. "I just figured since we used to be roomies anyway . . ."

"Charlie, you scared me to death," Jessica said in a mock-scolding tone. "What are you doing here?"

"I told you I'm having dinner with John?" Charlie said, and Jessica nodded. "Could I borrow something to wear? Maybe you could help me pick something out?" Charlie looked hesitant, like she was asking an immense favor, and Jessica gave her a puzzled frown.

"Yeah, sure, of course." Jessica tried to calm herself. "But, Charlie—it's not like you need my help choosing an outfit these days." Jessica gestured at Charlie's clothing: she was wearing her habitual combat boots—or a more elegant version of them—but she had paired them with a medium-length black skirt and a dark red, scoop-necked blouse. Charlie shrugged and shifted her feet.

"I just think—he might like me better if you help me pick an outfit, instead of me dressing myself, you know? John doesn't seem to like my new look."

"Well, Charlie . . ." Jessica stopped, choosing her words carefully. "It won't do either of you any good to pretend nothing has changed," she said firmly. "Wear what you have on, you look great."

"You think so?" Charlie said, looking doubtful.

"Yeah," Jessica said. She brushed past Charlie to go into her room, stepping cautiously past her, and Charlie followed, pausing in the doorway like a vampire waiting for an invitation. Jessica looked at Charlie and was suddenly set at ease, as if their friendship had never been interrupted. Jessica grinned. "So, I mean, are you nervous?" she asked, going to her dresser for her hairbrush, and Charlie came in and sat down on the bed.

"I feel like I have to prove something to him, but I'm not sure what," she said, tracing the flower design on Jessica's bedspread. "You were right, by the way."

Jessica turned around, brushing her hair absently. "He wants to see you tonight. I think that's a great start," she offered. "Just let him spend some time with you. He's been through a lot. Remember, from his perspective, he saw you die, right in front of his eyes."

Charlie laughed, a soft, forced sound, then was silent. "I'm just worried about him. And I can't even help him, because"—she broke off—"Jessica, do you remember him telling me something important that night?" Something in her tone changed: it was subtle, just a hint of strain. Jessica kept her expression neutral, pretending not to notice.

"Something important?" Jessica asked.

"Something . . . that I would remember. *Should* remember." She kept her eyes on the bedspread, still tracing the pattern like she was trying to memorize it. Jessica hesitated. She could still see it all, as vivid as the present, though it gave her a sick feeling in the pit of her stomach. *Charlie was trapped in the twisted, broken Freddy suit, with just her arm free; John was holding her hand*—Jessica shuddered, that terrible, singular crunching sound echoing in her head.

"Jessica?" Charlie asked, and Jessica nodded briskly.

"Sorry." She cleared her throat. "I don't know, you and John were alone together for a few minutes. I'm not sure what he said. Why?"

"I think it's important to him that I remember," Charlie said, back to tracing the bedspread. Jessica watched her for a moment, suddenly ill at ease in her own bedroom. As if sensing it, Charlie stood and met her eyes.

"Thanks, Jessica," she said. "Sorry again for breaking in. I mean, I didn't break in, the door was unlocked—but you know what I mean."

"No problem, just . . . announce yourself sooner next time?" Jessica smiled, feeling a rush of warmth for her friend.

She hugged Charlie good-bye at the door. Charlie walked a few steps and picked the apple up off the ground, then handed it back to Jessica.

"I think this belongs to you." Charlie smiled, then turned to walk away. When she had closed the door, Jessica sighed. The anxiety that had risen while Charlie was in her room had not abated. She leaned back against the door, replaying what had just happened. *Why would John want Charlie to remember the last thing he said to her?* She tossed the apple a few inches into the air, then let it fall back into her hand.

"He's testing her," Jessica said to the empty apartment.

Outside Jessica's building, Charlie stopped in the parking lot, frustrated. *What did he say that was so important?* She walked across the baked pavement to her car. Charlie climbed into her car, slamming the door shut with more force than she needed to. She stared petulantly at the steering wheel. *They're lying to me,* she thought. *I feel like a little kid, with all the grown-ups keeping secrets from me. Deciding for me what I should and shouldn't know.*

She glanced at her watch—the clock in the car was either an hour ahead or an hour behind, and she could never remember which. She had about twenty minutes before she had to meet John. "I can't show up early," she said plainly, "then he *really* won't believe it's me." Trying to shrug off her bad mood, Charlie put the car in gear and pulled out of the lot.

When she got to the restaurant, she could see John through the window, seated at the same table they had sat at last time, all the way in the back. He was staring into space, as if he were deep in thought, or completely zoned out. She followed the hostess to his table, and it was only when she was standing right beside him that he seemed to realize she was there. When he did, he stood hastily. Charlie started to move toward him, but he sat back down, and she quickly sidestepped and did the same.

"Hi," she said with an awkward smile.

"Hi, Charlie," he said quietly, then grinned suddenly. "You're dressed a lot nicer than last time we were here."

"It probably just seems that way because I'm not covered in dirt and blood this time," Charlie said lightly.

"Right." He laughed, but there was a quick instant of appraisal in his eyes. *That was a test.* The thought sent something cold through the pit of her stomach. She had known it would happen, but knowing did not make it easier to have his eyes, usually so warm, look at her with calculation.

"What was that movie we saw?" John asked, seeming to fumble at an answer. "Last time I visited, we went to that theater down the street, didn't we? It's on the tip of my tongue."

"*Zombies vs. Zombies!*" Charlie said.

"Right, I knew it was about zombies," John said thoughtfully.

"So, what have you been doing since then?" Charlie asked, attempting to shift the topic. "Are you still doing construction work?"

"Yeah," John said, then cast his eyes down at the table. "Actually, maybe not. I just got fired."

"Oh," Charlie said. "I'm sorry."

He nodded. "Yeah. I mean, it was my fault. I showed up late, and—there was some other stuff—but I really liked that job. Well . . . it was *a* job at least."

"There have to be other building sites," Charlie said.

"Yeah, I guess." He looked at her searchingly, and she looked back, trying not to shrink under scrutiny. *Believe me,* she pleaded silently. *What will it take for you to believe me?*

"I've missed this," she said instead.

He nodded, his eyes softening for a moment. "Me too," he said quietly, though she knew it was only half true.

"You know I didn't leave because of—it wasn't because of you," Charlie said. "I'm sorry if it seemed like it was; I just had to get away from everything and everyone. I—"

"Are you folks ready to order?" the waitress asked brightly. John straightened his posture and cleared his throat. Charlie looked down at the menu, glad of the interruption, but the pictures of food looked strange, as if she had heard food described, but never seen any. "Miss?" The waitress was looking at her expectantly.

"I'll have the same," Charlie said quickly, and shut the menu. The young woman frowned confusedly.

"Oh, uh, okay. I guess I should order then." John laughed.

"Anything will be fine." Charlie sat patiently. "I'm sorry. I'll be right back." She got up from the table hastily and headed for the bathroom, leaving John to take care of things.

Walking into the bathroom, she was struck with a jarring sense of déjà vu. *I've been here before. Trapped in a box, I was trapped in a box*—Charlie slammed the door shut and locked it. *I'm not trapped.* She ran her fingers through her hair, though it didn't really need adjusting, and washed her hands; she was just killing time, stealing a moment away from John's scrutiny. Every time he gave her that level, untrusting look, she felt exposed.

"I am Charlie," she said to her reflection, smoothing down her hair again nervously. "I don't have to convince John that I'm me." The words sounded thin in the small room. *Who else would I be?* Charlie washed her hands again, straightened her shoulders, and went back out into the dining room. She sat down and put her paper napkin in her lap, then looked John squarely in the eye.

"I still don't remember," she said abruptly, seized by an obstinate recklessness.

John raised his eyebrows. "What?"

"I don't remember what you said to me that night. I know it's important to you—I know maybe it's why you think what you think about me, but I just . . . don't remember. I can't change that."

"Okay." He slid his hands off the edge of the table and let them rest in his lap. "I know—I know that. Um, a lot happened that night. I know." He sighed for a moment but then smiled almost reassuringly. Charlie bit her lip.

"If it's that important, why can't you just tell me?" she asked gently. Instantly, she could see that it was the wrong thing to say. John's features hardened; he drew back from the table slightly. She looked down at the napkin in her lap; she had been shredding the corner of it without noticing. "Never mind," she said, her voice barely above a whisper, letting several long minutes pass. "Forget I said anything." She looked up, but John didn't respond.

"Excuse me for just a minute. I'll be right back." He got up and left the table.

She stared at his empty chair. The waitress approached and cleared her throat; Charlie heard her, but did not move. She wasn't sure she could move. *This is going horribly. Maybe I'll just sit here forever. I'll be a statue of myself, a monument to Charlie-that-was. Charlie-that-will-never-be-again.*

"Miss?" The waitress sounded concerned, and it was enough for Charlie to, with herculean effort, turn her head.

"Is everything all right, miss?" the waitress asked, and it took Charlie another long moment to comprehend the question.

"Yes," she said at last. "Could I have another napkin?" She held up the first, half-shredded, as evidence of her need, and the waitress went away. Charlie turned back to John's empty chair.

John slid back into view and sat down, breaking the line of her vacant stare.

"Everything okay?" he asked. She nodded.

"The waitress is getting me another napkin." Charlie gestured vaguely in the direction the waitress had gone.

"Right." He opened his mouth to go on, but before he could speak, the waitress returned, carrying Charlie's napkin, along with their food. They were both silent as she placed it in front of them, and John smiled at her. "Thanks," he said. Charlie stared at her plate: it was some kind of pasta. She took her fork carefully but didn't start to eat.

"Can I ask you something?" John finally said, and she nodded eagerly, setting the fork back down. He took a deep breath.

"That night, how did you survive? I—There was so much blood . . ." He stopped, at a loss for words. Charlie looked at him, at the familiar face that had somehow turned against her. She had been trying to piece together a story for him, but now she just spoke.

"I don't know," she said. "I—There's time missing, when I try to think about it my mind—flinches away, like it's hit something sharp." The distance in John's eyes faded a little as she spoke. "I'd been in a suit before," she went on. "I think I must have figured out how to get away somehow, or at least how to position myself." She looked anxiously at him, and his gaze sharpened.

"I still don't understand. How did you manage to get away . . . undamaged?" He looked her up and down again, seeming to examine her.

Charlie's breath caught in her throat, and she turned away from him, staring fixedly out the window at the parking lot.

"I didn't," she said tightly.

John didn't answer, searching Charlie's half-turned face for a spark of something he could recognize—or *not* recognize. She was saying all the right things, in all the right ways, and her hints—more than hints—at the unshakable trauma she had gone through that night made his stomach clench. As she gazed off into the middle distance, her jaw was clenched; she looked like she was fighting something off, and John was seized with a sudden urge to go to her, to hold out his hand and offer his help. Instead he picked up his fork and began to eat, looking down at his plate instead of at her.

She knows what I'm doing, he thought, chewing grimly. *She's giving me the right answers. Some detective I've turned out to be.* John took another bite and stole a glance at her; she was still looking off at the parking lot. He swallowed and cleared his throat.

Before he could speak, Charlie turned back to him. "After that night, I had to get away," she said. Her voice was hoarse, and her face was strained, her features seeming harsher than before. "I had to leave everything behind, John. *Everything.* My whole life has been haunted by what happened here, and the last couple of years . . . even before that, too. It's just been my whole life." She met his eyes briefly, then looked away, blinking rapidly like she was holding back tears. "I wanted be somebody different; I had to or I'd go insane. I know it's a cliché to think you can change your life if you change your hair and your clothes"—she gave an ironic half smile and flipped her long hair over her shoulder—"but I couldn't be *your* Charlie forever, that naïve little girl, scared of her own shadow; *living* in a shadow. Honestly, I don't even know what you saw in that girl—selfish, scatterbrained, *pathetic.*" She said the last word so caustically that she almost shook with it, a sour look coming over her face as if loathing for her past self had overwhelmed her.

"I never thought you were any of those things," John said quietly, and looked down. He ran his fork along the rim of his plate, not knowing what to say. He made himself look up; Charlie's face had softened, and now she seemed anxious.

"But it's still me." She shrugged, her voice breaking. He couldn't answer; he didn't know where to start. Charlie bit her lip. "You still think it, don't you?" she said after a moment. John shifted uncomfortably in his seat, ashamed, but Charlie pressed on.

"John, please, I don't understand. If you think I'm not me, then . . . what do you think? Who can you possibly think I am?" She looked utterly bewildered, and again John felt himself wavering.

"I think—" He gestured graspingly at the air, catching nothing. "Charlie, what I saw—!" he exclaimed, then stopped short, remembering they were in public. He glanced around, but no one was looking at them: the restaurant was not busy, but everyone there was occupied, the guests talking to the people they came with, the staff talking among themselves. "I saw you die," he said, lowering his voice. "When you walked into that diner the next day, Charlie, I wanted to believe it was true—I *still* want to believe it, but I—I saw you die," he finished helplessly. Charlie shook her head slowly.

"I'm telling you that I'm alive, how can that not be enough? If you want to believe me, why don't you?" The pain in her voice sent a pang of guilt through him, but he met her eyes calmly.

"Because I'd rather know the truth than believe something just because it would make me happy."

Charlie looked at him searchingly. "So, what do you think is the truth? Who do you—" she swallowed, and started again. "Who do you think I am, if I'm not me?"

John sighed. "I've thought about it a lot," he said at last. "Almost constantly, actually." Charlie nodded slightly, barely moving her head, like she was afraid she would spook him. "I thought about a lot of things, I guess—theories—um . . ."

"Like what?" Charlie asked gently.

"Well . . ." John's face was getting hot. *I should never have agreed to see her.*

"John?"

"I—I guess maybe I thought you might be Sammy," he mumbled; she looked puzzled for a moment, like she had not quite heard him, then her eyes widened.

"Sammy's dead," she said tightly. John looked up at the ceiling and put his hands to his temples.

"I know," he said, and met her eyes again. "But, *Charlie,* look: I don't know that. Neither do you. The last thing . . . you remember, of Sammy, what was it?"

"You know the answer to that," she said in a low, level voice.

"You saw him being taken," John said after a moment. She made no response, and he took it as license to continue. "You saw him being kidnapped, not killed. By Dave, or Afton—Springtrap. So, what if he wasn't killed? What if

Sammy was *raised* by William Afton, twisted, and brought up by a murderous madman to replace you—to replace Charlie—after her death? Also, Sammy could be short for Samantha. I forgot that part. Sammy could have been a girl all along." Charlie was motionless across the table; she scarcely looked like she was breathing. "I know how it sounds when I say it out loud," John added in a rush. "That's why I mostly don't." Charlie had covered her face with her hand, and her shoulders were shaking. He broke off as she looked up: this time she was laughing. There was a manic edge to it, like it might turn back into crying at any moment, but John tentatively tried to smile.

"Oh, John," she said at last. "I don't even—You know that's crazy, right?"

"Is it crazier than anything else we've seen?" he argued without much conviction.

"John, you took me to see the grave yourself, remember?"

John paused and looked confused for a moment, trying to reconcile what he'd just heard.

"You took me yourself, to Sammy's grave."

"I took you to the cemetery, but I never saw Sammy's grave, or your father's," John corrected.

"Then go look sometime." Charlie's voice was patient. John felt immediately foolish.

"Aunt Jen warned me not to come back to Hurricane." Charlie looked down at the table. "She's three for three at this point. Have you heard from her, by the way?"

"From your aunt?" John asked, disconcerted by the sudden change of subject. "I figured you were living with her after you moved out of Jessica's place."

"Yeah," Charlie said.

"You were living with her?"

"Have you seen her?"

"Why would I have seen her?" John asked slowly, suddenly feeling a bit lost in the conversation. He had seen Jen twice: once as a child, and once on that terrible night, crouched beside the twisted, broken Freddy suit in a pool of Charlie's blood. But Charlie didn't know about either. "You know I've never actually met her," John said, watching Charlie's face. Her expression was pensive, and did not change.

"I just thought she might try to get in touch," Charlie said idly.

"Okay. I'll let you know if she does?" John offered.

"Please do, thanks," Charlie said. It was only then that she seemed to register his confusion. "I haven't seen her in a while. She rescued me that night," she said. "She took me home and cleaned me up, made sure I was okay." She flashed John a quick half smile, and he returned it warily.

"I thought you said you didn't remember anything from that night," he said, trying to keep his tone from sounding accusatory.

"I said there was a lot I don't remember. But mostly that's what Jen told me. Honestly, the first thing I remember is her waking me up the next morning, telling me to put on the dress she had for me." Charlie made a face. "She always wanted me to dress more like a girl. Of course, the joke was on me; it turns out after a few near-death experiences, there's nothing I wanted more than a makeover."

John smiled, and she batted her eyelashes exaggeratedly. He laughed in spite of himself.

"So, you think she might be looking for you?" He paused, unsure how to phrase the next part. "Do you want her to find you?" he asked at last, and she shrugged.

"I'd like to know where she is."

"She's not at the house where you're living? When did she leave?"

"Everybody leaves eventually," Charlie said in a sardonic tone, and he laughed again, less heartily.

You didn't answer my question.

Charlie glanced at her watch: like everything else she now wore, it was a smaller, feminized version of the one she used to have. "There's a good zombie movie starting in about fifteen minutes, I think," she said brightly. "The new theater isn't far from here. What do you think, should we see if the old formula still works?"

What does that mean? John held back a smile. "I can't go to the movies," he said with real reluctance. "I've got somewhere that I need to be."

"Another time?" Charlie said, and he nodded.

"Yeah, maybe."

As he walked back to his car, John noticed a crowd outside the new pizzeria. *I guess everybody likes the circus*, he thought. He wandered closer, trying to see where Charlie had gone, but she was nowhere to be seen. Suddenly, like noticing hidden figures in a picture, John realized that the crowd around him was dotted with clowns: painted faces, white billowy costumes, noses of all shapes and colors. They were everywhere. He backed out of the throng, tripping on an oversize shoe and almost falling off the sidewalk.

When he was free of the crowd, John took a deep breath and looked back at the restaurant, noticing for the first time the banner strung over the front entrance. GRAND OPENING: COME DRESSED AS A CLOWN AND EAT FREE! it read, hanging between the gigantic faces of two grinning clowns. He looked around. More people were arriving, many of them in costume, and John felt the hair on the back of his neck stand on end. He glanced behind him, but there was nothing sinister, besides the clowns. He forced himself to look at them individually: people had dressed with varying degrees of enthusiasm—some had structured bodysuits, wigs, and enormous feet; others had simply painted their faces and worn polka-dot T-shirts. Still, his sense of unease did not abate.

They're just people in costumes, he scolded himself, then laughed abruptly, startling a woman standing nearby. "People in costumes. That's never gone wrong for me," he muttered, walking away from the crowd to find his car.

Driving home, John found himself agitated; twice he looked at the speedometer and saw that he'd gone dangerously over the speed limit without noticing. He tapped his hand restlessly against the steering wheel, thinking of the next day. *What then?* Seeing Charlie had rattled him more than he had realized. After months of solitary scribbling, going over and over his bizarre theories, he'd been forced to put his conviction to the test, to ask her questions and watch her answer, and ask himself as he did, *Are you her? Are you my Charlie?* Now that it was over, it felt unreal, like a dream that lingered too long, unwelcome in the waking world. As he approached the turnoff that would take him home, he sped up, driving straight on past it.

John parked his car a few blocks away from Clay Burke's house. He pulled the keys out of the ignition and jangled them nervously in his hand for a minute, then opened the door decisively and got out. When he got to the house it was dark except for a single window, which he thought was Clay's office. *I wonder if Carlton's gone back to school*, he wondered, unsure whether he was hoping for his friend's presence, or his absence.

He knocked and waited, then rang the bell. A long moment later, Clay opened the door.

"John. Good," he said, and nodded, seeming unsurprised by his presence. He stepped aside to let John in, and ushered him into the study. "Do you want some coffee?" he asked, gesturing at the mug on his desk.

"It's a little late for me," John said. "I'll be up all night."

Clay nodded. "I'm substituting lesser vices," was all he said. John glanced around the room. The last time he had been here they'd used the desk as a barricade against an army of angry animatronics.

"You fixed the door," he observed.

"I fixed the door," Clay said. "Oak. Reinforced. What brings you here?"

"I saw Charlie." Clay raised his eyebrows, but didn't say anything. "She said something: she asked if I'd heard from—" John stopped, seized by a sudden sense that he was being watched. Clay had his head tilted to the side as though sensing something as well.

Silently, Clay made his way to the closed window, positioning himself beside one of the long, pale green drapes, and peered outside. "Everyone is a little on edge with all these weirdos walking around in face paint," he said, but he kept his voice low. He pulled the drapes together, then walked back toward John. "Have a seat," Clay offered; there were two dark green upholstered chairs and a matching couch along one wall. John sat on the couch. Clay grabbed his desk chair and dragged it across the rug so they were only a few feet apart.

"What did Charlie ask you?" Clay began. John glanced at the window again; he felt as if waves of dread were emanating from it, rolling into the room like an unseen fog. Clay looked back over his shoulder, but only for a second. John cleared his throat.

"She asked about her aunt Jen. If I'd seen her. I thought you might know something?" he finished uncertainly. Clay looked lost in thought, and John wondered for a moment if he should repeat himself.

"No," Clay said finally. "Did Charlie say why she was asking?"

John shook his head. "She just said she wanted to know if I'd heard from her. I don't know why I would hear from her, though," he said. He was choosing his words carefully, as if saying the right ones in the right order would unlock a door in Clay's mind, and convince him to tell John what he knew. Clay just nodded thoughtfully. "Did you ever meet her?" John asked.

"Never a formal introduction, no," Clay said. "She was a bit older than Henry, I think." Clay got quiet for a moment and tilted his glass from side to side, swirling the last few sips at the bottom. "When he moved here, Henry was something of a recluse; we all knew he'd lost a kid." Clay sat up slowly. "Didn't see them for a while, even Charlie, and then . . ." Clay let out a pained sigh. "Jen was around for about a year, and she was the one watching the kid. Jen stuck to Charlie's side like glue. I guess Henry just didn't trust people anymore, and I can't blame him."

"I always kind of got the impression . . ." John paused, choosing his words again. "Charlie always gave me the impression that she was kind of cold."

"Well, like I said, after something like that," Clay said. "I was surprised when Jen took Charlie, after Henry died," he went on.

"What about Charlie's mother?" John asked hesitantly. It felt intrusive to pry, worse because Charlie was not here: he felt like they were talking about her behind her back.

"No, Charlie's mother ran off before her and her father moved to Hurricane," Clay said. "Henry never said anything bad about her mother. He pretty much never said anything about her at all, but I asked one day, just out of curiosity. Maybe it was the detective in me; I couldn't help myself. He thought a long time before answering me, then he gave me this sad look, and he said, 'She wouldn't know what to do with my little girl.' I backed off the subject after that. I mean, I knew they'd lost another kid. I guess I assumed Charlie's mother had had some kind of breakdown, or else just found herself unable to care for a child so much like the one she'd lost. I think it should be said, though, to her aunt Jen's credit, Charlie seems to have turned out all right." He smiled and gave a nod. "She's a bit odd, but she's a good kid."

"She's unique, for sure," John said.

"Unique, then," Clay said drily. The walls trembled briefly as a strong wind passed over the house. John cast his eyes around the room uncomfortably, then lit on something familiar in the corner, tucked away between the end of a bookshelf and the wall.

"Is that Ella?" John asked, pointing. Clay looked blank for a moment.

"The doll? That turned up in the rubble of Charlie's old house. The rest got hauled away, but I kept that."

"Her name is Ella," John said. "Charlie's dad made her, she used to go around on a track, carrying a tea set."

"I asked Charlie if she wanted it," Clay said. "She wasn't interested."

"She wasn't?" John repeated, alarmed. Clay shook his head absently.

"I have a hard time believing that," John said incredulously as he held the old toy in his arms, and Clay came back to attention.

"Well, tell her that it's here if she ever wants it."

"I will," John said, setting the doll back down. Clay glanced at the window again and looked preoccupied. "Is something wrong?" John asked.

"Not at all," he said.

John raised his eyebrows. "Are you sure about that?"

Clay sighed. "A child was abducted this morning."

"What?"

"A little girl, she disappeared sometime between midnight and six a.m." Clay was stone-faced; John searched for words and came up empty. "It's the second one this month," Clay added quietly.

"I haven't heard anything about that," John said. He glanced at the window again as the wind began to howl outside, then looked back at Clay, and immediately the knot of fear took up its post behind his head again. "Do you have any leads?" John asked the first question he could think of. Clay didn't answer for a long moment, and John asked the next question. "Do you think it has something to do with— I mean, missing kids, it's not the first time that's happened here."

"No, it's certainly not." Clay was staring into the space between them as if there was something there he could see. "I don't see any way that it could be connected, though; Freddy's has been destroyed at this point."

"Right," John said. "So, you don't have any leads?"

"I'm doing the best that I can." Clay lowered his head and ran his hand though his hair, then sat up straight again. "I'm sorry. It's got me on edge; I feel like I'm reliving those days: children, the same age as my little boy—the same age as you back when—getting snatched one after another, and there was nothing I could do to stop it then, either."

"Michael," John said quietly.

"Michael. And the others. There never seems to be a shortage of evil in this world."

"But that's why we have you, right?" John smiled.

Clay snorted. "Right. I wish it were that simple."

"You said two kids were missing?" John said, his eyes drawn again toward the sound of the wind dragging branches and leaves against the side of the house.

Clay stood up and went to the window, almost defiantly, and opened it wide. John startled at the sound of the window cracking. John could see from where he sat that Clay seemed to be scanning the area for something under the guise of getting some air.

After a moment, he pulled himself back inside and shut the window, then drew the curtains closed. "It might not be as bad as it looks now, John. There's usually a normal explanation, and most kids turn up, one way or another. Two weeks ago, there was a little boy named Edgar, whatever. Two and a half years old."

"What happened?"

"His parents have been fighting about custody for over a year. His father ends up losing that fight—only gets to see the kid once a month, supervised visits, which I can tell you was for good reasons. Edgar disappears, surprise, surprise. He was found a few days later, alive and well; spontaneous road trip with his dad. Most kidnappings, it's one of the parents."

"Is that what you think is happening here?" John asked skeptically.

"No." Clay didn't take long to answer. "No, I don't," he repeated, sounding graver.

He took a deep breath and leaned forward. "And it doesn't help that the whole town's obsessed with this new restaurant, dressing up like clowns—it's a waste of time for my officers to be doing crowd control, or clown control, as it were."

"Can I do anything?" John asked, though he couldn't imagine what kind of help he could be.

"Not a thing," Clay said. "If I'm right, I may need you. And I'll need—" He stopped.

"Charlie," John said. "You'll need Charlie."

Clay nodded. "It's not fair to ask that of her," Clay said. "Not after everything she's been through. But I will if I have to."

"Yeah," John said. Clay was staring at the space between them again, and John felt suddenly like he was intruding. "It's getting late," he said.

"Yeah, well, watch yourself out there," Clay said, hastily standing. "Do you want to take my gun?" Clay said lightly. He smiled, but there was tension in his face, as though he were half hoping John would take it.

"Don't need it." John grinned. "I've got these guns." He held a tight fist in the air and threatened the room before letting himself out.

"Okay, tough guy, see you soon," Clay said grimly.

John started back toward his car: it was pitch-black now—it had been dark when he arrived, he realized, but now he *noticed* it. The streetlamps didn't go far, the pools of light beneath him swallowed up only a few feet out. His footsteps landed hard; and there seemed to be no way to quiet them. The distant roar of the highway was too faint to provide cover, and the wind was silent for the time being, as though it had temporarily gone into hiding. Something moved a few yards ahead of him, and John stopped dead: coming down the road was another costumed moviegoer, but there was something off about this one. It was heading in his direction, walking in the middle of the road at an even pace. John stayed where he was between two of the tall, thin saplings planted along the sidewalk, his eyes glued to the approaching figure.

As it came closer, a chill gripped John's spine: The clown's movements were feminine, but wrong. She walked like something mechanical, yet graceful. His breath caught in his throat as the clown glided toward him like a wraith. The creature was staring straight ahead as it passed; John waited, hoping to stay out of its line of sight. As she grew closer however, her eyes drifted toward him, her head turning only slightly as though to acknowledge his passing.

John stared back, at first admiring the sleek and controlled beauty of her face, split down the middle through some trick of costuming. John instinctively took a step back—he had seen monsters before—and prepared to run, or fight, if necessary. But just as his heart began thudding against his chest, she looked away again and slipped back into the dark as gracefully as she had appeared. John watched for a moment, then continued to his car. He checked his rearview mirror, but there was no one in sight. As he drove home, he checked the mirror more often than he needed to. His thoughts kept returning to those shiny, penetrating eyes: the clown had looked at him like she knew him; like she could see right through him. "Relax," John said to the empty car. "It was just some weirdo in a costume." Saying the words aloud, however, did not make them any more convincing.

Clay went back to his office and stopped by the window, drawing aside the curtains slightly to make sure John had made it around the corner and out of sight. Clay sighed; he sat down at his desk, picked up the case file on the second missing child, and began to review it. The information he needed just wasn't there, but it didn't stop him from returning to it over and over again. His officers had diligently done their jobs: they'd gone to the right places, talked to the right people, and asked all the wrong questions. *They just don't know what I know.*

There was a sound from down the hallway, a distinct creak. Clay's eyes lifted, and he set the file carefully back on his desk.

"John?" he called, but there was no response. With practiced calm, Clay quietly reached for the gun he kept in a holster under his desk and flipped the safety off. He went to the open office door and paused, listening for another noise from the dark hall. Nothing came. Clay pulled the door shut, snapping the deadbolts into place.

Clay stepped back into the center of the room and stood, listening. A moment passed in silence and his eyes dropped, his shoulders feeling at ease, but suddenly his eyes lifted again, and his jaw clenched. He took one deliberate step back, focusing directly on the center of the door ahead of him. He lifted and steadied his gun, and took aim. Several minutes passed, but Clay's eyes never wavered. There was something in the hall.

$\star$ $\star$ $\star$

John let his front door fall shut behind him with a heavy thud and tossed his keys on the kitchen counter. He sat down heavily on the couch, letting his head fall back, weighted down with fatigue. After only a moment, he lifted his head back up: the strange noise was coming from his bedroom again. It sounded a little like the sounds the rabbit's head had been making, but something had changed, though he couldn't pinpoint how. It sounded like a voice, then static, a voice, then static. Something was being repeated.

John's bedroom door was almost all the way closed, and he got up from the couch and approached it slowly from the side, putting his feet down silently one after the other, the rubber soles scarcely tapping the floor. He eased the door open: the sound was louder now, more distinct: the voice continued, garbled and muffled. John turned on the light and went to Theodore's head. He bent over so his eyes were level with Theodore's plastic ones, and listened. The rabbit's head stared back, muttered words, broke into static, then a moment later repeated. John grabbed a notebook and pen off his bed and closed his eyes, concentrated on the sounds.

After a minute, he began to hear words. "Shining?" John whispered. "Shining—something. Silver?" He continued to listen, but he couldn't make out the rest. John gritted his teeth and opened his eyes, glaring at the stuffed rabbit's head as it continued to repeat the same incoherent phrase. John drew in a long breath, then let it out, trying to release the tension in his neck, in his jaw, in his back. He sat down on the bed, put the pen and paper down, and closed his eyes once more. *Just listen.* The sounds repeated, again and again. Suddenly, they resolved, like song lyrics after the thousandth play: John understood.

"Shining Star? Silver . . . something. Silver Reef? Shining Star, Silver Reef."

"Shining Star, Silver Reef," Theodore repeated. John got up again, putting his ear to Theodore's nose, trying to make sure he had it right. "Shining Star, Silver Reef . . ." the rabbit intoned. John raced back to his car.

When he reached Clay's driveway again, John stopped dead: the front door was gaping open, light from inside the house spilling into the yard. He ran up the steps, calling, "Clay! Clay, are you here?" He ran inside, still shouting, and made for Clay's office just a few steps past the front hall.

"Clay!"

John dropped to his knees beside Clay; he was on the floor, one side of his face slick with his own blood, more pooling beneath his head. His eyes were closed. John grabbed his wrist and pressed his fingers against the veins, hoping for a pulse: after a few frantic seconds, he found it, and relief washed through him, but it was momentary. "Clay?" John repeated, jostling him lightly. Clay didn't respond. John looked around with alarm; the new door, the one Clay had described as "reinforced," was in pieces. What was left of the door was still hanging in place by the upper hinge. Hastily, John pulled Clay out into the hall as best he could.

He glanced back toward the office: the chair was over-turned, and everything that had been on the desk littered the carpet. He patted Clay's shoulder. "You're going to be okay," he said hoarsely, and he went to the office phone and dialed 911. As he waited for an operator, he looked nervously back at the demolished door. Another surge of wind rushed through the front door and out the open window, seemingly to carry with it whatever horror had happened here.

CHAPTER FIVE

The hissing sound continued; there was no place to get away from it. Their pain came at random, for no reason they could discern, and they clung together in their confusion.

"Hold still," a voice said, and they trembled with fear, for they knew the terrifying voice well. Frozen like a frightened animal, trying to hide but completely exposed; inner, bloody screams silent to the world. The shadow blotted out the light from above. "Keep wiggling, and I will keep taking the parts of you that wiggle," the voice growled. The hissing grew louder, and with a sudden snap, and a flash of shocking pain, the shadow withdrew, holding something in his hands. "I'll be back soon."

★　　★　　★

"I was gone for less than an hour," John said in a low voice, leaning in so Jessica could hear him over the sound of the hospital waiting room's TV. "I came back, and he was lying there. If I had just stayed with him a little longer . . ." He trailed off, and Jessica gave him a sympathetic look. He grabbed his backpack off the floor and put it in his lap, touching the front pocket to reassure himself that Theodore's head was still where he'd stuffed it.

"Do you think it was just someone with a grudge?" she asked, then flushed. "I don't mean 'just,' like it's not a big deal, but I mean, I'm sure Clay made his fair share of enemies, being the police chief. It probably didn't have anything to do with . . ." She glanced around and lowered her voice. "Anything to do with *us.*"

John looked down at the backpack in his lap. "The door . . . was *shredded*, Jess."

Jessica looked nervously down the hallway, like she was worried Clay might hear them. "Well, regardless, it's not your fault."

A heavy silence settled in between them, only punctuated by the half-crazed voices coming from the TV, which was showing a montage of ghastly faced clowns. For a moment, John was distracted, searching for a glimpse of the apparition who had silently passed him in the street, but she was not among the crowd.

"People are going crazy this weekend," Jessica said, recalling his attention. "Dressing up in those costumes—did you hear about the kid who got kidnapped?"

"Yeah," John said. "Clay told me about it. Actually, when I went to see him—" John broke off as a nurse in blue scrubs walked up purposefully.

"John, Jessica?" she said as if she already knew the answer.

"Yeah, that's us," Jessica said, with a hint of anxiety.

The nurse gave her a smile. "Chief Burke wants to see you. I tried to tell him visits are supposed to be immediate family only right now, but, well. Chief's orders."

The room was only a few doors down the hallway, but the bright lights and slick, grayish surfaces were disorienting. John squinted to ward off the offensive glare. Jessica was in front of him, and he bumped into her before he realized she had stopped just short of Clay's door.

"What's the matter?" he asked, confused as to why she was standing still.

She turned around and moved close to whisper: "Can you go in first?"

"Yeah, of course," he said, understanding. "He's not that bad, Jess, I promise."

"Still." She made a concerned face and stepped back so John could approach the doorway.

The door was open: He could see Clay, apparently asleep. He was in a hospital gown, and with the blood cleaned from his face, his skin looked sallow. A line of black stitches ran from his forehead to his cheekbone, splitting his eyebrow.

"He almost lost that eye."

Jessica jumped. The nurse had apparently followed them.

"He looks pretty out of it," John said quietly. "Are you sure he wanted to talk to us?"

"He's drifting in and out," the nurse replied in a normal tone of voice. "Go ahead, it won't hurt him to talk for a bit."

"Hey, Clay," John said awkwardly as he approached the bed. "Carlton and Marla are on their way. They should be here soon." Jessica looked sideways at the elderly woman asleep in the other bed, and the nurse stepped past her, closing the curtain between the two patients.

"Privacy, if you can call it that," the nurse said drily, and then left, closing the door partway behind her.

As soon as she was out of the room, Clay's eyes opened. "Good," he said. His voice was reedy, and he didn't lift his head from the pillow, but his eyes were sharp. "Don't pull any plugs just yet, I'm still here," Clay said lightly, and John gave him a wry smile.

"Okay, not yet," he agreed.

"How are you feeling?" Jessica asked.

"Get my jacket," Clay said, pointing to the enclosure's only chair, where a dark gray sport coat was draped over the back. Jessica hurried to get it, and Clay fumbled around with it for a minute, finally extracting a long white envelope from the inside breast pocket. He held it out to John, sitting up slightly; John took it and Clay fell back on the pillow, breathing heavily.

"Take it easy," John said, alarmed.

Clay nodded weakly, his eyes closed. "It has to have a range," he mumbled.

"What?" Jessica leaned in beside John, and they exchanged a worried look.

"It has to have a maximum range." Clay's head lolled to the side and his breath slowed: he seemed to be drifting out of consciousness again.

"Should we get the nurse?" Jessica looked to John, who peered at the monitor, then shook his head.

"His vitals look okay."

"You're not a doctor, John!"

"Shut the door a little more?" John said, ignoring her. Jessica did as he asked begrudgingly, leaving it a few inches ajar. John turned the envelope over: It was unaddressed, sealed, and heavy. He opened it, and something small fell out: Jessica moved to grab it, and John took out the rest of the contents: It was a stack of photographs, about an inch thick. The top one was of him and Charlie in the restaurant only the night before. It seemed to have been shot from outside the building, through the front window. John continued to browse the photos: Each one tracked through his evening with Charlie until they had parted ways: eating, coming out of the restaurant, and saying good-bye, the pictures all taken from a distance. In some the image was askew, or the figures blurry—the photographer had not been interested in composition. There was a last shot in the sequence: Charlie walking away toward the crowd by the new pizzeria; John could make out the back of his own head in the bottom corner of the photo. He quickly put it behind the others and kept looking. The next sequence showed Jessica and Charlie in a clothing store, coming in and out of a dressing room in various outfits, talking and laughing. The pictures seemed to have been taken from the other side of the store—the edges of some were obscured by fabric, as if someone had been hiding behind a rack of clothes.

John felt a stab of angry revulsion. The restaurant pictures were bad enough, but this seemed far more intrusive, an invasion of an intimate moment. He glanced at Jessica; she had moved to the window, holding something up to the light, and after a moment John realized that it was a strip of film. He squinted over her shoulder, and she lowered it, turning to face him.

"All the pictures on this are of us," she said quietly.

He held up the stack of pictures. "These, too."

Jessica held out a hand silently: He passed her half the stack and they each sorted through their share. The photos covered several more moments in time: there was a set of Jessica and Carlton meeting Charlie at a café; John showed one to Jessica and she nodded. "That's when Charlie first got back," she said. Her brow furrowed, and she held up a shot of her, Charlie, and Marla coming out of a building. "This is my apartment complex," she said, her voice tense. "John, this looks like somebody hired a P.I. to follow all of us around. How did he get these? And *why?*"

"I don't know," John said slowly, looking back down at the photo in his hands, the last in the stack. The picture had been taken at night, outside, but the figures were clear: He himself was facing the camera, his hands shoved into his pockets. The despair on his face visible even at a distance. Charlie had her back to the camera; she was hugging herself so tightly that he could see her fingers gripping the back of her dress, a contorted, useless comfort. *Charlie.* His head was too tight, his chest ached. John reflexively bent the photo and put it in his pocket, then turned his head to make sure no one had noticed. Jessica said nothing.

John cleared his throat. "The reason I went to see Clay was that I wanted to show him something."

"What is it?" Jessica stepped closer. John went to the door and peered out, then snuck a glance behind the curtain at the elderly woman. She was still asleep. He took off his backpack and got Theodore out. Jessica yelped, then slapped a hand over her mouth. "Where did you get him?" she demanded.

John took a step back, startled by her sudden, searing scrutiny.

"What's wrong with you?" he asked.

"It's weird. I always hated that thing." Jessica fluttered her hand by her face. "Charlie's robotics experiments always creeped me out, but it's kind of nice to see it."

"Well, this one has an interesting secret."

"Don't let Charlie see it; she's been throwing away things like that, anything from her dad. It's probably some kind of five-step grief-acceptance thing, but still."

"No, I'm not going to show her this. This is going to sound crazy, but Theodore's been . . . talking to me, and yesterday—" He didn't have to continue. A garbled, static-filled noise retched from the rabbit's head, and Jessica winced. Before she could say anything, the sound changed.

Now that he knew the words, they were perfectly clear; Jessica tilted her head to the side, listening intently.

"Is he saying, 'Silver Reef'?" she asked.

"Shining Star. Shining Star, Silver Reef." Theodore was still repeating the phrase, but John shoved him back into his backpack and covered him with a mostly clean T-shirt, muffling the sound. Remembering the pictures, he bundled them back into the envelope and added them to the bag before zipping it back up. "You got it quicker than I did," he told Jessica. She nodded absently, a faraway look in her eye.

"Silver Reef," she repeated.

"Does it mean anything to you?" he asked with a spark of hope.

"It's a town near Hurricane," she said.

"Maybe Charlie's family used to live there?" John said. Jessica shook her head.

"No. It's a ghost town. Nobody lives there."

"Jessica! John!" Marla's voice pierced the quiet, and they turned to see Carlton beside her, his face pale and tense. He brushed past the others and went straight to the bed.

"Dad, are you okay?" He hovered beside Clay, reaching out to touch his hand, then pulling away. "Is he okay?" he glanced back at the others, and Marla hurried forward, examining the monitors.

"He's okay, Carlton," Marla said, putting a hand on his shoulder, and he nodded sharply, not taking his eyes off Clay's still face.

"He'll be fine," John said, trying to sound confident. "He was just awake, talking. The nurse said he's going to be okay."

"What happened?" Carlton asked quietly, and John shook his head.

"I don't know," he said helplessly. "I got there too late." Carlton didn't answer, but pulled a chair up beside the bed and sat down. He rested his chin on his fist, hunching over.

"It'll be okay," Marla repeated, then glanced around the room with a puzzled expression. "Where did she go?"

"Who's with you?" Jessica asked alarmingly, looking to John. John was looking at the door: Charlie had stopped just outside the room.

"Charlie. Hey, come in," he spoke loudly, wondering with guilt if she had heard any of the conversation that had taken place. She stepped into the room, but hung back. John glanced at his backpack, on the floor at the foot of Clay's bed. The noise seemed to have stopped, to his relief. When he looked up, Charlie gave him an embarrassed half smile.

"I don't like hospitals very much," she said softly. "Is he okay?" She didn't turn her head, and John realized that she was deliberately staying where she couldn't see Clay.

"He's going to be," he said. "He's doing okay." She nodded, but stayed where she was, looking unconvinced.

"He's lucky you were there!" Marla exclaimed. "John, you must have saved his life."

"Um, maybe," he said. "I don't know." He squeezed her hand, then let go of it. He turned back to Charlie; she gave him a small, tight smile, her arms folded. The nurse came in, and Marla intercepted her, pulling her aside for an update on his condition and Jessica took the opportunity to lean in. "John, I'm going to leave. I've got classes this afternoon. Pick me up at seven, don't be late."

"Right," John whispered. Jessica made her way past everyone and through the door. Charlie watched her until she was out of sight, then she looked at John again, making eye contact for only a moment before turning her attention back to the nurse. John glanced around the room: with Jessica gone, he felt suddenly untethered, less at ease among these people than he already had been. Without another word, he slipped out the door, ignoring the soft sound of Marla calling his name.

He was only a few feet down the hall when Jessica caught his arm. "John!"

"Hey!" he protested, then saw there was someone next to her, a slight, blonde woman who looked like she had been crying, her red eyes the only color in her washed-out face. "What's wrong?" he asked warily.

"This is Anna," Jessica said. "Clay . . . Chief Burke was— is—helping her to . . ." She cleared her throat. "Her son is missing. Chief Burke was helping."

"Oh," John said awkwardly. "I'm so sorry, ma'am." Anna blew her nose into a crumpled tissue.

"I was just at the station and I overheard . . . they said Chief Burke was here, and I just needed to know he's okay. Is he okay?" she asked anxiously.

"He's going to be fine," Jessica said, and Anna nodded, not seeming convinced.

"When I went to report that Jacob . . . was missing, the desk sergeant had me fill out paperwork, he asked me about my ex-husband and said he had probably taken Jacob. I told him, that man would never take Jacob, he wouldn't know what to do with him!"

"Okay," John said, shifting uncomfortably. "We don't work for the police department—"

"I know that," she said quickly, shaking her head. "I'm sorry, I can't think straight, it's just I overheard the nurse in the waiting room talking to you before. Chief Burke was there when the sergeant was telling me to call my ex-husband; he took me aside and asked me questions, he said he was going to find my son, and I believed him."

"He's a good officer," Jessica said softly. "He's a good person. He'll find your son." Anna pressed her hand to her mouth, stifling a sob as she began to cry again.

"Is he really going to be all right? I heard . . ." She broke off, and John put a hand on her shoulder.

"He's going to be all right," he said firmly. "We just saw him; he talked to us." Anna nodded, but didn't look convinced. Jessica gave John a helpless glance. He racked his brain for something to say. "He will find—Jacob, was it?" he asked, and Anna nodded tearfully.

"Anna!" An older woman rounded the corner briskly, and Anna turned at the sound of her name.

"Mom," she said, the strain in her voice easing slightly. Her mother wrapped her arms around her, and Anna held on tightly, crying into her shoulder.

"It'll be all right," Anna's mother whispered. *Thank you*, she mouthed silently to John and Jessica, and they nodded, exchanged a glance, and headed for the hospital entrance.

As soon as they were in the parking lot, Jessica let out a gasp like she had been holding her breath, and hugged John fiercely. He put his arms around her, surprised. "It'll be all right," he said, and she pushed him away.

"Will it?" she asked, her eyes bright with tears. "It's nice to tell that poor woman that Clay will find her son, but, John, you and I both know that when kids go missing in this town . . . they don't get found." John shook his head. He wanted to argue with her, but there was something leaden in the pit of his stomach.

"It doesn't have to end like that this time," he said without conviction, and Jessica straightened, wiping her eyes like it was a gesture of defiance.

"It can't. It can't end like that again, John. If that little boy is mixed up in all this, we have to find him and bring him home. For Michael."

John nodded, and before she could answer, she strode to her car and drove away, leaving him alone in the parking lot.

That night, John had barely stopped in front of Jessica's building when she came running out. She opened the car door and jumped in with lightning speed. "Go," she said urgently, and he hit the gas.

"What's wrong, what happened?" he asked.

"Just drive, hurry."

"Okay, put on your seat belt!" he scolded as they veered around a corner.

"Sorry! Everything is fine," she said. "I just don't like thinking someone could be out there stalking me."

"Yeah," he agreed, peering into the rearview mirror. "But it's dark out; we should be okay."

"That doesn't make me feel better."

"So, what do you think?" John said after a moment. "Did you notice anything about the photos?"

"That they're enough to get a restraining order in most states?" she joked, but there was real anxiety in her voice.

"None of them were of just one of us," he said. "And none of them were just you and me, or just you and Marla."

"You mean it's about Charlie," Jessica said, understanding immediately.

"Isn't everything?" John said drily. The words sounded bitter, though he had not meant them to, and he glanced at Jessica, trying to gauge her reaction. She was staring out the window like she hadn't heard him.

In less than half an hour, they were at the ghost town. John stopped the car beside a wooden sign reading WELCOME TO SILVER REEF, and got out; Jessica followed. It was an odd mix, even in the dark: in the distance they could see the crumbling walls of buildings that would never be restored, and close by were the places rebuilt for tourists: a church, a museum, and a few others John couldn't make out.

"John, we're going to get killed out here," Jessica said, briefly losing her balance on the loose dirt and gravel.

"When exactly did people last live here?" John asked quietly.

"Late eighteen-hundreds I think. Silver mining town, hence the name."

The town appeared even more abandoned than they were expecting, possibly closed to tourists for the season, but on distant hills there were scattered lights. John turned in a circle, wishing Theodore had been just a little more forthcoming. "What does 'Shining Star' mean, anyway?" he muttered to himself. He looked up: the night was clear, and the sky was awash in stars, with no city lights to drown them out.

"It's beautiful," Jessica murmured.

"Yeah, but not helpful," John said, rubbing the back of his neck. He turned around again, and then he saw it. "Shining star," he said.

"What?" Jessica turned, then squinted and tried to follow his eye line.

A few yards back the way they'd come was a wooden archway leading into a field; at the peak of the arch, was a single silver star.

The field was wide, sloping upward, and at the top of the hill, John could see the outline of a house. It was scarcely visible: had it not been for the guidance of Theodore's mumbling head, it wouldn't have stood out from anything else in the canopy of silhouettes. With wordless agreement, they passed under the star, leaving the remains of the town behind them. The black field soon consumed their line of sight in all directions, with only the faint discoloration of a winding gravel path to guide their steps.

As they made their way up the hill, a small, squarish one-story house came into view; there were windows on each outfacing wall, but only one was lit, in the back. They slowed their pace as they reached the front door: there was only one concrete step, unusually high and wide. John reached out a hand to help Jessica up. She didn't really need it, being five times the athlete that he was, but it still seemed polite. The front door was unwelcoming, the little, lightless lamps almost hidden, offering no help. John looked around for a doorbell and couldn't find one, so he knocked. There was no sound of movement from inside. Jessica leaned to the side, trying to see through the windows. John had raised his hand to try again when the door creaked open, and a tall, dark-haired woman peered out, staring at them coldly.

"Aunt Jen?" John asked meekly, stepping back instinctively before he could stop himself. He recognized her, but standing face-to-face, he felt almost as though they had come to this house at random. Jen tilted her head, her dark eyes fixing on him.

"I'm someone's aunt Jen, yes," she said drily. "But I don't believe I'm yours." She stayed where she was, one hand on the doorframe and the other on the knob; she was blocking the entry as if she thought they might try to force their way in.

"I'm a friend of Charlie's," John said, and a ghost of an expression flickered on her face.

"And?" she said.

"I'm John. This is Jessica," he added, realizing she had not yet spoken. Jessica would usually have jumped in as the social director, but she was leaving this to him, looking back nervously as though she suspected someone was creeping through the dark. John glanced back at her, and she gave him a little, encouraging nod to go on. "I'm here because I got a message," he said. She waited patiently, and John took off his backpack and took Theodore out; Jessica reached forward to take the empty bag, and he held the rabbit's head up. Jen showed no surprise, only curling her lip slightly.

"Hello, Theodore," she said calmly. "You've seen better days, haven't you?"

John smiled reflexively, then hardened his features.

"Shining Star, Silver Reef," John said, but Jen didn't react. "I have to say, this is a strange place to call home," he said, though what he wanted to say was, *You owe us an explanation.*

"A message." She looked at Theodore's head, then looked accusingly over her shoulder, though all that was visible behind her was a dark hallway.

"Did you want us to come here? I don't understand," John pressed.

"Why don't you come inside," Jen said, stepping back, then closing the door with haste as soon as they were inside. The house was spare: the furniture was dark and plain, and there was little of it. The walls were thick with layered wall-papers, rich with vintage designs from decades past, but there was nothing hanging on them, though John saw nail holes and marks where decorations had once been. Jen ushered them through a living room with only two chairs and an end table, into a small room almost entirely filled by a square, black-stained dinner table. There were four matching chairs, and Jen pulled out the one closest to the door, then sat down.

"Please," she said, gesturing to the other chairs. John and Jessica made their way around the table to face her, as she stared into the middle distance.

"So, is this where Charlie grew up?" Jessica asked awkwardly as she sat down.

"No."

"So, then you moved here recently?" John asked suspiciously, refusing to believe someone would select this house by choice.

"How is Charlie?" Jen said slowly. "Did she know about the message as well?" Jen made a discreet glance at the window behind them, then focused back on John.

"No," John said plainly. Jen nodded; she was still staring into space, and he had a sudden but profound impression that there was something in the room that only she could see.

"We want to help Charlie. Is there anything going on that we need to know about?" Jessica asked, and Jen snapped to attention.

"Charlie is my concern. She's my responsibility." Jen spoke with an air of pure self-assurance, and something in it must have struck Jessica: she straightened, lifting her chin to match Jen's posture.

"Charlie's our friend, she's our concern, too," Jessica said.

There was silence, and John flicked his eyes back and forth between the two women, waiting. A long moment passed, the two of them staring at each other, immobile, and John realized he was holding his breath.

"Jen," he said, plunging in. "A friend gave us pictures someone had been taking of Charlie, and of us." He unzipped his backpack, and that noise snapped Jessica and Jen out of their staring contest. He pulled the pictures Clay had given them out of their envelope, leaving the film, and placed them in front of Jen on the table. "If you want to take responsibility for Charlie, look at these and tell me if they mean anything to you."

She began going through the stack, peering intently at each photo, then putting each aside, making a second, neat pile of discards. "Why don't you ask your detective friend what they mean?" she asked.

"Because last night our detective friend was nearly murdered," John said. Jen didn't respond, and continued her methodical progress through the pictures. When she had gone through all the pictures, she looked up at John. Her expression had softened slightly; the hostility had given way to something else, a discomfort, and fear.

"Is this all?" she asked. "Is there anything else?" She cleared her throat.

"He said something before he lost consciousness."

"And what was that?"

John looked to Jessica briefly, then back to Jen. "'It has to have a range. It has to have a maximum range.'" He looked at her expectantly, but she showed no sign of recognition.

"I don't know what that means," she said. She put her chin in her hand, staring down again at the first picture in the stack, then she shook her head. "I know you mean well." She leaned back in the wooden chair, looking from John to Jessica and back again. "I should tell you to go away, to forget her. All these years . . ." She trailed off, then gave each of them a piercing look. "Secrets petrify you. You harden yourself against the world to keep them safe, and the longer you keep them, the harder you become. Then one day you look in the mirror, and you realize you've turned to stone." She smiled sadly. "I'm sorry."

"You're not going to tell us anything? We're here to help. We're Charlie's friends!" Jessica insisted.

"If I didn't plan on telling you anything I wouldn't have anything to be sorry about," Jen said, her mouth almost forming a smile. John collected the photos to put back in his bag.

"If you have something to tell us—do it now, or we're leaving. I may not know much, but I know that girl isn't Charlie, or she is under some kind of influence." He waited for a response, but none came. "She isn't herself," he added, sounding more desperate than before. Jen looked up at them: her rigid face had broken, tears were in her eyes.

A knock came from the front door, and even Jen startled. She looked to the door, then back to John and Jessica. Her face was grave. "That way," she said in a voice barely above a whisper, pointing down a narrow hallway. "Close the door behind you." The knock came again; John touched Jessica's arm and nodded, and they got up from the table, careful not to let the chairs make noise as they dragged across the floor.

The hallway was dark, the only light coming from the room they had just left, and John kept a hand on the wall for balance. After a second his eyes adjusted, and he could see an open door at the end of the hall.

"John, come on," Jessica whispered, grabbing his arm briefly as she brushed past him and hurried into the room.

"Yeah," he said, and stopped moving as his fingers touched the frame of a door.

"John!" Jessica hissed. John tried the door. It opened easily; he peered in, and recoiled.

Someone's in there!

"John!" Jessica whispered urgently as the knock at the door came again. John didn't move.

It took only a second for him to register that the figure in the closet was not a person. It was about his height, with a roughly human shape, but it resembled nothing that had ever been alive. John stepped closer and took his keys from his pocket. He switched on the keyring penlight, and swept it up and down quickly. His heart stopped. It was a skeleton, metal and naked wires, encased in nothing. Its arms hung at its sides, and its head was bowed, exposing its open skull, the circuits silent and lightless. Its face was bare and metal.

"John!" Jessica was standing behind the door at the end of the hall, holding it open just a crack as she waited for him. John closed the closet door, blinded again in the darkness, and walked toward the sound of her voice like a beacon. His steps took ages, the air like molasses, as the thing in the closet echoed in his mind like a gunshot, drowning out everything else.

In a daze, John reached the end of the hall as Jessica beckoned frantically. She grabbed his arm and pulled him inside, carefully closing the door behind him.

"What's wrong with you? John, what was in that closet?" she whispered, still holding on to his arm, her nails digging in, bringing him closer to reality.

"It was . . ." He swallowed. *It was holding a knife.* "It was the machine Charlie's father built to kill himself," he said hoarsely. Jessica's eyes widened, and she stared at him like he was a ghost.

The knock came again, much louder, and they both jumped. This time they could hear Jen's footsteps walking toward the sound. Jessica bent and pressed her ear to the keyhole. "Do you see anything?" John whispered. The front door creaked as it opened.

"Charlie," John could hear Jen say. "What a nice surprise." Jessica twisted around in her crouched posture.

"Charlie's here?" she said, scarcely whispering, and John shrugged.

"Aunt Jen, it's so wonderful to see you again," Charlie's voice came through faintly, but clear. Jessica stayed where she was, listening for more, but John was restless, and he looked around the room.

They were in a bedroom—at least, there was a bed—but it was mostly filled with cardboard boxes and old-fashioned wooden trunks. John stumbled around them for a moment, then froze, looking as though something had just occurred to him. He knelt quietly and opened one of the chests, moving slowly to make no sound.

"John, what are you doing?" Jessica whispered angrily.

"Something isn't right here," John breathed, glancing at the door. "Come on, this might be our only chance to find out what she's up to." John shuffled through some of the papers in the first chest, then closed the lid and flipped up the top of a nearby cardboard box: It was filled with computer parts and mechanisms he didn't recognize. A second and third held massive tangles of electric cable. "This looks like stuff I'd expect to find in Charlie's room," he murmured to himself.

"Shhh!" Jessica hissed, pressing her ear back against the door to the hall.

"What's going on out there?" John said under his breath. "I can barely hear anything."

Jessica shook her head.

"Let me know if you hear someone coming." John moved to a large green chest, the paint almost entirely worn off. There was no lock. John knelt beside it, found the handle, and heaved it open, then shuddered, falling back and pushing himself away.

"Jessica," he gasped, moving back to the chest and leaning over it.

"Shhhh!" Jessica hissed from the door, listening intently.

"Jessica."

"What, John? I'm trying to listen."

"It's . . . it's Charlie," he said hoarsely. "In the chest."

"What?" Jessica whispered. She turned around in annoyance, her face falling. She dropped to her knees and crawled to the chest, where John had gone back to looking down at what lay inside. Charlie was curled up in the fetal position; she looked like she was sleeping, with a pillow under her head and blankets surrounding her. Her brown hair was a mess; her face was round; and she was wearing light gray sweatpants and a sweatshirt, both too large for her. John stared, his heart pounding so hard he could hear nothing but the rush of his own blood, not daring to hope, until: she took a breath, and then another. *She's alive.* John reached down into the trunk and touched her cheek: it was too cool. His mind snapped out of its first shock. *We have to get her out of here; she's sick.* He stood and reached awkwardly into the trunk, then gently, cautiously, lifted her out. He looked down at her in his arms, astonished, all his thoughts wordless, except, *Charlie.*

Don't let me go—let go of me, what's happening? Someone touched her cheek, a brief, startling spot of warmth. It was gone just as quickly, leaving her colder than before. *Come back*, she tried to say, but she could not remember how to make the words come out.

"Charlie." *That's my name, someone is saying my name.* Charlie tried to open her eyes. *I know that voice.* Someone's arms reached down under her, lifting her from the cramped, dark place she'd been so long that memories of somewhere else seemed like dreams. She still couldn't open her eyes. A woman said something. *I know them.* She couldn't remember their names.

The first voice came again, it was a man's voice, and she felt its reverberation as he pulled her against his chest, holding her like a child. Warmth radiated from him; he was solid and alive. Even standing still, he was filled with movement: She could hear his heartbeat, just beside her ear. *I am alive.* He said something else, and the rumble of it shook her whole body; the woman answered, and then she was jostled painfully. *We're going somewhere.* She still couldn't open her eyes.

"It's gonna be okay, Charlie," he whispered, and the sleeping world began to pull her down again. *I want to stay!* She began to panic, then as she slipped into unconsciousness again, she grabbed hold of the last words he'd said. *It's gonna be okay.*

John clutched Charlie to his chest, then relaxed his grip anxiously, afraid of hurting her.

"How are we going to get her out?" Jessica whispered, and he glanced around the room. There was a window, but it was high and narrow: getting all three of them through it would take time.

"We'll have to run for it," he said in a low voice. "Wait until . . . *she* leaves." Jessica met his eyes, her face written over with all the questions he had been asking himself for the last six months.

A scream ripped through the silence between them, and John came alert. Someone screamed again, and the room shuddered with impact from somewhere in the house. John looked around wildly for an escape, and his eyes lit on a closet door. "There," he said, nodding toward it. Another bang came, and the wall beside them shook; another scream, and then a scrabbling sound, like an animal scratching at the door. "Hurry," John whispered, but Jessica was already clearing a path. She moved ahead of him, moving aside boxes as quickly and soundlessly as she could, and he carried Charlie carefully behind, his whole being focused on holding her safe. Jessica shoved coats on hangers aside, making room, and they crammed themselves into the space.

"It's gonna be okay, Charlie," John whispered. Jessica closed the door behind them, then stopped, her hand on the knob.

"Wait," she whispered.

"What?"

Jessica ran back across the room carelessly, her steps thudding on the wood floor.

"Jessica, what are you doing?" John hissed, shrinking back farther into the recess of the closet, awkwardly shielding Charlie's head from hangers and hooks with his elbow. Jessica reached the window, snapped open the lock, and threw it open with a loud bang. John gaped as Jessica raced on tiptoe back to the closet, this time making no noise. She nestled in beside him, leaving the door open just a crack, and rested a hand on Charlie's shoulder.

Within an instant, the bedroom door opened, and someone stepped through. The light from the rest of the house filtered in dimly, and through the tiny crack in the door, they could barely make out a silhouette in red, walking purposefully across the room. The figure paused for a moment, looking outside, then with a rush of movement too quick to follow, vanished out the window.

John stood stock still, his heart pounding, half expecting the mysterious figure to appear again in front of them. Charlie's unconscious weight was starting to drag on his arms, and he shifted uncomfortably, trying not to jostle her.

"Come on," Jessica said. He nodded, though she couldn't see him. Jessica pushed the door open cautiously, and they were met with silence. They made their way to the hall, and stopped short again: Jen was slumped on the floor, blood spattering the wall behind her like an abstract mural, and pooled beneath her, trickling across the floor in little rivulets. John raised his hand to cover Charlie's face. There was no doubt that Jen was dead: her eyes glazed and dimmed with the marble stare of death, her stomach laid open.

"We have to go," he said hoarsely, and they turned from the grotesque scene and hurried out of the house. They ran headlong down the hill. John stumbled on the uneven gravel, barely catching himself, and Jessica turned back. "Go," he grunted, and clutched Charlie tighter, slowing his pace just a little.

At last they reached the car, and Jessica opened the back door and got in, then scooted over to the far side and reached out to help him put Charlie inside. Together they laid her across the back seat, placing her head in Jessica's lap. John started the car.

As they sped through the night he kept checking the rear-view mirror, reassuring himself: Charlie still slept, as Jessica twined her fingers in her hair, looking down at her face in wonder. John met her eyes in the mirror and saw his own thoughts on her face: *She's here. She's alive.*

Charlie raced down the hill, exhilarated, almost leaping— she felt like if she went fast enough she might take off and fly. Her heart was beating in a new rhythm; the night air was cool and fresh, and all her senses felt heightened: she could see anything, hear anything—*do* anything.

She reached the bottom of the hill and took off up the next one—she had parked her car behind it. She smiled into the night, picturing Aunt Jen's face in the moment it had dawned on her what was about to happen. That smooth, near-impermeable calm had ruptured; the cold-blooded woman had become a soft, frightened animal in the space of an instant. *At least she had the dignity not to beg,* Charlie thought. *Or maybe she just knew it wouldn't help.* She shivered, then shrugged.

They had been having pleasantries, then Charlie gave Jen a wide, cruel smile, and Jen screamed. Charlie advanced on her, and she screamed again; this time Charlie choked off the noise, grabbing Aunt Jen by the throat. She lifted her off her feet, and slammed her into a door with such force it clattered in its hinges. Her aunt tried to crawl away, and she caught her by her hair, now sticky with blood, and threw her into the wall again. This time she did not try to run, and Charlie crouched beside her and put a hand around her throat again, taking her time now, relishing the feeling of her aunt's pulse beneath her fingers, and the terrified look in her eyes. Jen opened and closed her mouth, gawping like a fish, and Charlie watched for a moment, considering.

"Is there something you'd like to say?" she asked mockingly. Jen made a tiny, pained nod, and Charlie leaned in close so she could whisper, keeping an iron grip on her throat. Jen took a thin, rattling breath, and Charlie reluctantly lightened the pressure enough to let her speak.

Her aunt wheezed for a moment, trying twice to speak before the words made it out. "I've always . . . loved you . . . Charlie."

Charlie pulled back and gave Aunt Jen a calmed look. "I love you, too," she said softly, and then she ripped open her stomach. "I really do."

Charlie reached her car; she was running so fast she ran a few yards past it before she could stop. She wanted to keep running, to keep this feeling alive. She opened and closed her fists; the blood on them was tacky and growing uncomfortable. She started the car and opened the trunk to get the first-aid kit she always carried. Standing in the beam of the headlights, Charlie took out some gauze and hydrogen peroxide and carefully wiped her hands clean finger by finger. When she was done, she examined them and nodded, satisfied; then she got in her car and sped off into the dark.

CHAPTER SIX

ohn was counting Charlie's breaths, *one-two, three-four, in-out,* each intake of air a marker of the time going by: that this was real, that she was not going to vanish. Hours had passed, and the sky outside was lightening, but still he could not take his eyes off her. His bed was narrow; she was curled on her side as she had been in the trunk, her back pressed against the wall, and he was perched on the edge, careful not to touch her. Jessica had taken a brief nap on the couch, and now she was up again, pacing the short length of his bedroom.

"John, we have to take her to a hospital," Jessica said for the second time since she awoke, and he shook his head.

"We don't even know what's wrong with her," he said softly. Jessica made a frustrated noise in her throat.

"That's all the more reason to *take her to a hospital*," she said, biting the words off individually.

"I don't think she'll be safe."

"You think she's safe here?"

John didn't answer. *One-two, three-four, in-out*—he realized he was counting her breaths again, and he looked away. He could still hear her breathing, though, and the count went on *nine-ten, eleven-twelve . . .* He could feel her presence beside him; even though they weren't touching, he had a constant awareness that she was close by.

"John?" Jessica prompted, and he looked first at Charlie, then at Jessica.

"Clay said something," he said.

"At the hospital?" Jessica frowned. "Something else?"

"No, before that. He had Ella at his house."

"That creepy doll from Charlie's bedroom?"

John hid a smile, remembering. *Jessica will like Ella*, Charlie had once confided to John. *She dresses like her.* But when Charlie had spun the wheel at the end of her bed, the one that made Ella glide out from the closet on her track, proffering her little tea tray, Jessica took one look at the toddler-size doll, screamed, and ran out of the room.

"Yeah, the creepy doll," he confirmed, his thoughts returning to the present. Jessica made an exaggerated shudder.

"I don't know how she could ever sleep, knowing that thing was in the closet."

"It wasn't the only closet," John said, furrowing his brow. "There were two more; Ella was in the littlest one."

"Well, it wasn't the location that creeped me out; I'm fine with closets . . . I take that back, I didn't like the last one we were in," Jessica said drily.

"I wish I could go back to that house—"

"Charlie's old house? It collapsed; it's gone," Jessica interrupted him, and he sighed.

"Ella turned up in the wreckage, but Clay said Charlie wasn't interested in keeping her. It seemed so unlike her; her father made that doll for her."

"Yeah." Jessica stopped pacing and leaned against the wall, letting everything sink in. "You were right, John." She opened her hands in a helpless gesture. "The *other* Charlie, she's an imposter; you were right. So, what do we do?"

John looked down again at Charlie, who stirred in her sleep. "Charlie?" he whispered.

She made a plaintive sound, then was still again.

John glanced thoughtfully at his dresser. After a moment, he went to it and began digging through the top drawer.

"What are you looking for?" Jessica asked.

"There was an old photo, one I found when Charlie and I were looking through her dad's stuff. It was Charlie when she was little. I know it's in here somewhere."

Jessica watched him for a moment, then leaned over as something caught her attention. She crouched beside the dresser and pulled at the corner of something sticking out from underneath. "This?" she asked.

"Yeah, that's it." John took the picture carefully and studied it.

"John, I realize you're having a sentimental moment right now, but we really need to get Charlie to the hospital." Jessica peered over his shoulder. "What is all of that stuff behind her in the picture? Cups and plates?"

"She was having a tea party," John whispered. "I have to go to Clay's house," he added after a moment.

"Clay's still in the hospital."

"I have to go back to his house. Stay here. Take care of Charlie."

"What's going on?" Jessica demanded as John grabbed his car keys from the dresser. "What am I supposed to do if *Not-Charlie* shows up? You saw what she did to Aunt Jen; she was probably the one who got Clay. And now she's gonna be after Charlie, too, *our* Charlie." John stopped, rubbing his temples with one hand.

"Don't let her in," he said finally. "Bolt the door after me, push the couch across the door. I'll be back."

"John!"

He left. He waited on the stoop until he heard the dead-bolt fall into place, then hurried to his car.

*   *   *

John pulled into Clay Burke's driveway too fast, slamming on the breaks and skidding onto the lawn. He rang the doorbell and waited long enough to confirm that no one was there, tried the knob and found it locked, then tried to act casual as he strolled around to the back of the house. He didn't think the neighbors could see through the hedges separating the houses, but there was no reason not to be careful. The back door off the kitchen was closed as well, so he made his way along the outside wall, looking for a window that would open. The living room was where he found it: the window was unlocked, and after a few minutes of fiddling, he was able to get the screen up, then haul himself over the sill, scraping his back against the window frame as he squeezed through.

He landed in a crouch, and stayed there for a moment, listening. The house had a thick hush, and a closed-up, stale smell; Carlton must have slept at the hospital. John got up and went to Clay's study, not bothering to be quiet.

He balked when he saw the wreckage: he hadn't forgotten the scene: the door smashed, the furniture upturned, and papers scattered over the floor like carpeting, but it was still a shock to see it. There was also a dark stain on the floor where he'd found Clay lying. John stepped over it carefully and went into the office.

He scanned the room quickly: only one corner remained undisturbed: Ella was standing there almost concealed behind a standing lamp, her tea tray steady in front of her.

"Hey, Ella," he said suspiciously. "Do you have something that you want to tell me?" he said as he turned his attention to the clutter in the room. There were three empty cardboard boxes beside the desk, and he went there first: it looked like their contents had been dumped out in one big pile. Sifting through quickly, he saw that they were all related to Freddy Fazbear's: photographs, papers of incorporation, tax forms, police reports, even menus. "Where do I start?" he murmured. He came to a photograph of Charlie and her father: Charlie was smiling; her father was holding her on his hip, pointing to something in the distance. He set it down and kept looking. Among the papers and photos were other things; the random computer chips and mechanical parts that seemed to turn up everywhere. He checked his watch; he was getting nervous at leaving Jessica alone with Charlie so long. He looked at Ella in the corner. "You know what I'm looking for, don't you?" he asked the doll, then sighed and went back to the pile.

On his hands and knees, he surveyed the area, and this time noticed a small cardboard box beneath Clay's desk. It was only a few inches across, sealed with packing tape, but a corner had ripped open, spilling out part of its contents: John could see a bolt and a small strand of copper wire stuck to the tape on the outside. He crawled under the desk and grabbed it, then ripped the hole wider, not bothering with the tape. He stood and dumped out the rest of it on Clay's desk; it was filled with more wires and parts. John shook the box and it rattled, and he banged on it until the thing that was stuck came out: a square circuit board attached to a tangle of wires. He studied it for a second before putting it aside and dropped the box, then spread the parts across the desk's surface in a single layer, then sat down and peered at them one by one, hoping for something familiar.

It took less than ten seconds to find it: a thin disc about the size of a half-dollar coin. His heart skipped, and he held the thing up, squinting at it until he saw the tiny words engraved along the edge in flowing, old-fashioned script: AFTON ROBOTICS, LLC. He swallowed, remembering the incapacitating nausea the last disc produced in him; he also remembered the more substantial effects the disc was capable of.

John glanced back at Ella, then stood and approached her. He knelt beside her, holding the disc firmly in his hand, with his thumbnail under the switch on its side. John's balance wavered. He set his jaw firmly and flipped the switch.

In an instant, Ella was gone. In her place was a human child, a toddler. She had short, frizzy brown hair and a round face set in a happy smile; her chubby hands gripped the tea tray determinedly. Only her absolute stillness indicated that she was not alive. That, and her vacant eyes, staring sightlessly ahead.

"Can you hear me?" he asked softly. There was no movement; the little girl was no more responsive than Ella. He reached out to touch her cheek, then pulled his hand back suddenly, revolted: her skin was warm and pliable—alive. He stood and went back to the desk, keeping his eyes on the girl. John clawed at the tiny switch again, flipping it back, and the toddler shimmered and blurred for a second, then the image solidified: Ella stood calmly in her place again, nothing more than a large toy doll. John sat down heavily. "Maximum range," he muttered to himself, recalling Clay's brief moment of consciousness at the hospital. But the photographs he'd insisted on giving them hadn't revealed anything. *Or had they?*

He went to Clay's desk and picked up the phone: There was a dial tone; it had not been damaged when the place was ransacked. He dialed his own number. *Please pick up, Jessica,* he thought.

"Hello?"

"Jessica, it's me."

"Who's me?"

"John!"

"Right, sorry. I'm a little jumpy. Charlie's fine—I mean, she's still asleep; she's not worse."

"Good. That's not why I called, though. I need you to meet me at the library—bring the envelope Clay gave us, it's in my backpack."

"All the pictures are gone," Jessica said. "We left them at Jen's house when we fled for our lives, remember?" she added with a hint of sarcasm.

"I know. We don't need the pictures. There was a roll of microfilm in the envelope."

There was a pause on the other end, then, "I'll see you there."

John turned to look at Ella, scratching his thumb thoughtfully across the surface of the disc. "And you; you're coming with me," he said quietly to Ella. He picked her up gingerly, repelled by what he had seen, but she felt just like the doll she seemed to be. She was large enough to be awkward to carry, so he placed her on his hip like a human child, and left through the front door. He stowed the doll in his trunk, put the picture of Charlie and her father in the visor, and pulled out of Clay's driveway.

When John got to the library, Jessica was already in conversation with the librarian, a middle-aged man with an irritated expression.

"If you want to use the microfiche reader, I need you to tell me what you want to look at. Would you like to see the index of our archives?" he asked. It sounded like he had asked the question several times already.

"No, that's all right, I just need to use the machine," Jessica said. The librarian smiled tensely.

"The reader is for looking at microfilm; what microfilm do you want to look at?" he asked very slowly.

"I brought my own," Jessica said breezily.

The librarian sighed. "Do you know how to use the machine?"

"No," she said after a moment's thought.

John stepped forward quickly. "I know how to use it; I'm with her. Can you just let us into the room?"

The librarian nodded wearily, and they followed him to a small back room, where the microfilm reader was set up. "You thread the film through here," he said, "and turn the knobs to advance it." He gave John a suspicious look. "Got it?"

"Yes, thank you for your help. We are very appreciative," John said as he glared at Jessica.

As the door closed behind the librarian, Jessica pulled the film out of her pocket and handed it over. "Okay, what are we looking for?" she asked excitedly, clapping her hands with anxious energy.

"Slow down, okay?" John said wearily. "We almost got killed, we don't even know what's wrong with Charlie, and now you're giddy like we're looking for hidden treasure."

"Sorry." Jessica straightened her posture.

"I think these are the same pictures," John said as he unwound the film and threaded it carefully through the machine. He flipped it on, and the first picture appeared: Jessica and Charlie, picking outfits in a clothing store. He clicked through the next few; they all matched what he remembered of the photos, though the order was different—chronological, he supposed.

"They're the same, and they're not any clearer, either," Jessica said.

"What?" John went back, trying to see what Jessica had noticed that he hadn't.

"They're not any clearer. Charlie is still blurry," Jessica pointed out.

"She's just in motion," John explained.

"In all of them?"

"The picture is clear," he said again, growing agitated. "She's just walking." Despite his words, he stopped and began to go through the pictures more slowly, studying Charlie's appearance in each one. Jessica was right: Charlie was blurry in all of the pictures, even some where she appeared to be standing still. John clicked through the photos fast, confirming it: there was Jessica and Charlie in a clothing store; Marla with them outside Jessica's apartment; Charlie hugging herself as she spoke to John at the Burkes' house that first night—Charlie was blurry in all of them. John flipped ahead quickly to the last set: himself with Charlie—the false Charlie—sitting in the restaurant where they'd had dinner.

The reel ended on the final picture from that night: Charlie nearly lost in the crowd, turning back one last time.

She was barely visible, far more distant here than in any of the other pictures, only recognizable by the color of her dress and hair.

"I still don't see the point," Jessica said impatiently. John grasped the lens and turned it; the picture shrank. "These are the same pictures." She turned away and sighed.

"This is the point," he said, slowly turning it back the other way. The film was high-resolution and the image continued to enlarge as he zoomed closer to Charlie.

"What is?"

John kept zooming in; Jessica gasped, stepping back from the machine. John let go of the lens. "It has a maximum range," he said softly. The figure that filled the screen was elegant and feminine, but it was not human. The face was exquisitely sculpted and was split down the middle, a thin seam outlining where the two halves met. The limbs and body were segmented plates, their color almost iridescent.

"It looks like a mannequin," Jessica gasped.

"Or a clown," John added. "I saw her," he said wonderingly. "The night Clay was attacked, she was on the road. She looked at me . . ." The eyes in the photo were difficult to see, and John leaned closer to the screen, trying to make them out.

"It's the imposter, it's the other Charlie," Jessica breathed. John snapped off the projector, blinking as the haunting figure disappeared. He took the disc from his pocket and handed it to Jessica. She turned it over in her hand, her eyes widening. "Is this hers?"

"No," John said shortly. "But I'm guessing that our mutual friend has one just like it, messing with our heads when we're around her and making us see her as Charlie." He leaned back against the table. "I think Clay took those pictures; I think he suspected something like this but needed to prove it."

"I don't understand."

"These things, these discs, send out signals that overwhelm your brain, causing you to not see what's really in front of you. Now, that wouldn't work on a camera, obviously, but Henry thought of that, too."

"So, the frequency or whatever it emits causes the image to blur," Jessica said, catching on.

"Exactly, but it has a maximum range. The signal fades; that's why he captured these from a distance. He suspected that whatever was causing the illusion must have its limits." John began putting the film back into his bag. "That's why she looks human in the other pictures, at least, human enough when blurred."

Jessica studied the disc again for a moment before John took it back. "I still don't understand," she said. She looked around as though suddenly afraid of being caught.

"I think it's exactly what I suspected," he said. "Except I was completely wrong."

"Oh, that makes perfect sense," Jessica quipped.

"I had all these theories about Charlie," John said. "And even though I may have been wrong about the details, I suspected that Charlie, *our* Charlie, had been swapped out with an imposter. But it wasn't a twin brother, or a twin sister. Afton swapped her out with . . . *this*."

"A robot?" Jessica said skeptically. "Like from Freddy's? John, that was different. People, kids, had been murdered. *Those* robots were haunted. I don't even believe in hauntings, but those things were haunted! Robots like what you're talking about don't exist, at least . . . not yet. Plus, she knew everything Charlie did, how could Afton have programmed that?"

"She didn't know everything, though. She blamed all the gaps in her memory on the near-death experience; her personality changed—everything changed—and we all believed she had just turned over a new leaf," he said bitterly.

"You didn't," Jessica said, and he met her eyes.

"Yeah, but I wanted to. Something just wasn't right."

Jessica was quiet for a moment. "Why did she kill Jen?" she said abruptly.

"What?"

"Why would she kill Jen?" she repeated.

"Charlie's aunt Jen knew her better than anyone," John said. "She must have known she couldn't fool her."

"Yeah, maybe." Jessica bit her lip, then her face took on a look of alarm. "Or she went there—"

"To find Charlie," John cut in.

"John, we left her alone; we have to go back."

John was already out the door, running headlong across the library to the exit. Jessica ran after him. They both got into John's car and he hit the gas, clenching his jaw as they sped toward his apartment.

CHAPTER SEVEN

Have you forgotten something?" the man snapped, and the woman gave him a level stare.

"I forget nothing."

"Then why are you not already on your way?" He lifted his arm weakly and gestured toward the door.

"Time is running short," she said. "I do not understand why we are spending our time—*your* time—pursuing this thing. I am better used here."

The man was silent.

"We are seeing results," she added, but he shook his head.

"We are seeing nothing." He held up a finger before she could protest. "Anyone can discover a fire already burning, but Henry found a unique spark—created something truly different, something he didn't deserve, or intend, to stumble upon." He gave the woman a sharp look. "You will bring it to me." The woman cast her eyes to the floor, and when she spoke there was something pleading in her voice.

"Am I not enough?" she asked softly.

"No, you're not," he said firmly, looking away.

The woman paused, then walked out the door, not looking back.

Neither of them spoke as they sped toward John's apartment. He gripped the wheel until his knuckles turned white, trying not to imagine what they might find.

When he turned into the lot, he let out a shaky breath: the few cars belonged to his neighbors, and his door was intact. He gave Jessica a curt nod, and they got out of the car. Jessica followed close behind and stood beside him, facing the parking lot, as he unlocked the door. Jessica jabbed him in the side hard with her elbow just as he was about to turn the key, and he jerked it back from the lock. "OW! What the . . . ?" He whirled around angrily to Jessica, then immediately straightened his posture and threw on a big smile.

"Charlie!" he blurted. The elegant woman approached them, and John reflexively took a step back. "Where did you come from? I mean, we didn't see your car. What a nice surprise," he added hastily. The woman who was not Charlie smiled easily.

"I've been out walking, I wanted to clear my head. I realized I was near you and thought I'd stop by. Is that okay?"

John nodded, stalling for time. "Of course! It's great to see you!" John blurted, painfully aware that he was overselling. "My place is a mess, though. Bachelor pad, you know?" He forced a grin. "Do you and Jessica mind waiting out here while I clean up a little?"

Charlie laughed. "John, you saw my dorm room last year—I can handle a little mess!"

"Well, unlike you last year, I'm not working on a crazy brilliant science project, so I have no excuse," he said.

Jessica jumped in. "How about that project, Charlie? Did you keep working on it? How's it looking?"

Charlie turned to Jessica as if seeing her for the first time. "I lost interest," she said. John seized his chance: he unlocked the door, slipped inside, and locked it behind him before the imposter could follow. In his bedroom, Charlie, *his* Charlie was still curled up on his bed, her back pressed against the wall; she didn't look like she'd moved since he left.

"Charlie," he whispered. "I'm sorry, but I have to move you, now. I'll be careful." He scooped her up with care. She was warm in his arms, and her eyes twitched beneath her lids: she was dreaming. John held on tightly, looking around the room for a place to hide her—his failure to furnish the place beyond the essentials was working against him. John carried Charlie out into the living room: the couch was at an angle to the wall, leaving a tiny, triangular space behind it. John set Charlie on the couch temporarily, took a blanket that had been in a heap on the floor, and tossed it down into the space, giving her at least a little cushion. Then he climbed over, picked her up, and lifted her over the back, settling her on the floor. He barely fit, even standing, and he kept his eyes behind him as he climbed back over the couch, afraid of kicking her. There was another gray blanket draped over the end of the couch, something left by a previous tenant, and he grabbed it and spread it over Charlie, covering her face.

Someone knocked on the door. "John?" Jessica called. "Are you almost done *cleaning*?" There was an edge of panic in her voice. John looked around. There was no evidence of a mess, or him having just hurriedly cleaned one. He rushed to the bedroom and grabbed some laundry from his laundry basket, then carried it with him to answer the door.

"Sorry," he said, aiming for a sheepish expression. "I don't get a lot of guests." Jessica smiled nervously and the other Charlie flashed a grin as she pushed in past him.

"Looks pretty nice," she said, turning to him. "How's the neighborhood?"

". . . Fine," John managed, disconcerted to be face-to-face with her, moments after the real Charlie. This time he could see the differences—he could have written a list. The impression that this woman, with her glamorous allure, was simply Charlie, grown into her beauty with grace and new self-assurance, was gone. Now, the individual features stuck out on her face like warts—each one a marker that this was not *Charlie*. Nose too narrow, cheeks too hollow. Eyes too far apart. Hairline too high. Eyebrows at the wrong angle. The disparities were minute, millimeters or less: the only way to be sure would be to look at Charlie and her robotic double side by side. Or one right after the other. The imposter Charlie gave him a subtle smile and shifted her balance, as though about to come closer. John cleared his throat, hunting for something to say, but Charlie had already looked away and was now glancing around the living room. Behind her, Jessica was giving him a questioning look, probably wondering where the real Charlie was. John ignored her: Not-Charlie strode past him into his bedroom, and he followed quickly.

"Right!" John bolted into action. "So, this is my bedroom," he said, as if the tour had been his own idea.

"Nice," Charlie murmured, surveying the room. She turned in a circle, taking it all in, then went to the dresser, and turned to inspect the room again from there.

"So, hey, we should all go hang out later or something!" Jessica said suddenly, but Charlie didn't answer. Instead, she knelt slowly and peered under the bed. Jessica and John exchanged a nervous glance.

"Not much to see. It's just me here." John laughed. Jessica elbowed him and made a disapproving expression. *I'm being too obvious again*, he realized. John could feel his pulse in his throat, immediately regretting what he'd said. *Please don't look around.* Charlie went into the bathroom and glanced around it, opening the medicine cabinet and examining the contents. Jessica gave John a perplexed look, then it occurred to her. *She's looking for signs that someone's been injured.* Charlie began to close the cabinet, then caught sight of her own reflection and paused, her hand still on the cabinet door, looking at herself. She was still for a long moment, then her eyes darted to John in the mirror, and she made a face.

"I hate mirrors," she remarked, then turned away and pulled back his shower curtain.

"I know right? They add ten pounds," John said mildly.

"I think that's cameras," Jessica corrected.

"Well, mirrors add at least five," John whispered.

"Maybe you just need to lose weight."

"Are we really having this conversation now?"

They continued to watch Charlie. "She's searching," Jessica whispered. "She's not even trying to hide it."

John worried. Charlie paused and opened the bedroom closet, then crouched down to look in the open space under his hanging shirts and jackets. She stood and went back into the living room: Jessica followed, sprinting to get ahead of her and sitting on the couch quickly, crossing her legs. Charlie went to the kitchenette and opened the refrigerator, then closed it.

"Are you hungry?" Jessica asked. "I'm sure John has something you can eat."

"No, thank you. How have you been, Jessica?" Charlie asked, crossing the room to the couch. John's whole body went rigid as he willed himself not to run across the room and yank her away. Instead, he opened the fridge himself, forcing himself to breathe as, from the corner of his eye, he watched her sit down beside Jessica.

"Anybody want a water? Or a soda?" he called.

"Yes, please," Jessica said with a strain in her voice, coughing loudly. John grabbed two cans and brought them over. Jessica took hers eagerly. "Thank you," she said with too much emphasis, and he nodded.

"Yeah, of course." He smiled stiffly at Charlie, and she looked back: every moment she was there, he felt more and more like his skin was about to crawl off his bones. He would have thought it was a side effect of her chip, except it had not happened until he knew what she was.

"Sit down, John." Charlie smiled, gesturing to the arm of the couch beside her.

"Sorry I don't have chairs and stuff. I never meant to live here long-term," John explained nervously.

"How long have you been here?" Charlie's familiar voice was like tin.

John sat down beside her. "Since—everything. This is where I lived when I first came here."

"Oh." She glanced around the room again. "I guess I don't remember it."

"You never saw it," he said, unable to keep the coldness from his voice. Jessica shot him a warning glance, and he took a deep breath. Charlie began scanning the room again. She stared straight ahead, her face taking on a look of concentration. Her eyes swept up and down the room in strokes, her head and torso slowly turning until she was looking almost directly behind her: in a second, she would see the gap behind the couch. "Charlie, I had fun the other night," John said quickly, forcing himself to mean it. "Do you want to have dinner again tonight?"

She turned back around, looking surprised. "Yes, of course—that sounds great, John. Same place?"

"Same place. Around seven?"

"Sure."

"Great!" Jessica declared, and stood. "Anyway, I have to go," she said. "Want to walk out with me, Charlie?" She glanced nervously at John, and he got up quickly.

"I can give you a ride if you need one," he volunteered, "I know you said you were walking."

Thank you, Jessica mouthed from behind her back.

"No," Charlie said. "I think I'll keep walking. I'm not parked too far away. It's really nice outside."

"Okay, then," John said. Charlie moved gracefully across the living room and let herself out. Jessica let out a long breath like she'd been holding it. They went to the window and, silently, they watched the imposter go, until she had disappeared around a bend in the road.

"What if she comes back?" Jessica said. "I don't want you alone with that *thing*," she finished, practically spitting the last word. John nodded in vigorous agreement.

"I don't want to be alone with her, either," he said.

Jessica looked thoughtful for a moment. "I won't be gone long," she said. "We need help. And if you don't think Charlie should go to the hospital, then the hospital has to come to her."

"Marla?"

"Marla." And with that, she went to the door quickly. John walked out with her, and watched uneasily as Jessica got in her car and drove off. Then he went back inside and shut the door, locking and bolting it. *A lot of good this will do*, he thought as he slipped the chain into place.

"Charlie?" he called softly. He didn't expect an answer, but he wanted—felt almost compelled—to talk to her. "Charlie, I wish you could hear me," he went on, going to the bedroom closet and pulling out all two of his other blankets. "I think it's safer for you to stay where you are than in the bedroom." He pulled the couch a little farther from the wall, trying to figure out how best to make her more comfortable. At a loss, he grabbed a pillow and leaned down, reaching to remove the blanket that covered her face.

"Sorry I've only got the one pillow," he said, trying not to lose his balance.

"'S okay," came a muffled murmur from beneath the blanket, and John fell back, tumbling over the seat and barely catching himself before his head hit the floor.

"Charlie?" he cried, then lowered his voice as he climbed back up. "Charlie, are you awake?" There was no answer. This time he did not try to climb into the space behind the couch, and bent over to see. She was stirring, just a little. "Charlie, it's me, John," he said, his voice hushed, but urgent. "If you can hear me, hold on to the sound of my voice." He stopped, as she sat up and pulled the blanket off her face.

He stared down at her, as astonished as the moment when he first saw her. Her face was red, and her hair was sticking to her skin after being under the blanket; her eyes were barely open; she blinked rapidly in the light, looking down and away. John leaped up and rushed to shutter the front window blinds. He closed the bedroom door and pulled the kitchen curtains. The apartment, never bright at its best, was nearly dark. He hurried back to Charlie's hiding place, grabbed one end of the couch, and pulled it out farther, enough for him to crawl behind with her. She was still sitting, leaning against the wall, but she looked limp, like she wouldn't be able to do it much longer. He reached out to steady her, but when his hand touched her arm she made a distressed, high-pitched noise, and he drew back instantly.

"Sorry. It's me, John," he repeated, and she turned her head to see him.

"John," she said, her voice thin and rasping. "I know." Her breathing was ragged, and talking seemed to take effort. She reached out feebly with one hand.

"What do you need?" he asked, searching her face. She reached out farther and then he understood; he took her hand.

"I won't ever let go of you again," he whispered. She smiled faintly.

"Could get awkward," she whispered. She opened her mouth as if to go on, then sighed, shuddering. John scooted closer, alarmed.

"What's—" She took another breath. "Wrong with me?" she finished in a rush. She opened her eyes, looking at him plaintively.

"How do you feel?" he asked, avoiding the question.

"Tired . . . everything hurts," she said haltingly, her eyes drifting shut, and he clenched his jaw, trying to keep his face neutral.

"I'm trying to help you," he said finally. "Look, you have to know—there's someone, something, out here impersonating you; saying that she is you." Her eyes snapped open and she squeezed his hand suddenly: she was alert. "She looks just like you. I don't know why, I don't know what she's after, but I'm going to find out. And I'm going to help you."

"Afton," she breathed, her voice barely audible, and John quickly reached over the couch to grab the pillow he'd brought.

"Can you lift your head?" he asked, and she did, slightly, letting him slide the pillow into place. "We know it's Afton," he said, picking up her hand when she was settled again; she squeezed it lightly. "I have one of the chips. Afton Robotics. Charlie, I've got this. Clay's helping, and Jessica, and we're getting Marla to help you get better. It's going to be okay. Okay?"

But Charlie had drifted back into unconsciousness; he had no idea how much she had heard, or understood. Her hand had gone limp in his own.

Someone that looks like me . . . Never let go . . . John? Charlie struggled to order her thoughts: things that had made sense a moment ago were losing their shape, drifting out of reach in a dozen directions like petals on the water. *The door . . .*

"It's going to be okay," John said, but she didn't know if he said it in her head or in the world. She felt herself slipping back into the dark; she tried to hold on, but the exhaustion was weightier than she was, pulling her inexorably down with it.

★　★　★

Charlie glanced at the door again. *He's late, or I'm early.* She picked up the fork in front of her and ran her thumb over the smooth metal; the tines hit her water glass with a clear *ding!* and she smiled at the sound. She hit the glass again. *How much does he know?*

Charlie struck the glass again, and this time she noticed several other patrons turning to look at her in confusion. She smiled politely, then set her fork down on the table and folded her hands in her lap. Charlie took in a breath and composed herself.

As John approached the restaurant he could see that *Not-Charlie* was already there. She had changed her clothes. He hadn't really registered what she had been wearing before, but now she had on a tight, short red dress—he would have remembered that. He stopped on the sidewalk, just out of her sight, steeling himself. He couldn't get the other image out of his mind, the painted face with the soldering line splitting it down the middle. Charlie was sitting back in her chair; there was nothing in front of her but a water glass. She had ordered food when they last met here, but John couldn't picture her actually eating it. He couldn't remember noticing her *not* eating, either.

"Stop stalling!" came a crackling voice from his waist, and he jumped. He extricated the walkie-talkie from his jacket pocket and turned away from the restaurant before speaking into it, just in case Not-Charlie looked out.

"I'm not stalling," he said.

"You shouldn't be able to hear us," Jessica's distorted voice reminded him. "Did you tape the button down?"

"Right, hang on." John examined the walkie-talkie: The tape he had placed over the button to transmit had come loose. He replaced it, flattening it down against the uneven surface with his fingernail. He slipped the device back in his pocket and went inside.

John glanced briefly around the restaurant as he entered. Jessica and Carlton were huddled together in a high-backed booth, out of Charlie's sight. "Can you both still hear me?" John whispered. Carlton's hand raised above the back of the booth momentarily with a triumphant thumbs-up, bringing a real smile to John's face. John turned his attention back to Charlie, who had not yet noticed him.

She lifted her head abruptly from the menu as he approached the table, as if sensing his presence. She flashed him a bright smile.

"Sorry I'm late," John said as he sat down.

"That's usually my line," Charlie joked, and he grinned uneasily.

"I guess so." He looked at her for a moment: he had rehearsed things to say, but his mind had gone blank.

"So, I heard you and Jessica visited that old ghost town." Charlie giggled. "What's that place called again?" She leaned in and rested her chin on her hand again.

"Ghost town?" John said unevenly, trying to keep his expression neutral. It took everything he had not to turn and look at Jessica and Carlton behind him. Charlie was looking at him expectantly, and he took a sip of water. "You mean Silver Reef?" he said, setting down the glass carefully.

"Yes, I mean Silver Reef." She was smiling, but her face looked tight, like there was something ravenous waiting just below the surface. "That's a strange place to go, John." She cocked her head slightly. "Just out seeing the sights?"

"I've always been a . . . history buff. The, the gold rush—"

"Silver," Charlie corrected.

"Silver. Yes. That too. Just fascinating times in history." John was tempted to turn and see if Jessica approved of his reply or if she was scrambling out of her seat to flee the restaurant. "You didn't know that about me, did you?" He straightened his posture. "I love history: historic towns, places." He cleared his throat.

Charlie picked up her water glass and drank; she set it down so he could see the red lipstick mark she left. John drew back slightly and looked elsewhere, searching for anything he could lock eyes with but her. "Why were you there?" Charlie asked, recalling his attention.

"I was—" he started, then paused, taking a moment to gather his thoughts. "I was looking for an old friend," he said, his answer calm. She nodded, then met his eyes. He blinked, but forced himself not to look away. He had seen eyes like those before: not the madness of Springtrap, or the uncanny, living plastic of the other robots, but the stark, brutal gaze of a creature bent on survival. Charlie was looking at him like he was prey.

"Did you find your old friend?" she asked, her tone warm, and out of place.

"Yes. I did," John said, not flinching from her stare. Charlie's eyes narrowed, the facade between them growing thinner by the moment. John leaned forward on his crossed arms, resting all his weight on the table between them. "I found her," he said in a low voice. There was a brief flare of something on Charlie's face—surprise, maybe, and she leaned in closer across the table, mimicking his pose. John tried not to flinch as Charlie's arms slid closer to his.

"Where is she?" Charlie asked, her tone as soft as John's. Her smile was gone.

"I don't know what it will take to show these people what you really are," John said. "But I can try all sorts of things before you make it out that door." He grasped his soda glass, not looking away from her. "I'll start with this glass of soda, then I'll try a chair over the back of your head, and we'll go from there."

Charlie tilted her head, as though taking in his posture. He knew his hand was twitching, and his face was red. His heart was racing; he could feel his pulse pounding at his throat. Charlie smiled, then stood and gently leaned over the table. John set his jaw, keeping his eyes fixed on her. Charlie kissed his cheek, placing a hand on the side of his neck. She kept it there as she moved away, watching his eyes. Charlie smiled, her fingers resting on his pulse for a scant moment before letting them drift away. John snapped back in his seat as if she'd been holding him in place.

"Thank you for dinner, John," she said, the words sounding almost giddy. She slowly let her hand recoil, as if relishing the moment. "It's always so wonderful to see you." She turned away, not waiting for a response, and went to pay the bill.

There was a long pause. "She's gone." John's voice came over the walkie-talkie. Jessica looked to Carlton; he seemed slightly in shock, staring after Charlie like he'd been hypnotized. "Carlton!" Jessica hissed. He snapped out of it, shaking his head.

"She looks hot!" Carlton said.

Jessica reared back and slapped Carlton as hard as she could.

"You idiot! You're supposed to be watching his back, not watching *her* butt! Besides, she put your father in the hospital!"

"No, no, I know. Very serious . . ." He trailed off, obviously distracted.

"Why did I even bring you along?" Jessica scooted out of the booth and got to her feet clumsily.

"Where are you going?" Carlton asked.

"I have an idea; stay here." Jessica sighed. "You take my car."

Carlton called after, but she didn't stop to answer, merely threw her car keys behind her. Carlton made his way over to John's booth.

"Hey. Are you okay?" John didn't turn at the sound of Carlton's voice beside him.

"No. Not really okay." John leaned back in his seat, looking up at the plaster ceiling, then finally turned to look at Carlton. "Where's Jessica?" John asked instantly.

"I'm not sure, she ran out . . ." Carlton gestured toward the parking lot, and John turned just in time to see Charlie pull out onto the road and drive away.

"She did something stupid, didn't she?" John said wearily. Carlton met his eyes, then they both ran for the door.

Jessica kept low and snuck to the back exit of the restaurant; she could see Charlie was still standing at the front desk taking care of the bill. Jessica slipped out the back door and ran around the perimeter of the building, her high heels clacking on the sidewalk. She yanked them off and threw them into the bushes, then kept running, barefoot.

"Jessica, what are you doing?" she muttered to herself. As she rounded the corner of the building into the parking lot, she spotted Charlie's car and made a beeline for it. The front door was unlocked. Jessica quickly popped the trunk, shut the door, and slipped inside, not closing the trunk lid all the way.

A minute later there was noise from inside the vehicle, and Jessica strained to listen: it sounded like voices. No, *a* voice, she realized after a few minutes. Charlie was talking, but there was no one answering her. Jessica concentrated, trying to isolate the sounds, but she could make out nothing: whatever Charlie was saying, it was unintelligible from the trunk. Jessica balanced herself carefully, trying to lay as flat as she could while bracing her arm in the air to hold the latch of the trunk. If she didn't hold it tight enough, it would visibly bounce and Charlie would notice it. But if she pulled it too close, the trunk might shut, and she would be trapped.

After about ten minutes, the car stopped short; Jessica was thrown back against the wall, almost losing hold of the latch. Regaining her balance, she held very still, listening. The driver's side door opened; then closed a moment later. Jessica heard the faint sound of Charlie walking away, crunching over gravel, then silence. Jessica sighed in relief, but did not move. She began to count: "One Mississippi . . . two

Mississippi . . ." she breathed, barely a whisper. There was no sound but her own hushed voice as she counted all the way to sixty, then stopped and scooted closer to the trunk door. She gently eased her grip of the trunk handle, letting the hood rise slowly.

The car was parked in the center of a large parking lot, illuminated impossibly bright by streetlamps. The light was tinged with red, and Jessica turned to see a large neon sign directly overhead, flooding the lot with brilliant reds and pinks and blocking her view of anything beyond. The air buzzed loudly with the noise of what must have been a hundred fluorescent bulbs. Jessica squinted and raised a hand to shade her eyes: the enormous, smiling face of a little girl stared down at her, glowing neon against the night sky. She was made up to look like a clown: her face was painted white, and her cheeks were marked with round, pink circles, her nose a matching triangle. Her bright orange hair was tied up in two pigtails on either side of her head, and beside her were fat, red letters outlined in yellow. Jessica peered at the backward sign for a moment before the letters made sense: CIRCUS BABY'S PIZZA. The glare of the light began to hurt her eyes, and she looked away, then ran toward the dark building at the edge of the lot, blinking to get the afterimage of the neon sign out of her head. She stumbled through a row of hedges to press into a white brick wall, which seemed brand-new. She lowered her hand from her face, her eyes adjusted to the light, and she saw a long row of tall, vertical windows along the face of the wall.

She went to the nearest one and pressed her face to the glass, but the tint was too dark to see even a shadow of what lay behind it. Jessica gave up on the windows and walked quickly to the back of the building, keeping close to the brick wall. The neon whites and reds faded as Jessica made her way around back, sinking into darkness.

There was more parking in the back, though it, too, was unoccupied. A single bulb flickered above a plain metal door, throwing off a sickly yellow color, which seemed to stick to everything. Trash cans lined the wall, and two Dumpsters enclosed the small area, shielding the door from outside view. Jessica crept toward the door, careful not to step on anything. She gave it a gentle pull, but it was sealed shut. She balanced against the frame as she pushed herself up onto her toes, and grinned. She could see inside.

Inside was a dimly lit room. Charlie was there: she was in profile, talking to someone just beyond Jessica's view, though she could not hear either voice. Jessica inched along the ridge, trying to see the other person, but all she could make out was the blur of movement as someone gestured. After a few minutes, her calves began to ache, and she eased herself back down off her toes and flexed her feet. She sighed and pushed herself up on her toes again, then pressed her face closer, cupping a hand over her eyes to block the outside light.

It was no use—the room was empty, or at least, the light had gone off. Jessica stepped back and reluctantly turned to find another place to peer inside—then screamed, slapping a hand over her mouth though she was too late to stifle the sound.

Charlie smiled. "Jessica," she said innocently, "you should have told me you were coming here, you could have ridden with me."

"Right, well, I ran outside to catch you, but you'd already left." Jessica stepped back, her heart racing. Every fiber of her being was telling her to run, but she knew she would never make it past the imposter who stood before her.

"Do you want to come in?" Charlie asked, still speaking like they were friends.

"Yeah, I'd love to; I just couldn't find the door." Jessica gestured back toward the parking lot. Charlie nodded.

"It's on the other side," she said, taking a step closer. Jessica stepped back again.

"What brings *you* here, anyway?" Jessica asked, trying to sound calm. *Does she not know that I know? Will she let me leave if I play along?*

"I can show you," Charlie said. Jessica kept her face blank; her muscles were so tense they were beginning to fatigue, and she breathed in deeply, trying to relax. But Jessica was suddenly aware that Charlie was steering her closer to a wall where she would be pinned.

"It's late, though; I should get going," Jessica said, making herself smile.

"It's not late," Charlie protested, gazing at the sky. Jessica hesitated, grasping for an excuse, and Charlie's eyes darted back to Jessica as she took another step forward. She was close enough for Jessica to feel her breath on her skin, but Charlie was not breathing.

Charlie smiled broadly, and Jessica drew back, her head pressing painfully into the brick wall. Charlie's smile grew wider and wider, elongating impossibly, then suddenly her lips were split at the middle as a wide seam appeared, bisecting her face from top to bottom. Jessica shrank back, curling in on herself instinctually, and as she did Charlie seemed to grow taller, her limbs segmenting at the joints like a moveable doll. Her features slowly paled and faded away, replaced by the iridescent, clown-painted metal face they had just been able to make out in Clay's pictures.

"Do you like my new look?" Charlie asked, her voice still soft and human. Jessica inhaled shudderingly, afraid to speak. The creature Charlie had become looked at her searchingly. For an instant, an acrid, chemical scent filled the air, then Charlie moved swiftly toward Jessica, and the world went dark.

CHAPTER EIGHT

can't see.

Jessica closed her eyes and opened them again, but the darkness remained. She tried again, realizing with a rising panic that she could not move. The air stank of something rotten, turning her stomach, and she forced herself to breathe deeply. *I'll stop noticing it if I breathe.* She tried again to move, testing to see what was restraining her. She was confined in a sitting position: Her wrists were tied together behind her, her arms pulled uncomfortably around the back of a wooden chair and her ankles bound to its legs. She pulled against the restraints, almost tipping the chair over as she struggled to free herself, but she could not break away. Then there was light.

Jessica stopped moving. She blinked in the sudden brightness, her vision resolving. Charlie's imposter stood in the light of the window, revealed in her true form: She was undeniably an animatronic, but she was nothing like any other Jessica had ever seen. She was human-size—the same size as Charlie—modeled on a human woman, of sorts, her bifurcated face painted with rosy cheeks and a bright red nose, and her enormous, round eyes were rimmed with long, black lashes. She even had hair, two silky orange pigtails sprouting from the sides of her head, gleaming unnaturally in the light—Jessica couldn't tell what her hair was made of. She was wearing a red-and-white costume—or rather the metal segments of her body were painted to look like a costume; at her waist, a red skirt stuck out playfully. She was standing very still, and she was staring straight at Jessica. Jessica froze, afraid to breathe, but the creature just tilted her metal head to the side, watching. Her animatronic face looked familiar, but she still felt fuzzy and couldn't recall where she'd seen it.

"I don't suppose you'd give me a hand with these?" Jessica lifted her feet the quarter inch the restraints would allow. The animatronic smiled.

"No, I don't suppose I would," she said, her voice alarmingly unchanged. Jessica shrank back, revolted at the sound of her friend's voice coming from this singular new creature.

"Who are you?" Jessica asked.

"I'm Charlie."

Jessica looked around the dimly lit room helplessly. Apart from the chair, the only object she could see was a gigantic, old-fashioned coal-burning furnace, with a warm orange glow emanating from the thin vents in its door.

"At least," the creature began, "part of me is Charlie." She held her hand out in front of her, studying it. Jessica looked up and suddenly it was Charlie standing in the light of the window, looking confused and innocent. "It's strange," the animatronic said. "I have these memories. I know they don't belong to me; and yet at the same time, they do." She paused, and Jessica returned to wrestling with the knots. "I know that they don't belong to me because I don't *feel* anything when they come to mind. They are just there, like a long road you walk on, lined with billboards of things happening somewhere else."

"Well, what *do* you feel?" Jessica muttered, trying to drag out the conversation as her survival instincts kicked in.

The animatronic girl's eyes darted toward her. "I feel . . . disappointment," she said, her voice growing more tense. "Desperation." She looked out the window. "A father's disappointment, and a daughter's desperation," she whispered.

"Henry?" Jessica gasped. The girl looked back at her.

"No. Not Henry. He was more brilliant than Henry. I watched my father work from a distance, a great, great, distance." Her voice trailed off. Jessica waited for her to go on, half forgetting that she was trying to escape. "I see everything clearly now," the animatronic continued. "But in my memories . . . things were much simpler, which made it so much more painful. Now I know that people are all fading, fragile, inconsequential. But when you are a child, your parents are everything: They are your world, and you don't know anything else. When you are a little girl, your father is your world. How tragic and miserable such an existence is." Jessica felt a wave of dizziness and looked up to see that the animatronic now appeared as the clown again, but the image passed. Suddenly, it was Charlie in the light, but the moment's disruption in the illusion was enough to remind Jessica of where she was—and that she had to get away.

The animatronic girl stood beside the only window in the room. There was a door nearby; she was closer to it than the animatronic, not that she could count on outrunning her. *What else am I going to try?* Tentatively, keeping her eyes fixed on her captor, Jessica started working her wrists back and forth, trying to loosen the rope that held her. The girl watched, but did not move to stop her, so Jessica kept going.

"That's the flaw, and the greatest sin of humanity," the girl said. "You are born with none of your intelligence, but all of your heart, fully capable of feeling pain, and torment, but with no power to understand. It opens you up to abuse, to neglect, to unimaginable pain. All you can do is *feel*." She studied her hands again. "All you can do is feel, but never understand. What a sick power it is that you are given."

The ropes only seemed to tighten as Jessica pulled at them, and Jessica felt tears of frustration pricking at her eyes. *No wonder she doesn't care if I try to escape,* she thought bitterly. *If I could just see the knots . . .* She stopped moving and took a deep breath, then closed her eyes. *Find the knot. Ignore the robot.* Jessica fumbled with her right hand, searching for the end of the knot, bending her wrist painfully. At last, she found the end of the rope and grasped it: the rope tightened, but she inched her fingers along until she came to the base of the knot, then began to carefully push the end of the rope up through the final loop.

"I wanted so desperately to have been the one on that stage, but it was always her. All of his love went into her."

"You're talking about Afton." Jessica stopped, and Charlie nodded confirmation. "William Afton never made anything with love," Jessica snarled.

"I should rip you in half." Charlie's appearance flashed, the animatronic's face and body seeming to break, then reassemble in an instant. For a moment her expression wavered, a vulnerability showing on her face, but she quickly collected herself. "She was his obsession."

The animatronic twisted her hair around her fingers. "He worked on her day and night, the clown baby with bright orange pigtails. Petite enough to be sweet and approachable, but large enough to swallow you whole." She laughed.

Jessica pulled the rope a last time: She had managed to undo the first knot. Breathing heavily with the effort, Jessica opened her eyes: The animatronic had not moved from the window—she seemed still to be watching with a kind of amused interest. Jessica gritted her teeth and closed her eyes, and started on the next knot.

"I wanted to be her," the girl whispered. "The focus of his attention, the center of his world."

"You're delusional." Jessica snickered as she struggled with the rope, trying to keep her distracted. "You're a robot; you're not his child."

The animatronic pulled a chair away from the wall, and sat with a pained expression. "One night I snuck out of bed to see her. I'd been told not to a hundred times. I pulled the sheet away. She was gleaming bright, beautiful, standing over me. She had happy red cheeks and a lovely red dress."

Jessica paused in her work, confused. *Who is she talking about?*

"It's odd, because I remember looking down at the little girl as well. It's strange seeing through both sets of eyes now. But as I said, one is no more than a data tape, a record of my first capture, my first kill." The animatronic's eyes flared bright in the darkness. "The little girl approached me and pulled the sheet away. I felt nothing; it's no more than a record of what happened. But there *is* feeling, my feeling as

I pulled the sheet away, and stood in awe before this creature my father loved, this daughter he had made for himself. The daughter who was better than me, the daughter he wished I had been. I wanted to be her, so badly." Charlie's appearance faded, revealing the painted clown, and Jessica sighed as a wave of nausea and dizziness passed over her again. "So, I did what I was built to do," the girl said, and stopped talking. The room was silent.

When the last knot slipped loose and the rope fell to the floor, Jessica's eyes popped open in surprise. She leaned forward, moving her numb, tingling arms down to her ankles as she watched the girl, who simply continued to observe her. Jessica undid the knots that held her ankles quickly—they were looser, done carelessly, and she put her feet flat on the floor, her stomach fluttering. *Time to run.*

Jessica ran for the door, propelling her wobbly knees and sore ankles through sheer force of will. There was no sound from behind her. *She's going to be right behind me!* she thought wildly as she reached the door and turned the knob. She yanked it open with overflowing relief—and screamed.

Close enough to touch was a mottled face, swollen and misshapen. The skin looked too thin, and the bloodshot eyes, staring angrily at her, quivered as if they were about to burst. Jessica jerked away, stumbling back into the room. Her eyes darted to his neck, where two rusting lengths of metal protruded from his skin. He stank of mold: the furry suit he wore was covered in it, turning the cloth green, though as Jessica took in the whole of him, she knew it had once been yellow.

"Springtrap," she breathed, her voice shaky, and his lips twitched into something that might have been a smile. Jessica ran to the chair she'd been tied to, putting it between them as if it would do any good, then horribly, Springtrap began to laugh. Jessica tensed, grasping the chair's wooden back, ready to defend herself, but Springtrap just kept laughing, not moving from the spot where he stood. He cackled on and on, rising to an impossible pitch, then he broke off abruptly, his eyes snapping to Jessica. He shuffled closer, then, inexplicably, he began to caper in a grotesque dance as he sang in a thin, unsteady voice.

Oh, Jessica's been caught
Oh, Jessica she fought
But now she's going to die!
Oh my!

Jessica glanced at the animatronic girl in the corner, who looked away as though disgusted. Springtrap danced closer, circling Jessica as he repeated the verse, and she hefted the chair between them, watching for a chance to strike. Jessica tripped over her own feet trying to get out of his way. *Even for him, this is insane.* He danced closer and away, the words he sang degenerating into syllables of nonsense, interrupted by maniacal laughter. Jessica held the chair steady, ready to swing it. Suddenly, Springtrap froze in place.

Jessica's arms wavered, and she set the chair down with a thud. Springtrap didn't move, even his face was completely motionless. *Like someone turned him off.* She had barely finished the thought when his whole body went limp, collapsing on the floor with a clatter. He flickered, then Springtrap faded away, leaving in his place a blank, segmented doll. Jessica whirled to look at the animatronic girl: she was still watching without expression.

"Enough theatrics." A rasping male voice came from the open door. "Jessica, isn't it?" The voiced wheezed. She squinted, unable to make out anything in the dim light.

"I know that voice," she said slowly. There was a whirring sound coming from the doorway, and soon Jessica could see something roll into the room, an automated wheelchair of some sort. He was dressed in what looked like white silk pajamas and a black robe of the same cloth, covering him from chin to toe, black leather slippers on his feet. Behind him, three IV bags hung from a wheeled stand, the tubes extending up under the sleeve of his pajama shirt. His head was bald, covered in ridged pink scars. Where there were no scars, there were strange pallets of plastic, molding, and metal, pressed into his head as though fused to it. He turned his head slightly and Jessica saw that while one eye was perfectly normal, the other was simply missing: the gaping socket was dark, and shot through with a thin steel rod that glinted in the light. He was painfully thin, the bones of his face visible, and as he gave Jessica a small, twisted smile, she saw tendons move like snakes beneath the surface of his skin. She had to fight to keep from retching.

"Do you know who I am?" he asked.

You're William Afton, Jessica thought, but she shook her head, and he sighed, a rattling sound.

"Come here," he said.

"I'll stay where I am," she said tightly.

"As you like." He shifted his weight carefully, the wheel-chair letting out a whir as it moved forward slowly. The animatronic girl started toward him and he waved her off, but the gesture threw off his balance, and for a moment he appeared as though he might fall to the side, but he gripped the arm of the chair with a pained expression, righting himself.

"So what was the dance routine for?" Jessica asked loudly, and he looked at her as though surprised she was still there. Then, he raised his hands to the knot on his robe, his fingers struggling clumsily to undo it.

"I thought you might like to see me as I was. A familiar face," he said, and smirked. He held up a small disc in his hand and clicked it on. The blank doll on the floor suddenly looked as it had a moment ago, with the bloodied, duplicate William Afton stuffed inside the rabbit suit.

"Time changes all things," he went on, clicking the disc off again. "As does pain. When I called myself Springtrap I was ecstatic with power, delirious over my newfound strength. But pain changes all things, as does time." He opened his robe to reveal his torso.

At the center of his chest was a mass of twisted flesh, crossed with neat, diagonal lines of black stitching thread; rippling out from the wound were the marks of the spring-lock suit, some scarred over years before, and some scarcely healed, the skin a shiny, angry red. He raised a hand to the wad of stitches, careful not to touch it. "Your friend inflicted this new wound," he said mildly, then bent his head slightly forward, calling her attention to his neck. She took an involuntary step closer, and gasped.

His skin was gone, she thought at first, the innards of his neck laid open to the air. *But the blood . . . he'd be dead.* Jessica took a long, slow breath, feeling light-headed as she tried to make sense of what she saw. The wound had been covered with something else, plastic, maybe: she could see where the surrounding skin had fused to it, healing red and ugly. Through the clear material, whatever it was, she could see his throat—she didn't know enough about anatomy to name the parts, but they were red and blue, blocks of muscle and strings of veins or tendons. Wedged in among them were things that never belonged inside a human body; small scraps of metal, embedded in the tissue. There were too many to count. The man moved, and they glinted in the light. Jessica gasped, and he wheezed, clearly struggling to breathe with his neck turned the way it was. Something caught her eye as he moved, and she leaned in closer: she was almost touching him now, and the smell was awful: a noxious perfume of disinfectant. She peered through the clear shield and saw it: a spring, its coils wrapped tightly around what looked like three veins, the sharp ends plunged deep into red muscle tissue.

Jessica stepped back and almost tripped on the fallen mannequin that had been Springtrap. She kicked away the jumble of limbs, recovering her balance, and looked into the man's mutilated face again.

"Yeah, I know you. Didn't you used to be a mall guard?" she said. His fists clenched, and his eyes darkened with fury.

"Spare me. Dave the guard was a character, one concocted on a moment's notice to play you for a fool, you and your friends. It was insulting. It doesn't take a great thespian to pretend to be an idiot night guard, as long as you can get around inconspicuously. I have not been inconspicuous for some time. It hardly matters now anyway, as this is all that's left of me." His voice gargled with despair.

"Come sit with me, Jessica." The animatronic girl dragged his IV stand with one hand, helping him back to a corner, where more medical devices and a reclining chair awaited. Jessica eyed the door, bracing herself to move, when the quiet was broken by what sounded like a child's scream in the distance.

"What was that?" Jessica said. "That sounded like a kid."

The man ignored her and settled back into the furnished chair. The animatronic girl busied herself with the machines around him, attaching electrodes to his bare scalp and checking the IV bags. A monitor began to beep at slightly irregular intervals, and he waved his hand. "Turn that off. I can't stand the sound of it. Jessica, come closer."

Stay alive. Play along, Jessica thought to herself as she warily picked up the chair she'd been tied to, carried it over to the man, and sat. Jessica trained her eyes on the animatronic girl as she strode across the room, gripped a handle, and pulled a long table straight out of the wall as if they were going to view a body in a morgue. Jessica clasped her hand over her mouth as fumes of oil and burning flesh washed over her. There was something lying on the table, covered with a plastic sheet.

Jessica leaped up again and backed away. "What is this? Who did you murder now?" she demanded.

"No one new," William spurted, almost as though he was trying to laugh. The plastic crinkled; something was moving inside.

"What have you done?" Jessica gasped.

The animatronic girl took a cotton ball from a bag nearby, wetted it from the bottle in her hand, and wiped it thoroughly up and down the metal fingers of one hand, then dropped it into a trash can at her feet. She took another piece of cotton and repeated the process, continuing over the surface of her hands and forearms up to her elbows. *She's sterilizing herself.* Jessica turned to the man in the chair, keeping the girl in her peripheral gaze. Behind him the animatronic girl was sterilizing a scalpel, using the same care she had taken with her hands.

"Here I thought you'd cheated death," Jessica said, almost feeling sorry for him.

"Oh, believe me, I have. You have only seen one fraction of what was done to me, the shrapnel that even dozens of surgeries—and I have had dozens—could not remove." He slowly rolled up the sleeve of his pajama shirt, revealing two staves of metal embedded in his arm, both dotted with ragged pieces of gray rubber. "Parts of that costume have become part of me." The animatronic girl took what looked like a pair of scissors out of the drawer and began to swab them clean, dabbing gently along every surface.

"But the fake blood." Jessica closed her eyes, shaking her head. *Charlie said that Clay found fake blood at Freddy's.* "There was fake blood; you faked your death."

Afton coughed, and his eyes widened. "I assure you, I didn't fake anything. If your police friend found fake blood . . ." He took a steadying breath. "It wasn't mine. I bleed, just like everyone else." He finished, and smiled, giving Jessica a moment to think before continuing.

"I gave you a monster." He gestured toward the collapsed doll that had been Springtrap. "But I assure you, I'm very, miserably, human." He paused again, a surge of anger crossing his face.

"My scalp was torn from my head when I escaped that costume, all but this piece here." He touched the small patch where hair still grew. "Scraps of metal are interwoven through every part of my body that has not been replaced with artificial tissue. Every movement causes me unimaginable pain. Not moving is even worse."

"I'm not going to feel sorry for you," Jessica said suddenly, braver than she felt. Afton took a breath and stared at her blankly.

"Do you believe that your pity will make any difference concerning what I do to you?" he asked with a steady tone. He tilted his head, leaning back as if taking a moment to relish the words, then his face lost the glint of cunning. "I am simply telling you, so that you can help with what comes next," he said tiredly. Jessica stood.

"You want me to be impressed by how much you've survived, and how much pain you're in. I don't care about you." She approached William's chair, then crossed her arms, glaring down at him from above. She glanced at the animatronic girl, who seemed poised to intervene, a half-swabbed scalpel in her hand, but Afton gave a subtle shake of his hand toward her, waving her off, seeming to enjoy the exchange. Jessica bent closer.

"William Afton," she said. "There is nothing in this world that I care less about than your pain."

Another child's scream came from somewhere nearby, and Jessica straightened.

"That *was* a little kid," Jessica said, a heady rush of adrenaline surging through her. She felt suddenly forceful, like she had some control of the situation. "You're the one who's been kidnapping those kids, aren't you?" she demanded, and Afton smiled weakly.

"I'm afraid those days are gone for me." He laughed, and looked fondly at the animatronic girl, who looked up at Jessica and smiled delicately. The girl straightened her posture and continued to stare; Jessica took a step back. All at once, the girl's stomach split open at the middle and out shot an enormous mass of wires and prongs. It reached its full extension and snapped open and shut with a steely clank. Jessica screamed, jumping back. The thing fell to the ground, then slowly recoiled back into the girl's stomach, which closed seamlessly. She smiled at Jessica, running her finger up and down the now-invisible line of the opening. Jessica averted her eyes.

"Baby, that's enough," Afton whispered. Jessica came to attention, her panic suddenly washed over with confusion. She looked from the girl to Afton, and back again.

"Circus Baby," she said, suddenly recalling the sign outside the restaurant. The animatronic girl smiled wider, her face threatening to split in half. "You're not as cute as you are on the sign," Jessica said bitingly, and the girl stopped smiling instantly, turning her body toward Jessica like she was aiming a weapon. A high-pitched ringing rose all around them, and Jessica edged backward. *That's her chip*, Jessica thought, bracing as if for impact. The animatronic girl held out her arms as though in a gesture of welcome.

Thin, sharp spines like porcupine's needles began to grow from her metal skin, each capped with a red knob like a pinhead, spaced a few inches apart, and extending from her face, her body, and her arms and legs. They grew slowly outward, lining up perfectly with one another to create a false contour all around her body. The girl looked expectantly at Jessica.

"Give it a minute," the girl said. "Let your eyes adjust."

The humming sound grew louder, rising higher in pitch until it became painful to hear. Jessica covered her ears, but it did nothing to dampen the sound. Suddenly, a new image snapped into place: where the smooth, slim redheaded animatronic had been was a gigantic, cartoonish child, her green eyes too large for her face, and her nose and cheeks painted a garish pink; she was a perfect image of the girl on the neon sign. Before Jessica could react, the childish image vanished, the needlelike extensions snapping back into the girl's body with a metallic snap. The humming stopped. The animatronic girl had returned to her former appearance. William Afton watched her with a gleam of pride.

Jessica turned again to the sleek, shiny girl standing at the man's side. "How did you create her?" Jessica asked, her eyes filled with curiosity for a moment before snapping herself back to the immediate danger surrounding her.

"Ah. A woman with a mind for science. You can't help but to admire what I've done." He braced himself on one arm of the chair, hoisting himself up to sit straighter. "Although . . ." He looked up at the gleaming girl for a moment, then turned away. "I can't take complete credit for this, unfortunately." He reclined his head again and let out a sigh. "Sometimes great things come at a great cost."

Jessica waited for him to go on, confused, then looked at the animatronic girl, recalling all that she'd said minutes before.

"I am a brilliant man, make no mistake. But what you see before you is a combination of all sorts of machinations and magic. My only real accomplishment was making something that could walk." He reached out and tapped the leg of the animatronic standing at his side; she did not react. "No small accomplishment. Although it's not happening as fluidly as you think. A lot of what you see is just in your head." He wheezed a laugh, then stopped himself, ending with a pained cough before going on. "That was Henry's idea not to try to reinvent the wheel. Why try to create the illusion of life, when your mind can do it for us?"

"She's more than an illusion, though," Jessica said plainly.

"Quite right," Afton answered thoughtfully. "Quite right. But that's why we're here—to discover the secret of that last ingredient, what you might call the spark of life."

"Is that why I'm here, too?" Jessica clenched her jaw.

"I believe you came here of your own free will, didn't you?" Afton said mildly.

"I didn't tie myself up."

"But I certainly didn't put you in the trunk of that car," he answered.

"We would rather have had your friend Charlie," he continued. "But we can find a use for you." He closed his eyes for a long moment, then opened them, meeting Jessica's eyes. "I have faced my own mortality, Jessica. I knew I was dying and through every broken fragment of my body, I was profoundly, immeasurably afraid. I fear it more than I fear life like this, even when every waking instant is pain, and sleep is possible only when induced by enough medication to kill most people."

"Everyone is afraid to die," Jessica said. "And you should be more afraid than anyone else, because if there's a hell, there's a hole at the bottom of it reserved for you."

Afton nodded with a moment of honest resignation. "In time, I'm sure that's where I will find myself. But the devil has knocked on my door before, and I've turned him away." He smiled.

"So, what? You want to live forever?"

William Afton smiled sadly and held out his hand to the animatronic girl; she went to him and put a protective hand on his shoulder. "Certainly not like this," he said. Jessica glanced at the robot girl, then back to the man in front of her, his body already riddled with mechanical parts.

"So, what, you're making yourself into a robot?" She laughed nervously, then stopped at his grave expression. "I didn't realize that you fancied yourself a mad scientist."

"No, that's science fiction," he said, unamused.

The plastic tarp moved again, and began to slide off the table, but stopped, not revealing what lay underneath.

"Everyone dies." Jessica blinked; the adrenaline was wearing off, and she was beginning to feel exhausted. Afton reached up and touched the mechanical girl's cheek, then turned his attention back to Jessica.

"The most terrible accidents sometimes bear the most beautiful fruits," he said, as if to himself. "Re-creating the accident—that is the duty and the honor of science. To replicate the experiment, and obtain the same result. I give my life to this experiment, piece by piece." He nodded at the girl, and she approached Jessica with deliberate steps. Jessica backed away, fear surging again.

"What are you going to do to me?" She could hear the urgency in her own voice.

"Please, enough. As a woman of science, at least try to appreciate what I've done," Afton said.

"I study archaeology," she said in a flat tone. He didn't respond; the girl stepped closer, giving her an unreadable stare.

The plastic tarp slid from the table, and Jessica startled and stared at what was underneath, but her terror turned to confusion in an instant. There wasn't a body, not human or machine. Instead there was a melted scrapheap, whose extensions could be interpreted as arms and legs, but with no defined mechanism of movement. There were no joints, no muscles, no skin or coverings, just masses of undefined tangles and cords, melted into one another and fused together. Most of it seemed fused to the table, burned and blackened at the edges where it touched the table itself, melting into it and seemingly inseparable from it.

"I don't understand." Jessica's mouth hung open, and she sat down again without thinking.

"Good girl." Afton smiled thinly. Jessica clenched her jaw. The animatronic girl went back to the table and took up the cotton balls and rubbing alcohol. She started with her fingers again, methodically wiping down each one. "Get on with it," Afton said impatiently. The girl did not break her deliberate pace.

"I touched you; I have to start over," she said.

"Nonsense, just do it. I've survived worse than this."

"The risk of infection . . ." she said calmly.

"Elizabeth!" he snapped. "Do as I say." The animatronic girl stopped moving at once, looking startled, and for a moment almost seemed to tremble. Jessica held her breath, wondering if anyone knew, or cared, that she had just heard the exchange. The girl immediately regained her composure, her eyes relaxing, then opened the drawer and took out a pair of rubber gloves, which she fitted easily over her metal hands. He settled back, and the girl came to him and bent over to press a button on the side of his chair. The chair made a pneumatic hiss and reclined, flattening out like a bed, and the girl placed her foot on a lever at the chair's base. She stepped on it, and the chair jerked upward. Afton made a pained grunt, and Jessica winced reflexively. The girl hit the lever again, yanking the chair up another inch, then stopped and flipped the monitor back on. It began to beep again at slightly irregular intervals, and she levered the chair up rapidly, jolting Afton's frail body as it rose. The girl darted her eyes from the monitor to Afton and back again, attentive to his vital signs. When the chair reached waist-height, she stepped back, apparently satisfied. Afton let out a rattling breath, then lifted his hand an inch to point at Jessica.

"Come closer," he said. She took a small step, and he curled his lips in a smile or a sneer. "I want you to watch what happens next," he said.

"What's going to happen next?" Jessica asked, hearing her own voice shake.

"How did the creatures at Freddy's move, of their own will, with no outside force controlling them?" he asked mildly. He tilted his head, waiting.

"The children were still inside. Their souls were inside those creatures," she said, the words brittle. She *felt* brittle, like if anything touched her now, she might easily break apart.

Afton sneered again.

"Oh, Jessica, come now. What else?" She closed her eyes. *What is he talking about?* "What else was inside them, to bind their spirits so inseparably to the bear, to the rabbit, to the fox? *How did they die, Jessica?*"

Jessica gasped, covering her mouth with both hands, as if she could stop herself from knowing, as long as she did not speak. "How, Jessica?" Afton demanded, and she lowered her hands, trying to steady her breath.

"You killed them," she said, and he made an impatient sound. She met his eyes again, not flinching from the empty socket. "They died in the suits," she said hoarsely. "Their bodies were bound inside, along with their souls."

He nodded. "The spirit follows the flesh, it would seem, and also the pain. If I wish to become my own immortal creation, my body must lead my spirit to its eternal home. Since I am still . . . experimenting . . . I move my flesh piece by piece." He looked thoughtfully over at the creature on the table. "More and more," he murmured, almost to himself, "it is a test of the strength of my own will. How much of myself can I carve away, and still remain in control?"

"Carve away?" Jessica repeated faintly, and he snapped his attention back to her.

"Yes. I will even allow you to watch," he said with a smirk.

"No, thanks," she said, shrinking back, and he wheezed a laugh.

"You will watch," he said, then gestured to the animatronic girl. "Keep an eye on her," Afton said.

"I have many eyes on her." The girl went to a cabinet and took out another IV bag: before she closed the door, Jessica caught a glimpse of more like it, and a shelf of what looked like vacuum-sealed cuts of meat. Her stomach flipped, and she swallowed hard.

Jessica started to squirm in her seat; there was a hissing sound coming from somewhere, and a smell of burning oil began to fill the room. The table where the mass of metal rested was beginning to glow orange at its center, and the mass on the table seemed to move slightly, although only out of the corner of Jessica's eye. Jessica snapped back to attention and turned toward Afton.

He appeared to be asleep: his chest rose and fell with slow breaths, and his eyes were closed; his eyelid draped loosely over the steel rod in the center of his missing eye, the thin skin hanging into the empty socket. The girl nodded, and moved to the table. Jessica swallowed, the rotten smell swelling around her. She had ceased to notice it, her nose tuning it out, but now it was everywhere, thickening the air with its miasma. *An operating theater . . . he's harvesting the kids for organs, transplanting them into himself?*

Jessica looked around the room, calculating—the scalpels were too far away to grab, and they wouldn't even scratch the animatronic girl's paint. If she ran, she would be dead before she was halfway to the door. Jessica forced herself to watch.

The animatronic girl went to William Afton's side, then checked the monitor again with care. She unbuttoned his pajama top and splayed it open, revealing his chest, and the mass of scars that had covered it since before he went by the name "Dave." The girl tugged the waist of his pants an inch lower, so that his torso was fully exposed, then nodded, took off her gloves, and replaced them with new ones. Then she took up one of the scalpels. Jessica looked away.

"You have to watch," the girl said, her voice chilling, a human voice stripped of human intonation. Jessica jerked her head up; the animatronic's eyes were on her. "He wants to see you watch," she repeated, the pleasant veneer cloaking her voice once more. Jessica gulped, and nodded, fixing her eyes on the scene before her. "I don't think you understand," the girl said. "Go wash your hands."

Shakily, Jessica got to her feet and went to the sink, feeling as if she might pass out at any moment. She turned the sink on and watched the water spiral down the drain, the shiny stainless steel gleaming through in the bright light.

"Wash your hands." Jessica obeyed, pushing up her sleeves above her elbows and washing her hands all the way up the forearms, foaming up the soap over and over as she had seen doctors do on TV. She rinsed them finally and turned to the animatronic girl.

"What am I doing?" she asked. The girl ripped open a plastic package and took out a towel. She held it out to Jessica.

"You're going to help."

Jessica took the towel and dried her hands, then put on gloves from the box the animatronic girl directed her to. "You know this thing isn't sterile, right?" she muttered, glancing at the mass on the table.

"Wait." Jessica gasped and took a step toward the table. From this angle, she could see more of its form. It was a melted mess, but she could recognize certain elements in the mass of fused scrap on the table. *A leg. A finger. An . . . eye socket.*

"I—I recognize these parts," Jessica said, but there was no answer. "These look like . . . endoskeletons, from Freddy's, the original Freddy's." Jessica began calculating in her head, measuring to herself how much this mass must weigh, and its size relative to the size of the endoskeletons she remembered.

Before she could think further, the creature on the table attempted to lift its leg, the makeshift knee bending partially. There was no mechanical device that she could make out—it seemed to be moving of its own will. After a second, it dropped back to the table.

"Where did you find these?" Jessica stepped back. "Where did you find these? What did you do? Why did you . . . melt them all together?"

"Hand me the scalpel," the girl said patiently. The surgical implements were laid out in a neat row on the rolling table, on a piece of paper, along with a set of curved needles, already threaded, and a small, kitchen-size propylene torch. The creature on the table tried again to lift its leg, and suddenly Jessica understood how it was able to move.

"They're still in there!" Jessica screamed. "The children— *Michael!*" The creature writhed pitifully, as if responding to her voice, and Jessica's heart wrenched. *They're in there, and they're in pain.*

"I guess I should have kidnapped Marla if I wanted a nurse," the girl said sardonically. "I told you, he wants you to watch. Look over here." Jessica obeyed, feeling her head go light as the girl pressed the scalpel into Afton's skin. *Don't pass out.* She drew the blade across his lower abdomen with steady, practiced hands, making a six-inch incision. She held out the scalpel, and Jessica stared for a moment before realizing she was supposed to take it. "He wants you to watch;

it's the only reason you're alive. If you don't watch, then there is no reason for you to be here. Do you understand?" Jessica steadied herself. *Breathe. Don't faint. Think about something else.*

John, Charlie—no, I'll start crying. Something else, something else . . .

Shoes. Black boots, knee high. The kind that look like riding boots. Italian leather. Jessica took the scalpel and set it down where it had been, and the blood dripped onto the paper, seeping into the fibers. Jessica took another deep breath.

The animatronic girl had one of her hands inside the incision, and was pulling it back, peering into the wound she had just made. "Scalpel," she said again, and Jessica picked up a new one and handed it to her. "Watch," the girl warned, and Jessica watched as she reached into the incision and cut something inside. Jessica flinched. *Shoes. Maroon clogs. Chunky heel, three inches. Patchwork stitching.* The girl held out the scalpel, her hand still inside Afton's body. "Take it; give me clamps." Jessica took the scalpel and replaced it.

"Clamps?" she asked, starting to panic as she searched among the instruments.

"They look like scissors, with teeth instead of blades. Open them and hand them to me, and do it fast."

Shoes. Jelly sandals, purple, sparkly. Jessica grabbed the clamps and tried to open them, but they were stuck together, hooked by an odd clasp at the top.

"Hurry up, do you want him to die?"

Yes, I do! Jessica wanted to shout, but held her tongue. She pinched the scissor handles together, and they came free. She handed them to the girl, relieved, and watched as she stuck the pointed end into the opening and pinched whatever she had been holding, clamping it shut. She took her hand slowly out of the wound and looked at Jessica.

"You have to be faster. Scalpel, then I'll need clamps right away."

Jessica nodded.

Shoes. Green suede kitten heels with a rhinestone strap at the ankle. She handed the girl the scalpel, then wrestled the clamps open as fast as she could, and was holding them out by the time the bloody blade was returned to her. She watched dizzily as the animatronic girl made another cut, severing something she could not see, and using the last set of clamps to hold it shut.

The table behind them began to hiss more loudly, and the orange glow intensified. Jessica took a step sideways to get away from the heat. The glow spread to the creature on the table, and parts of it seemed to turn from side to side.

"Hold out your hands," the girl said.

Platform sneakers. Denim. Hideous. Jessica held out her hands for the clamps, but the girl left them in place. Instead, she slid both hands into Afton's open body and lifted out a bloody object. *His kidney, that's his kidney. Black leather combat boots.*

Black leather combat boots. Charlie's black leather combat boots. The animatronic girl held the kidney up in the air for a moment, and blood dripped from it onto her face. *Charlie's boots. Charlie.* The girl turned to Jessica, and she shrank back.

"Hold out your hands," the girl repeated with cold insistence, and Jessica obeyed, fighting not to retch as the warm organ was placed gently in her hands. *It's meat; it's not part of a person; just think of it as meat. Platform sneakers. Stiletto boots. Penny loafers.* She watched in a daze as the girl took a curved needle and black thread and began to sew William Afton back together, starting with his innards, and ending with the first incision, making a row of Xs across the left half of his body. At last she finished, snipping the last thread off with practiced ease.

"What's next?" Jessica asked, her voice sounding faint against the rushing in her ears. *Yellow sneakers with a blue streak on the side. Those brown pumps Mom got me. Oh, Mom—*

"The next part is easy," the girl said, pulling the gloves off and picking the kidney up again with her hand and approaching the table where the mass lay.

"What are you going to do?" Jessica quivered.

"What did you think all of this was for?" the girl said softly. "He told you: piece by piece."

Jessica looked down at the creature on the table, glowing orange at its core, and dripping fluid from its various parts, the drops landing with a hiss on the hot surface.

"This is a transplant," she said.

The mass of melted parts for a moment looked human, its demeanor suddenly childlike as it squirmed, and its head turned to face Jessica. For just a moment, Jessica thought she could make out eyes looking back at her. Suddenly, the silence was broken as the animatronic girl clenched her fist around the kidney and slammed it against the creature's chest, pressing so hard that the metal underneath sank inward, embedding the kidney deep inside where it gurgled and hissed. More fluid seeped out the sides of the creature and burned on the table, as the girl wrenched it back and forth inside.

She pulled her hand from the cavity she had created, her hand charred black, and rested it at her side, extending and retracting her fingers as though making sure they still worked.

"Now, we are done," she said. She brushed past Jessica and went to the cabinet, and emerged with a long needle. She strode purposefully to William Afton's side, stopped with her fist raised over her head, then brought the needle down, plunging it into his chest.

A second passed, then he heaved an enormous breath and groaned. The girl pulled the needle from his chest and set it gently on the table beside him. William Afton opened his eyes, and his single eyeball moved back and forth between Jessica and the animatronic girl.

"Is it done?" he asked.

Jessica screamed. The intensity of it roused her from her daze and she screamed again, letting the sound drown out everything else. Her throat went raw, but she screamed again, clinging to the roar of her own voice; for an instant, she felt like if she kept screaming nothing worse could happen.

The air around the girl shimmered, and Jessica's vision blurred in front of her: something was moving. In a moment, her eyes cleared, and Charlie was standing in front of her.

"Jessica, don't worry! You can trust me," Charlie said cheerfully.

CHAPTER NINE

A hand was stroking her hair. The sun was going down over a field of grain. A cluster of birds were fluttering overhead, their calls echoing out over the landscape. "I'm so happy to be here with you," a kind voice said. She looked up and nestled against him; her father smiled down at her, but there were tears in his eyes. Don't cry, Daddy, she wanted to say, but when she tried to speak, the words did not come. She reached up to touch his face, but her hand passed through empty air: he was gone, and she was alone in the grass. Overhead the birds began to wail, and their calls sounded like human voices, breaking with despair. "Daddy!" Charlie screamed, but there was no answer, only the birds' lamentation as the sun vanished beyond the horizon.

It was dark, and he had not come back; all the birds were gone but one, and that one sounded more human with every cry. Charlie *stood unsteadily; by some trick of time she was no longer a child, but a teenage girl, and the fields around her had turned to rubble; she stood in the midst of a ruined place, but there was a single wall standing in front of her, and a door at the center of it. The birds were silent, but someone was crying on the other side of the door, crying alone in a small, cramped space. She ran to it, banging her fists on the metal surface. "Let me in!" she cried. "Let me in! I have to get inside!"*

I have to get inside! Charlie sat bolt upright with a ragged gasp, inhaling like she'd just escaped from drowning. *The doors—the closet.* She threw off the gray wool blanket and sheets, tangling herself in the process before she managed to get free. She was so hot she could barely stand it, and the wool had been scratching where it touched her chin. She felt strange, more alert: the world was in sharp focus, and it was jarring, as if she had been drifting in some kind of shadowy, half-conscious state for days. *Everything hurts*, she'd managed to whisper to John, but it had been somehow detached from her, there was some buffer between her body and her mind. Now, her mind clear, the buffer was gone, and she ached all over, a dull, constant pain that seemed to be everywhere at once. She leaned back against the wall. She had not woken to sleepy disorientation—she knew exactly where she was. She was in John's apartment, behind the couch. She was behind the couch, because . . .

"Someone is impersonating me," she said uncertainly, and the sound of her own voice was startling in the empty room.

She got to her knees, not quite trusting her legs, then steadied herself on the back of the couch, getting to her feet with effort. She straightened, and was instantly dizzy, her head swimming as her knees threatened to buckle under her. Charlie gripped the back of the couch determinedly, picking a point on the wall and staring at it, willing the room to stop spinning.

After a moment, it did, and Charlie realized the wall she was staring at was a door. *Doors.* The thought made her light-headed again, but she kept a firm hand on the couch and made her way around to the front, then sat down on it carefully. She glanced around the room—so far all she had seen was the corner behind the sofa. The shades were pulled down, and she could see that the front door was bolted. Charlie lost interest in the rest of it, her eyes drawn back to the other door. It was scarcely ajar, the room behind it dark, and Charlie shivered, echoes of her dream reverberating in her head. *Doors. Someone was on the other side, behind the door, somewhere small and dark; I was drawing them, doors; I had to find the door. Then . . .* She closed her eyes, remembering. They were running, desperate to get away as the building thundered around them, already falling to pieces, when she saw the door. *The door called to me; it was hidden in the wall, but I went to it, I knew exactly where it was. As I walked toward it, it was like I was on both sides—walking to it, and trapped behind it. Separated from myself. When I touched it, I could feel the beating of your heart, and then* . . . Charlie's eyes snapped open. "John pulled me away," she said, the memory solidifying as she let herself dwell on it. "I didn't want to go because . . ." She heard it, suddenly: the hiss and the cracks appearing in the wall. ". . . because the door had started to open."

Charlie stood, her eyes glued to the door in John's living room. She approached it as if propelled by the same instinctive force, her heart picking up its pace. "It's just the bedroom, right?" she murmured, but still she edged toward it slowly. She stopped in front of the door and reached out tentatively, vaguely surprised when her fingers touched real wood. She pushed it gently and it swung open easily, revealing a girl identical to Charlie.

A mirror.

She looked the same. Her face was pale and strained, but it was her face, and she smiled instinctively. In the haze of the last few . . . days? Weeks? She had been utterly disoriented, fading in and out of consciousness, pain finding her even in dreams. Charlie had not felt like herself, but there she was. She reached out to touch the mirror girl's hand. "You, are you," she said quietly.

Behind her came the unmistakable sound of a lock being turned, and she whirled around in sudden panic, losing her balance and catching herself on John's dresser. The front door opened and she shrank back, kneeling to let the dresser shield her. A clamor of voices burst in, all talking at once—there were too many to make out the words, until a familiar voice called, "Charlie?"

Charlie didn't move, waiting to be sure. Footsteps came to the doorway of the bedroom, then the voice again: "Charlie?"

"Marla!" Charlie answered. "I'm here." She started to get up, but her legs would not take her weight. "I can't—" she started, tears of frustration pricking her eyes as Marla hurried over.

"It's okay," Marla said hurriedly. "It's okay, I'll help. It's amazing you made it this far!" Charlie looked at her flatly, and Marla laughed. "I'm sorry," she said. "It's just—glaring at me like that you're so . . ."

"What?"

"Charlie."

"Who else am I supposed to be?" Charlie smiled as Marla took hold of her wrist with medical authority and began to silently count. She looked past Marla to Carlton, who came over quickly. John was standing in the door, but he made no move to join them, not meeting Charlie's eyes.

"I didn't want to crowd you," Carlton said, sitting down beside her and crossing his legs. "Charlie, I'm—" He broke off and swallowed, looking away. "I'm really glad to see you," he said to the floor.

"I'm glad to see you, too," Charlie said. She looked back to Marla, who nodded briskly.

"Your pulse is a little slow," she said. "I want to check it again in a few minutes. I want you to drink some water." Charlie nodded.

"Okay," she said bemusedly.

"Let's get her onto the bed," Marla said to Carlton, who nodded and, before Charlie could protest, scooped her up into his arms. Charlie glanced around for John, but he had disappeared.

Marla pulled the blankets back. Charlie felt the pull of sleep, like something standing behind her, gently tugging. She blinked rapidly, trying to rouse herself as Carlton set her down. Marla started to pull the blankets over her, and Charlie waved her hands, ineffectually trying to push them away.

"I'm too hot," she said, and Marla stopped.

"Okay," she said. "They're here if you need them." Charlie nodded. The tugging was growing stronger: if she just closed her eyes, she would slip back into the dark. Marla and Carlton were talking to each other, but it was getting harder to keep track of what they were saying.

A loud bang rattled the small apartment, and Charlie jolted awake, her heart thudding alarmingly. Almost instantly, Marla's hand was on her shoulder. "It's just John," she said.

"I think my heart rate is back up," Charlie said, attempting to joke, but Marla turned on her with appraising eyes, grabbed her wrist, and started to count again. "Marla, I'm fine," Charlie said, halfheartedly pulling away. Marla held on for another few seconds, then released her.

In the living room, John set something down on the floor with force. Carlton gave Charlie a concerned glance, then helped her off the bed, giving her an arm to lean on as they went out into the living room to join John. For a moment, the object was obscured, then they all moved aside so she could see the child-size doll. Charlie sat down on the floor, a little apart from the others.

"Ella," she whispered. Some tight, painful knot inside her chest began to loosen, and she felt herself smile. "John, how did you find her?" she asked. John knelt down behind the doll and looked up at her grimly, and her smile faded. "What's wrong?" she asked. He didn't answer her.

"Everyone, keep your eyes on the doll," he said instead, and took something out of his pocket. He flicked his thumb against the object, a tiny motion, and the air around Ella shimmered for a moment, blurring her. Charlie rubbed her eyes and heard Marla gasp. Ella was gone: standing where she had been was a little girl about three years old, dressed in Ella's clothes. The knot in Charlie's chest started to tighten again.

"What is this, John?" Marla asked sharply. John flicked his thumb again, and the shimmer passed over the girl, then she was a doll again, her vacant eyes staring placidly into eternity. Charlie darted her eyes from one to the next: Marla looked scared, but Carlton was fascinated. John, for some reason, seemed angry. Charlie shifted uneasily. John manipulated the object in his hand again, and the little girl appeared once more. Carlton crouched down to look at her, and Marla bent down to see, keeping her distance.

John stood, leaving them to stare at Ella, and knelt beside Charlie, giving her the same dark look he'd had since he brought in the doll. "What is this?" he asked harshly, and Charlie stared at him, hurt. John looked away with a pained expression, his face flushed. When he looked back at Charlie, the anger in his face had faded, but was not gone. "I need to know what this is."

"I don't know," she said. John nodded, and sat on the floor with her, carefully leaving a wide space between them. He opened his hand: in it was a small, flat disc. Charlie didn't move to touch it—there was something odd in his manner, something untrusting she had never seen in him before.

"Did you know?"

"No." Charlie tilted her head, staring at the motionless little girl.

"It's the same as Afton's creatures, though, isn't it?" John said. "Pattern projection, bombarding the mind; overwhelming the senses—"

"This one is different, though," Charlie cut in. She shivered, though she wasn't cold, suddenly unable to shake the memory of the twisted bear, his face stripped to the metal staves, the illusion sparking on and off as he loomed over them. "Can I see it?" she said, forcing herself back to the present. John held out the disc, and she took it carefully, watching him warily. He was giving off the sense of a brewing storm, and she was afraid of setting it off. Charlie held the disc up to the light, turning it back and forth, then handed it back.

"That's it?" John's eyes widened.

"What do you want me to say?" she cried.

"I mean, you can't tell me anything about it?"

"The others all had that inscription: *Afton Robotics*. This one doesn't. But I'd bet you noticed that."

"Actually, I didn't." John looked at her thoughtfully, then back down at the disc. He flipped the switch, and Marla yelped in surprise. "Sorry! It's a bit jarring if you aren't expecting it," he said, turning back to Charlie with a grin. She smiled, and as he met her eyes, his smile faltered, something troubling passing over his face. Before she could speak, it was gone. He grinned widely and winked at her, then flipped the switch—Marla cried out again, and Carlton laughed.

"Stop doing that!" Marla shouted from several feet away.

John ignored her, and leaned in closer to Charlie, hesitantly, like he thought she might run away. She turned to face him, a wave of nervousness washing over her. She ducked her head, letting her hair fall over her face, and he reached out and touched it gently, brushing a strand out of her eyes. He gave her a small smile and flipped the switch once, then again.

"That's enough," Marla called. "This is too weird for me."

John didn't seem to hear her; he was looking at Charlie with a new troubled expression.

"What is it?" she asked quietly.

"Nothing," he said. He touched her hair again, this time brushing it back from her face and tucking it behind her ear. "Hey," he said abruptly, changing his tone. "Do you remember your experiment from last year?" She nodded eagerly, then stopped, freshly aware of how long she had been away.

"My faces. But they must be gone, everything must be gone." She looked at John with anxious eyes, but he smiled.

"Nothing's gone," he said, and her heart lifted; she felt as if he had just given her a gift. "Jessica packed up all your stuff; she's got it in her apartment."

"Oh," Charlie said, darting her eyes around the room. "Jessica? Where is she?"

"Charlie," John said patiently, and she tried to focus on him; she could feel her attention waning, as if her mind were spreading thin, floating out like clouds. "The faces," John went on. "There was an earpiece so they could recognize you, right?"

She nodded.

"Could you make it work the other way?"

Charlie thought for a moment then met his eyes again. "You mean, make it so that the animatronics *can't* see you?" She frowned, her focus returning as she concentrated on the problem. "The earpieces emit a frequency that alerts the animatronics to you, it makes you visible. If you inverted that frequency . . ." She paused again. "I don't know if it would work, John. It might."

"It could make us invisible to them?"

"*Maybe*, but that's a big leap."

"How would I do it? Invert the frequency?"

Charlie shrugged. "Just switch the wires, and . . ."

"Charlie, what part of 'stay in bed' wasn't clear?" Marla asked good-naturedly, coming over to them. John stood, his mouth hanging open as though Marla had interrupted Charlie's answer, but she didn't seem poised to add more.

"Sorry," he said hastily.

"Be careful," Charlie said. She was beginning to feel light-headed again, and when Marla reached out to help her back to the bedroom, she did not protest.

John paused in the door, watching as Charlie curled up on her side, her eyes already closed. Marla raised her eyebrows, and he left, shutting the door halfway. In the living room,

Carlton was kneeling beside Ella—now in doll form again—and looking intently into her ear.

"Uh, Carlton?" John said dubiously, and Carlton sat back on his heels.

"Amazing," he said. "She looked human, like actually, for real, a human child."

"Yeah, I think that was the idea. Can we talk outside?" John asked brusquely, and Carlton looked at him in surprise.

"Sure," Carlton said with some concern in his voice.

"Come on." John headed for the door, and Carlton hurried after him. Once they were outside, John looked at Carlton for a moment, thinking.

"What's the idea?" Carlton asked with a hint of suspicion.

"Let me try to get this straight in my own head first," John said. "Last year, when she was still in school, Charlie had this experiment she was doing, something about teaching robots language."

"Oh yeah!" Carlton nodded enthusiastically. "She told me about it. Natural language programming. They listen to people talking around them, and to them, and they learn to talk, too. Didn't sound like it worked very well, though."

"Well, whatever. She had these earpieces—like, the robots would only talk to each other—they only recognized each other. You with me so far?"

"Um, I think?"

"Well, if you, Carlton, wanted to be *in* on the conversation, you would need to wear a special earpiece. The earpieces would make them recognize you. Otherwise, you were just part of the background, like they couldn't *see* you."

"Okay?" Carlton gave him a puzzled look, and John rolled his eyes.

"Wearing the earpieces included you in their conversation. It made you one of them, from their perspective."

"Hate to break it to you, but the big ones already see us . . . at least I'm pretty sure they do. See this scar?"

"Will you shut up for a second?" John said. "I asked Charlie, and she said we might be able to reverse engineer it. We can switch the wires, and instead of the earpieces *including* us, it would deliberately *exclude* us."

Carlton furrowed his brow.

"It could effectively make us invisible . . ." John prompted.

"Switch the wires," Carlton repeated. "It would mask us, and make us not a part of the world they can perceive."

"Right." John nodded.

Carlton waited for John to go on, then added, "What do you want me to do?"

"Go to Jessica's house. She's got all of Charlie's old stuff boxed up in a closet. If she's not there, she leaves her spare key under the welcome mat."

Carlton raised his eyebrows. "Under the welcome mat? That's a *horrible* place to leave a key!"

"It's a good neighborhood," John said defensively.

Carlton raised his eyebrows. "Yeah, it's a good neighborhood, John. Nothing bad ever happens here." Carlton slapped John on the shoulder as he headed for his car. "I'm on it!" he called.

John let out a sigh, then went back inside. Marla was sitting on the couch, staring at the television, which was not turned on.

"How is she?" John asked, sitting down beside her, and she shrugged.

"Okay, considering the circumstances." She turned away from the blank screen, looking distressed. "She was locked in a box! That's insane, she was locked in a *box*! Who knows for how long—days, months? She must have been fed, given water, or she'd have starved, but she has no memory of it, she just remembers drifting in and out of sleep. She *seems* healthy. I don't know what to say."

Impulsively, John hugged her, and she sighed, hugging him back tightly. She released him abruptly, looking away as she brushed at her eyes. John pretended not to see.

"Can I go sit with her for a minute?" he said when she straightened. "I won't bother her, I just want to sit with her and know she's there."

Marla nodded, her eyes brightening with tears again. "Don't wake her up," she admonished as he went to the door. He nodded, and slipped inside, closing the door behind him.

Carlton pulled into the lot outside Jessica's apartment building, glancing around for her car. It didn't seem to be there.

"Guess I'll be breaking and entering; sorry, Jess," he said cheerfully as he pulled into a spot, but a sense of dread had already set in. He wanted company, even on this small errand. "Let's see what skeletons Jessica has hiding in her closet." He drummed his hands on the steering wheel, tamping down his nerves, and got out of the car.

Jessica lived on the third floor. Carlton had only been to her place once, but he found it again easily. In front of her door was a welcome mat: it was dark green, the word WELCOME written out in black script. Carlton lifted the mat, but there was nothing under it.

For a moment he stared, at a loss for what to do next, then he flipped the mat all the way over: taped to the center was a key. "Thought you could outsmart me?" he murmured, peeling off the clear tape.

"Can I help you?" someone asked sternly from behind him. Carlton froze. The voice said nothing else, and so with deliberate movements he finished removing the key, set the mat back on the ground, and smoothed it back into place, trying to seem unconcerned. He put a pleasant expression on his face, stood, and turned to face an elderly man scowling at him from across the hall. He was wearing a faded button-up shirt and holding a hefty book, his finger marking his place.

"Do I know you?" the man demanded. Carlton forced a grin and waved the key in the air.

"Just visiting," he said. "I'm a friend of Jessica's." The old man peered at him suspiciously.

"She makes too much noise," he said, and shut his door. Carlton heard three locks snap into place, then silence. He waited a moment, then turned and hurriedly entered Jessica's apartment.

He shut the door carefully behind him and glanced around. The apartment was no bigger—or nicer—than John's, although it was definitely cleaner. Most of the furniture had probably come with the place, but Jessica had determinedly made it her own. The scuffed floor was as spotless as it could be made without an industrial sander, and Carlton looked guiltily down at his sneakers, thinking maybe he should have taken them off outside. Jessica had covered the worn-out couch in fluffy blankets and throw pillows; her textbooks were lined up neatly on a wide bookshelf made out of brightly painted wood planks, and above the shelf was a large corkboard full of photographs, cards, and ticket stubs. Carlton made his way over to it, curious. "Let's see what Jessica's been up to," he said, talking to himself just to fill the silence.

The corkboard was full of smiling pictures of Jessica with her friends; a graduation photo with her parents; ticket stubs from concerts and movies; two birthday cards, and a few postcards with enthusiastically—and illegibly—scribbled notes. Carlton let out a low whistle. "Somebody's popular," he muttered, then something else caught his eye: a child's drawing, pinned to the lower corner of the board. He bent down to look, and his throat caught: it was a crayon drawing of five children, smiling happily as they posed with a big yellow rabbit. In the bottom left corner, the artist had signed his name, and Carlton reached out to touch it lightly. "Michael," he whispered. He stared into the bright eyes of the yellow rabbit behind the children and his mouth went dry. *If only I could have warned you, somehow.*

He swallowed and straightened up, turning his attention deliberately back to the photos.

"She sure gets out a lot," he remarked, opening one of the cards to distract himself. HAPPY 15TH BIRTHDAY, JESSICA! it read, and he stepped back, feeling slightly ashamed as suddenly he understood. He glanced at the ticket stubs: they were all from shows in New York; the pictures with friends were all a few years old. Jessica's new life, here, didn't give her much in the way of mementos. Carlton turned away from the corkboard, wishing he had not intruded.

"The closet," he said loudly. "I have to find the closet with the stuff." There was a kitchenette, and past that a hallway, presumably leading to the bedroom. He found a light switch and flipped it on, and the closet appeared, halfway down the hall. He opened it, half expecting the contents to come tumbling down on him, but though these were Charlie's possessions, it was Jessica who had done the packing. Stacks of cardboard boxes filled the closet completely, each one labeled clearly: CHARLIE—SHIRTS AND SOCKS, CHARLIE—BOOKS, etc. At the very top of the stack was a long, flat box labeled, CHARLIE—WEIRD EXPERIMENT.

"Weird experiment; feels like the story of my life these days," Carlton whispered. He reached for it carefully, and had almost gotten it down when he knocked the corner against the box underneath it, sending, CHARLIE—MISCELLANEOUS to the ground. The box split open, spewing out computer parts and random bolts and scraps of metal, fur, and two unattached paws. Three plastic eyes bounced as they hit the floor, then rolled across the carpet, clacking against each other merrily.

"This is life or death; someone else can clean it up," Carlton decided. He stepped carefully over the rest of the mess, and carried the box into Jessica's bedroom. He set it down on her bed, careful of the pale blue spread, and dragged the spare key across the packing tape to cut it. He opened the box.

"Yikes." He startled. Two identical faces stood upright in the box, staring at each other with blank eyes. They were like unfinished statues: they had features, but they were not refined, and seemed incapable of expression. He started to lift them out of the box, then realized that they were attached to something. With care, he managed to extract the entire structure: a large, black box with knobs and buttons, and the faces on their stand, wired to it. It all seemed to be intact. Carlton eyed the wall socket by Jessica's bed for a moment, then grabbed the cord, and plugged the whole thing in. An array of lights came on, red and green, flashing on and off seemingly at random, then stabilizing: some off, some on. Several fans started to whir. Carlton looked at the faces: they were stretching, almost mimicking human movement. "Creepy," he whispered.

"You, me," said the first, and he jumped back, disconcerted.

"We, she," said the second. He stared, waiting for more, but they were apparently finished for the moment, motionless and silent. Carlton shook his head, trying to make himself focus, though all he really wanted to do was sit here and watch the two faces, and see what else they might have to say. *Or talk to them.* He went back to the box: the earpieces

John had described were wrapped up in a thin layer of bubble wrap. They looked like hearing aids, small clear pieces of plastic, full of wiring, with a tiny switch on one side. Carlton flipped the switch on one, and put it in his ear. Instantly, the faces turned to him, tilting up like they were looking straight at him. *Can they see me?*

"Hi?" Carlton said reluctantly.

"Who?" one asked.

"Carlton," he answered nervously.

"You," the other said.

"Me," said the first.

"You guys really love pronouns, huh?" Carlton said. There was no answer from the faces. He took out the earpiece and flipped the switch off, and simultaneously the faces turned back to each other. *Makes you visible. Right*, he thought with a shiver. He turned back to the earpiece itself, sliding his thumbnail into the thin seam that ran around the edge of the casing. It popped open easily, revealing a mess of wires and a tiny computer chip. "Just switch the wires, it's that easy," he muttered to himself. There was a lamp on a nightstand beside Jessica's bed, and he turned it on, holding the earpiece under the light. He stared at it, looking for a clue as to what John had been suggesting, angling the tiny object from side to side. At last he spotted it: a single, empty round input, outlined in red. "And why is nothing plugged in to you?" Carlton said triumphantly. He sorted through the other wires until he found one that matched it, the outline green. He quickly switched the wire to the red-lined plug and snapped the case back together, then switched it on and stuck it back in his ear. The faces did not move.

"What's wrong? Don't want to talk to me anymore?" he said loudly. There was no response. "Excellent," he said, satisfied. He took out the earpiece and put it in his pocket, then grabbed the other one as well. He unplugged the experiment and was about to pack it back into the box, when he felt a sudden prickling between his shoulders, as if someone was standing directly behind him. He could almost feel breath on his neck. Carlton held very still, scarcely breathing, then he spun around, his hands raised to defend himself.

The room was empty. He flicked his eyes from side to side, unconvinced that he was alone, but there was nothing there. "Just pack up and get out," he said weakly, but his heart was still pounding in his chest like he was fighting for his life. He took a deep breath, and went back to the experiment. Before he could touch it, the room dipped under him like a ship bobbing in the ocean, and he fell to his knees, clutching the bed frame to steady himself. His vision blurred: nothing was fixed in place anymore, everything in the room seemed like it was moving at various speeds and different directions. Carlton let go of the bed frame and sank to the floor as a piercing whine arose, quickly ascending to a pitch too high to perceive. He covered his ears, but it did nothing to ease the nausea. The room kept spinning, and his stomach lurched; he groaned, holding his head and closing his eyes, but the movement continued. He clenched his teeth, grimly determined not to vomit. *What is happening?*

Carlton . . . Carlton . . . Someone called his name sweetly, and he looked. One thing in the room was still: an enormous pair of eyes, staring at him as the room rocked sickeningly. He tried to stand, but as soon as he moved, dizziness and nausea overwhelmed him. He pressed his cheek to the cool floor, desperate for relief, but it only made the room spin faster.

"Carlton?"

The room snapped back into focus; everything stopped moving. Carlton didn't move, afraid of setting it all off again. "Carlton, are you okay?" said a familiar voice, and he looked up to see Charlie, bent over him anxiously.

"Charlie?" he said weakly. "What are you doing here?"

"John sent me to help. What were you doing with all this stuff?" she asked.

"I'm sorry, I hope I didn't break anything," he said, sitting up carefully. The nausea still lingered, but it was easing as he began to trust that the room had steadied itself. He glanced at Charlie, his vision still a little fuzzy.

"I don't mind, it's all junk anyway. But the way you were rolling around on the floor, you must have activated something, or electrocuted yourself, one or the other. Are you okay?"

"I think so," he said. He slumped back against the bed.

"Nausea? Room spinning?" she asked sympathetically.

"Terrible," he said.

She put a hand on his shoulder. "Come on, we need to get out of here." She stood and held out a hand to help him up; he took it, standing gingerly, the effects of whatever it had been were almost completely gone. He looked around the room, his vision clear.

"What exactly were you doing?" Charlie asked, and Carlton froze. Her voice was too hard, too . . . polished. He turned to her, keeping his face neutral.

"He didn't say? John thought you might want to have it, your old experiment. I think he wanted to surprise you with it," he said. He grinned. "Surprise!"

Charlie smiled.

"You know, your old experiment?" Carlton's mind raced. "The one with the robotic hand that could play the piano?" he added. "You remember?"

"Right. How sweet of you to come get it," she said, a flirtatious note in her voice, and Carlton's blood went cold. He nodded carefully.

"You know me. Always thinking of others," he said, glancing over Charlie's shoulder at the bedroom door behind her. It was closed. She took a step closer to him, and he stepped back instinctively. She looked surprised for a moment, then grinned, looking down and seeing the two faces in the box. He moved back again, startling when he hit the wall behind him.

"Carlton, if I didn't know better I'd think you were afraid of me," Charlie said in a low voice, stepping so close there was almost no space between them, pinning him to the wall. She reached out toward his face, and he set his jaw, trying not to flinch. She ran her fingers down his cheek, then traced the line of his jaw. He didn't move, his breathing shallow. Charlie brushed his hair out of his face and pressed closer to him, trailing her hand to the back of his neck. Her face was inches from his.

"Um, Charlie, you're not really my type, you know?" he managed to say.

She smiled. "You haven't even given me a chance. Are you sure?" she whispered.

"Yeah, I'm sure. I mean don't get me wrong, you're okay-looking, but let's be honest, you're nothing to write home about," he quipped, maintaining eye contact. "I mean, those boots with *that* skirt?"

Charlie's grin started to wane.

"Sorry, that was rude. I'm sure you'll find a guy someday who appreciates you for who you are." He tried to inch his way toward the door. "Now, if you'll excuse me, I'm late for quartet practice, so let me just get by you and I'll be on my way."

Carlton squirmed but Charlie didn't budge. "I promise I won't tell anyone that I rejected you. Just hit that gym and we can try again in a few years."

"Carlton, you're obviously flustered. There's only one way to really be sure how you feel," Charlie said softly. She leaned closer, and Carlton screwed his eyes shut. *The earpiece.* It was in his right pocket.

"Charlie, you're right, but maybe we should just talk for a while, you know. I rushed into my last relationship and I almost ended up dead in a moldy fur suit." *Just distract her until* . . . his fingers closed on the earpiece, and he pulled it from his pocket, opening his eyes at the same time.

Carlton screamed.

Charlie's face was splitting apart. Her skin had taken on a plastic cast, it was cracked at the middle, splintering into triangular sections. As he watched, her hand tightening around his neck, the triangles lifted up and pulled back like razor-edged flower petals, revealing an entirely different face, sleek and feminine, but definitely not human. The petals of what had been Charlie's face began to move along the round perimeter of the new face, beginning to look more like a saw blade than a flower. The animatronic girl pursed her metal lips, leaning in for a kiss as the blades spun closer and closer to Carlton's face. In a final burst of self-preservation, he yanked the earpiece out of his pocket and jammed it into his ear, flipping the switch.

The animatronic girl drew back at once, letting go of Carlton's neck with a surprised look on her metal face. She glanced around the room. He stared at her, frozen in terror for a moment, then he realized what was happening. *She can't see me.* He waited, watching as she took deliberate steps backward, her eyes darting back and forth. She stood for a moment, the plates of her face snapping back together to form the painted, glossy face of a doll, then suddenly a ripple of light passed over her and she appeared to be Charlie again, her face expressionless. After another minute, she turned and went to the bedroom closet. She peered in, pushing clothes out of it as if something might be hidden behind them, then stepped away. She went to the bed and grabbed a corner, then lifted it off the ground. She considered the empty floor for a second, then let the bed drop with a crash. Once more she scanned the room, and at last, she opened the door to the bedroom and let herself out. Carlton tiptoed behind her, following her into the hall. She stopped short in front of the hall closet, and he almost bumped into her, barely catching himself before they collided.

The animatronic girl ripped the boxes from the neatly stacked closet, tossing them haphazardly on the ground behind her. Carlton cautiously stepped back a few feet.

When the girl was satisfied the closet was unoccupied, she checked the bathroom, then walked out into the living room. With one last, dissatisfied glance around, the animatronic girl left Jessica's apartment, closing the door calmly behind her. Carlton rushed to the window, watching as she exited the building and walked away down the road, heading toward the town.

Once she was out of sight, Carlton heaved a sigh, gasping as if he had been holding his breath. He felt dizzy again, light-headed, but this time it was only fading adrenaline. He started to take the earpiece out, then thought better of it and left it in place. He patted his left pocket, reassuring himself that the second earpiece was still there, and he hurried out of the apartment and down to his car. He drove away urgently, heading toward John's house without regard for the speed limit, and hoping the animatronic girl was going the other direction.

Charlie heard the door close, and she turned toward it. The room was dark except for the light filtering in through the small, dirty window, and she squinted to see who had just come in.

"John?" she whispered.

"Yeah," he said in the same tone. "Did I wake you up?"

"It's okay, all I do lately is sleep, and dream." The last word was bitter on her tongue, and he must have heard it, too, because he sat down on the chair Marla had placed beside the bed.

"Is it okay if I sit?" he asked nervously, already there.

"Yes," she said. Charlie closed her eyes. The room was different now. Safer. "You said something," she murmured, almost to herself, and John leaned closer.

"Did I? What did I say?" He cleared his throat, his palms already sweating.

"You said . . . you loved me," she whispered, and he jolted as if someone had struck him.

"Yes," he said, his voice sounding choked-off. "That is what I said to you. You remember *that*?" Charlie nodded carefully, knowing her response was inadequate. He turned away from her for a second, letting out a forced breath. "It's true. I do!" he said in a rush, turning back to her. "I mean, you've been my friend since forever. Just like Marla or Carlton or Jessica. I would have said that to any of them. Well, maybe not Jessica. So, you remember some of that night, then?" he asked briskly.

"It's all I remember. And the door. John!" She grasped his arm, alarmed. "John, the door was opening, I think Sammy was inside—I could feel him there, his heartbeat . . ." She trailed off as another memory overwhelmed her, a moment in the strange, artificial cave under the restaurant that was so like Freddy's, and yet so unlike it. "Springtrap," she said. "I fought with him. There was a metal spike, and his head . . ." She could see him, gasping on the rocks as she ground the piece of metal torturously into his wound.

"I know; I saw it, too," John said, an uncomfortable shift in his eyes.

"He said, 'I didn't take him. I took you.'"

"What?" John gave her a puzzled look, and she sighed in frustration.

"Sammy! I asked him why, why he took my brother from me, and that was what he said. 'I took you.'"

"Well, you're here now. He's insane, anyway." John attempted a smile. "He probably just said it to hurt you, to confuse you."

"Well, it worked." She let her head sink back onto the pillow. "John, everyone's avoiding the question: How long has it been? I know it's been more than days, but how bad is it? A month?"

He didn't answer.

"Two months?" she ventured. "I know it can't be more than a year or you'd have a nicer apartment," she said weakly, and he winced. "John, tell me," Charlie insisted, hearing her own voice rising, her heart beating faster as she waited for him to speak.

"Six months," he said at last. She didn't move. She could hear the blood rushing in her ears.

"Where have I been?" she asked, her voice barely audible over the rushing sound.

"Your aunt Jen, you were with her, at least I think that's where you were."

"You think?"

"I'll tell you everything, Charlie, I promise—as soon as I understand it myself. There are things I just don't know," he finished helplessly. She lay back, staring up at the ceiling. In the dim light, the stains looked like they could be decorative.

"About your aunt," John went on, something awful in his voice. "I saw her that night."

Charlie looked sharply at him. "That night?"

"The building was coming down; you were inside, and I was trying to get to you, and she was just suddenly there— I don't know how she got in, or why."

"It was her house, technically," Charlie said, turning back to the ceiling. "Maybe she was there looking for me."

"And that makes sense to you?"

"I don't know what makes sense," she said steadily. "It doesn't make sense what I remember and what I don't remember. There's no one moment where suddenly it all goes blank. But I don't remember Aunt Jen being there."

"Okay," he said.

"I have to see her," Charlie said with sudden intensity. "She's the only one who knows how all of the pieces fit; she's the one with all the secrets. She's always tried to protect me from them, but now . . . secrets aren't protecting anyone."

She stopped: John looked stricken, his face stuck between expressions like he was afraid to move it. "John?" Charlie said, a knot forming in her stomach. John took a breath as if to speak, then hesitated; she could see he was searching for words. She gave them to him. "She's dead, isn't she?" Charlie said faintly. She felt like she was drifting off again, but she was not losing consciousness. John nodded.

"I'm sorry, Charlie," he said hoarsely. "I couldn't stop it."

Charlie looked back up at the stains. *I should feel something*, she thought. "You need your head clear," she whispered, echoing her aunt's habitual reminder.

"What?" John was watching her anxiously.

"Paperwork," she said more loudly. "She kept files on everything, locked up in cabinets. Whatever she knew, she wrote it down, or someone else did. Where was she?"

"A house, in Silver Reef, the ghost town," John stammered; he looked taken aback. "There were files there, boxes of papers."

"Then we have to go back there," Charlie said firmly. John looked as if he wanted to protest, but he just nodded.

"*She* might go back there, too, if she thinks you'll be there." John shared a worried look.

"We have to go."

"Then we go there," he said. Charlie closed her eyes, the decision releasing her into sleepiness. The door opened, and dimly, Charlie heard Marla and John whispering to each other. She took a deep breath, like she was going underwater, and let herself slip into the dark.

CHAPTER TEN

Hey!" Something poked Jessica's shoulder, and she shrugged it away and rolled over, still half-asleep. *"Hey, you okay?"* Something poked her cheek, much harder, and she opened her eyes and looked up to see a ring of children surrounding her, staring with wide eyes. Jessica screamed.

Someone grabbed her from behind, covering her mouth, and she struggled to get away.

"You have to be quiet," a desperate voice whispered, and she turned to face a red-haired girl of about seven, looking at her anxiously. "If you're not quiet, it'll come get you," she explained.

Jessica sat up carefully and put a hand on her head; it felt like it was stuffed with cotton, and her sinuses were burning. "Not again." *Chloroform, or whatever that gas was.*

"What?" the girl asked.

"Nothing," Jessica said, looking at the frightened faces that surrounded her. There were four children in all, two boys and two girls: There was the young redheaded girl with freckles on her nose, and a stocky, African American boy of about the same age, who looked like he had been crying before she arrived. He was sitting cross-legged with a young Latina girl of three or four on his lap, hiding her face in his shirt. Her fine brown hair had all but come loose from two long braids down her back, each capped with a pink ribbon, and the matching pink shorts and T-shirt she wore were stained and filthy. The last little boy, a skinny blond kindergartener with a massive bruise on his forearm, hung back a little from the rest, his hair hanging over his face. They were all looking at her like they expected her to do something.

"What is this disgusting place?" Jessica wiped her hands on her shirt and shook out her hair as though it might be full of spiders. She stopped in midshake, and turned to the kids as though seeing them again for the first time. Her mouth hung open slightly.

"You're the kids." She gasped. "I mean, you're the kids, the ones that were taken, and you're *alive*!" She suddenly remembered the mother at the hospital. *We have to find that kid and bring him home*, Jessica had insisted to John, the words sounding hollow even to her own ears. Now the kids were standing right in front of her. *It's not too late to save you*, she thought, filling her with new purpose. She looked at the little blond boy. "Are you Jacob?" she asked, her heart fluttering, and his eyes widened in response.

"Hey, it's going to be okay," she said, trying to believe her own words. "I'm Jessica." None of them answered her right away, instead glancing at one another, trying to reach some silent consensus. Leaving them to it, Jessica stood, surveying their surroundings.

It was a dank, brick-walled room with a very low ceiling, so low that Jessica couldn't fully stand upright. The room had exposed pipes all along the walls, some of them giving off plumes of steam. There was a large tank in one corner, probably a hot-water heater, and in the far corner was a door. Jessica went to it.

"Don't!" the redheaded girl squealed.

"It's okay," Jessica said, trying to make her tone soothing. "I'm going to get us all out of here. Let's just see if it's locked," she said, hearing her own voice ring out cheerful and hearty. She sounded patronizing; it was a tone she'd always despised in adults when she was a child. "I'll just check," she said more normally. She walked briskly toward the door.

"No!" three voices cried. Jessica hesitated, then grasped the knob firmly and gave it a twist. Nothing happened. Behind her, one of the children let out a sigh of relief.

"It's okay," Jessica said, turning back to them. "There's always another way out." She scanned their anxious, grimy faces. "What happened here?" she asked. The boy with the child on his lap looked at her suspiciously.

"Why should we tell you anything? You could be one of them."

"I'm in here, same as you," Jessica pointed out. She dropped down to sit beside him, putting herself on the children's eye level. "My name is Jessica."

"Ron," he said. The little girl on his lap tapped his shoulder, and he bent down as she whispered something in his ear. "Her name's Lisa," he added.

"Alanna," the redhead said, a little too loudly. The blond boy didn't say anything. Jessica eyed him, but did not ask.

"Hi, Ron, Lisa, Alanna, and, Jacob," Jessica said with excruciating patience. "Can you tell me what happened?"

"She ate me in her tummy," Lisa whispered. Instantly, Jessica felt the blood rush from her face.

"You mean the clown girl?" Jessica asked softly. "The robot girl?" The children nodded in unison.

"I was in the woods," Alanna said. She held her hand against her stomach, then mimed the clamp shooting out. "Chomp!" she said, her face deadly serious.

"I was riding my bike by my house," Ron said. "There was a woman in the road—she came out of nowhere, and I fell off the bike, I was trying not to hit her." He gestured to his knees, and Jessica noticed for the first time that they were scabbed over. *He's been here long enough for those to heal,* she thought, but held her tongue, afraid if she interrupted he would stop talking altogether. "When I got up, she was standing over me," Ron continued. "I thought she was trying to help. I told her I was okay, and she smiled, and then . . ." He glanced down at the girl on his lap for a moment, then went on. "I swear, honest, her stomach split right open, and there was this big metal *thing* that came out of it, and—" He shook his head. "She's not going to believe us."

"Did the thing grab you and pull you inside?" Jessica asked softly, and he looked up at her in surprise.

"Yeah," he said. "Did she get you, too?" he asked.

"No, but I've seen it happen," she said half-truthfully. "Then what?"

"I don't know. Next thing I remember I woke up in here."

"What about her?" Jessica gestured to the girl on his lap. He shrugged, looking briefly embarrassed.

"As soon as she woke up, she climbed onto my lap."

"Do you know her?"

"You mean from before?" He looked down at the little girl again.

"No, none of us knew one another before," Alanna said. Jessica looked at the little blond boy, and he looked away.

"Okay, well listen," Jessica said, and they all turned their eyes to her again. *Creepy. Like I'm really a grown-up or something,* she thought uneasily. She took a deep breath. "I've dealt with . . . *things* like this before."

"Really?" Alanna was suddenly skeptical; Ron watched her warily. Lisa opened one eye, then pressed her face back into Ron's shirt.

"I'm *not* with them," Jessica said hurriedly. "I'm locked in here with you because I got caught trying to find out more about them."

"Did you know about us?" Ron asked.

"Not much, but I'm glad that I found you—everybody's been looking for you. The people who took you, they're trying to hurt a friend of mine—they already have hurt her—and I came here to stop them, to save her from them. Now that I know you're here, I'm going to save you from them, too."

"You're locked in here, just like us," Alanna said, this time like she believed it. Jessica suppressed a smile, momentarily amused.

"I have friends out there, and they're going to help, we're going to get you out of this." Alanna still looked suspicious, but Lisa was peeking at her from behind her hair, loosening her grip on Ron's shirt for the first time. "I promise you, everything is going to be all right," Jessica said with a surge of confidence. She looked at the children with calm determination, surprised to realize she had meant every word.

"John! Charlie!" Carlton burst in to John's apartment, the door hitting the wall as it swung open.

Marla jumped, sitting up straight on the couch. "Carlton, what's going on?"

He didn't respond, scanning the room. Marla was alone; she had the TV on at a low volume. The door to John's room was closed, and he went to it. "No one's here," Marla said with a hint of disapproval, but Carlton rushed to look inside anyway. "John's not here; neither is Charlie," Marla called.

"Well, I ran into one of them," Carlton said grimly. "One of the Charlies, that is. The bad one. Where is John? Where's everyone?"

"John and Charlie went somewhere; they seemed to be in a hurry and they wouldn't say where they were going."

"Jessica?"

"I haven't seen her. She's probably at home."

"I was just at her apartment, she's not there." Carlton stared at Marla, palpable dread rising between them. "Charlie—the other Charlie, I didn't even hear her come in; she didn't knock or anything. It was like she knew Jessica wouldn't be there."

"Wait, shut up," Marla said suddenly, pointing to the TV.

"Marla, this is serious!" Carlton said with alarm.

"Look at this; they've been playing this commercial all day." Then the cartoonish face of a little girl, painted like a clown, filled the screen.

"Come dressed as a clown and eat for free!" said a booming voice, then the camera cut to the front of a restaurant.

"That—that's her!" Carlton shouted. "I mean the sign, the girl on the sign, the clown girl thing!" Marla leaned forward, squinting at the screen. Carlton stopped, thoughtful for a moment. "She was taller, and a little attractive. It was really confusing; so many emotions."

"They've been playing these all day. New restaurant, animatronic characters . . ."

"It's like the girl on the sign was all grown-up, and wanted to feed me pizza . . ." He trailed off.

"Carlton!" Marla yelled, snapping him back to the present.

"You know where it is? The new place?" he asked.

"Yes," Marla announced. She flipped off the TV and stood. "Let's go." Carlton looked her grimly up and down, then took the other earpiece out of his pocket.

"Put this in your ear," he said. "It's all we have; trust me."

"Okay." Marla snatched the earpiece out of his hand on her way out the door. "I guess you'll fill me in on the way?" Carlton didn't answer as he hurried after her, slamming the door behind them.

CHAPTER ELEVEN

As they drove through the ghost town, Charlie could feel John's eyes on her. She had not spoken since they got in the car, and she was beginning to dread the moment she would have to speak again. John made a sharp turn, jostling the car, and she jerked forward in her seat, pressing into the seat belt.

"Sorry," John said sheepishly. Charlie eased back again.

"It's fine," she said with a small smile. "I know this might be a strange time to ask, but, where is *my* car?"

"I'm afraid your doppelganger has your car." He eyed her nervously, and she forced a crooked smile and nodded.

"What would that police report look like, I wonder?" she said lightly, and John grinned.

John slowed to a stop, his expression fading. "This is it," he said quietly. Charlie opened her door and got out. They were at the bottom of a hill; John had stopped beside a narrow archway with a small, metal star at its crest. At the top of the hill was a small house.

"Okay, let's get this over with," Charlie said. She looked around nervously, half expecting someone to come running at them. "Let's go."

As they climbed the hill, John looked several times like he wanted to say something, but did not. When they reached the front porch, Charlie put a hand on his arm.

"So, she's still in there?" she asked. "Jen, I mean."

He nodded. "Yeah. At least, I think so. Are you sure you want to do this?"

"I have to."

"I'll go in first," he offered. "I can . . . cover her up, if you want me to." He looked at her, distressed. Charlie hesitated.

"No," she said finally, and grasped the knob firmly. The door wasn't locked, and Charlie scanned the room apprehensively as she entered. The place was in disarray, everything blended into everything else, and at first nothing stood out. Then they saw her.

There was a woman in the corner, by the hallway; she was huddled against the wall, curled over herself, and her dark hair hung thickly over her face. Charlie heard a sharp intake of breath, then realized it was her own. She held a hand out stiffly behind her, unable to say in words what she needed, but John saw, and took her hand, stepping close behind her.

"That's really her?"

"Yeah," he whispered. "Did you want to get closer?" John asked uncertainly.

Charlie shook her head. "No. It's not her anymore," she whispered, turning away, closing it off in her mind. She took a deep breath. "Where did you find . . . me?" She gestured to herself, to make sure John knew which Charlie she meant.

"That way."

John led her to the hallway, keeping wide of Jen's slumped body; Charlie forced herself not to look directly at her, allowing herself to see only a dark, hunched shape in the corner of her eye as she passed. At the end of the hall was the open door to a storage room, filled with trunks and cardboard boxes. The window was open, and it was not until she breathed fresh air that Charlie noticed the damp, moldy smell that had taken over the rest of the house.

"This one," John said. He was standing beside a large green trunk, its lid standing open.

"In here?" Charlie said bleakly, stepping over several boxes to get to him. She peered inside: there was a small pillow, and nothing else. "I was just in there?" she asked, somehow disappointed.

"Yeah. I mean, Jen must have had a reason. She must have known about the imposter. Maybe she put you there just before we arrived."

Charlie reached out and closed the trunk. "I want to look around."

"What are we looking for?" John asked, and she shrugged, opening another trunk.

"Anything," she said. "If there's anything useful, this is where it will be. We need to know what we're up against."

They searched in silence for a while. None of the boxes were labeled, and Charlie opened them haphazardly, sifting quickly through the ones containing paperwork, and setting aside the others unexamined. Those contained random assortments of household items—dishes and silverware, knickknacks Charlie recognized from childhood, even some of her old toys. She scanned a box of Jen's tax documents carefully, then replaced them, finding nothing that seemed to stand out. She reached for another box, then saw John giving her a funny look.

"What?" she asked. He smiled, and there was a hint of something sad beyond it.

"You read really fast," was all he said.

"Didn't anyone ever teach you how to speed-read?" she said briefly, then turned her attention elsewhere. Charlie abandoned the stack of boxes she had been going through and went to the far corner of the room. She shoved a precarious pile of neatly folded sheets and towels aside, and sat down cross-legged on the carpet. From here, she could not even see John, though she could hear him, shuffling through paper and muttering to himself under his breath. She swept her eyes up and down the stacks, one after another, then she saw it: *Henry*, written in her aunt's careful script. Charlie moved three overcoats and another box, and then it was in her hands.

She stared at the lettering for a long moment. The ink had faded over the years. Charlie traced it with her index finger, her pulse fluttering in her throat like her heart was trying to get out. *Daddy.* She opened the box, and saw it—on top was an old, green plaid flannel shirt, worn down as thin and soft as cotton. She picked it up as if it were something delicate, and pressed it to her face, inhaling through the fiber. It only smelled like dust and time, but the touch of the fabric on her face brought tears to her eyes. She breathed in and out slowly, trying to force them back, and finally regained her composure, though part of her howled out the unfairness of it, that she could not even take a moment to cling to his slight presence, and mourn. Self-consciously, Charlie put the shirt over her shoulders, letting it drape over her back as she leaned once more over the box. The rest of the box was stacked with smaller boxes, and she opened the first one to find a framed picture of herself with Sammy, infants in those few, precious years before everything was ripped apart. Under the picture was an envelope, addressed in her father's handwriting, to "Jenny." Charlie smiled and shook her head. *I can't imagine anyone calling Aunt Jen, "Jenny."* She opened the letter.

My Dearest Jenny,

I had an entire list of instructions written out for you; schedules and timetables, keys and procedures. You have indulged me so much, and it's only now, at the end, that I see how it has helped me get through these dark times, but also how ultimately empty it has been. I had everything so carefully planned; I've worked so tirelessly. I've warped and twisted my surroundings to the point where I can never be sure if I've completely settled back into reality, and even if I did manage to turn off everything planted in the walls to deceive myself, I think my mind would deceive me still. I don't need clinical testing of the long-term effects of these devices to know that I've undoubtedly done permanent damage to myself. I will always see what I want to see, but worse than that, there is the splinter, more like the stake, always deep into my heart reminding me more and more every day that what I see is a lie. Through your patience and your indulgence of me, you've tried to keep me happy, but it's also somehow brought me back from this world I've made for myself. I think maybe it would have been better for you to have not indulged me; then I could have excluded you from my bubble, convinced myself that you were crazy like everyone else. But instead, your unceasing love caused me to listen to you, to let you in, and the consequence of that was seeing the truth in your eyes, and letting that in as well.

I have my Charlie here with me. You will never have to indulge me in her again. Rather than taking joy in her, I have cried over her, so many countless tears. I have poured agony into her, until she serves as another reminder not of what I once had, but of the unbearable pain of what was taken from me. She has come to reflect my pain back to me; whereas I, for a time, took great comfort in her eyes, I now only see loss, endless, debilitating loss. Her eyes will never fill me again. In fact, they have emptied me.

Keep all the closets shut. Let them be tombs for my denial and my grievance. My only lasting instruction for you concerns the fourth closet. It is not enough to keep it shut, you must keep that one sealed and buried. My grief was already beginning to waken me to reality when I began what was to be her final stage. When I rose, slightly, from the depth of my despair, I saw that I had no choice but to cease my work, for I was only feeding my own delusion. My old faithful partner, who I can only hope now is in a grave of his own, took what I had begun, and made something of his own—something dreadful. He crafted my beloved work into something of his own, and endowed it with who knows what kinds of evil. I was able to stop him, and to seal away what he made, and you, Jenny, must ensure that the seal remains.

I would instruct you to demolish the house if I could trust that
it could be done effectively. Keep it, and make sure the world
forgets it. Then, someday, after many decades have passed and
no one remembers, fill it with every kind of flammable thing
and burn it to the ground, standing close guard to put a bullet
into anything that emerges from the rubble, no matter what, or
who, it looks like.

I'm going to be with my daughter.

Love always & to the end,

Henry

"Charlie?" John was standing behind her. Wordlessly, she held the pages out to him. He took them, and she moved aside the box the letter had been in and stared down at the next one. It was sealed with packing tape, but the sticky side was old and dry, the edges curling up from the cardboard. John shuffled the pages, still reading. Charlie shivered, despite the warm air, and she put her arms through the sleeves of her father's shirt and rolled them up to her elbows.

"Do you know what it means?" John asked quietly. Charlie looked up at him and shook her head. "Scoot over," he said with a small smile, and she did, making room for him in the little space among the boxes. He sat down facing her, crossing his legs awkwardly. He handed the pages back to her, and she scanned them again. "What did he mean about the closets?" John said.

"I don't know," Charlie said drily.

"Think," John protested. "It has to mean something."

"I don't know," Charlie repeated. "You were there; they were always empty. Except the one with Ella."

"You don't know that," John said softly. "There was one that was locked," he continued, almost to himself.

"It doesn't matter, does it?" Charlie said. "The house is gone. Unless you feel like digging through more rubble, this is all we have." She pried the box with the peeling tape out of the larger box and handed it to him. All that was left under it was a lockbox, which opened easily when she tugged at the lid. It, too, was filled with papers: on top was a fine-pencil drawing of a familiar face.

"That's Ella," John said, peering over her shoulder.

"Yeah," Charlie said. Her father had captured the doll's delicate features in exquisite detail, not only her face but her shiny, synthetic hair, and the tiny creases in her dark, starched dress. Her eyes were open wide, and their blank stare was at odds with the rest of the picture: a perfectly lifelike representation of something lifeless.

"I didn't realize he was such an artist," John said, and Charlie smiled.

"He said he drew things so he could see them, that it didn't work the other way around." She handed John the picture; below it was another, again of Ella, this time from the side. The next showed only Ella's face, in profile.

"He made Ella, right?" John asked, and Charlie tilted her head, considering the drawing.

Charlie sorted through the rest of the pile more quickly and shook her head, confused. "They're all of Ella."

John picked up the remaining cardboard box and ripped the tape off with sound like tearing cloth. It stuck to his fingers as he balled it up, and from the corner of her eye, Charlie saw him struggling to dislodge it. She paged through the drawings again.

"Look at the notes." She handed him the first drawing they had looked at, growing impatient as he peered at her father's meticulous, but tiny handwriting. He read it out slowly.

"Height: 81 cm; Head circumference . . ." He looked up. "It's just measurements." Charlie handed him another drawing. "Looks the same to me," John said, then flicked his eyes to the notations. *"Height: 118 cm."* John tilted the page as though he might be reading it wrong.

"This one says 164.5," Charlie said, holding up another, seemingly identical picture. "I don't understand," she said, setting the page in her lap. "Did he make another Ella?" She traced a finger along the line of Ella's hair, smudging the pencil mark, then a thought struck her. "I wonder if he was trying to make it up to me," she said.

"What do you mean?"

"If he was trying to give me . . . a companion; a friend, because of what happened." She met John's eyes, unable to say what she really meant.

"You mean Sammy? Because you lost your twin, he wanted to give you a doll that would . . . what, grow up with you?" John said incredulously, and she nodded, relieved that he had made sense of her half-spoken words.

"Maybe," Charlie said softly. His eyes were pinched with worry, and he looked away, studying the drawings in his hands again.

"It doesn't really make sense, though, does it?" Charlie said. "What would I do with a five-and-a-half-foot doll on a track?" She reached for the letter again, holding it like a talisman though she did not need to read from it. "Was there a bigger version of Ella in the locked closet?"

John's eyes searched the air without a target in the silent room for several long moments, then snapped back to attention. Charlie was quietly looking down at her own hand, slowly curling her fingers, then uncurling them. The silence dragged on, smothering, then John grabbed Charlie's hand, startling her.

"I saw your blood."

"What?" Charlie said, startled.

"I saw your blood that night. You bled. I don't think Ella bleeds, do you?" The statement was absurd, but John was watching her uneasily, as if he expected a response. Seconds passed, and Charlie did not know what to say. "I thought you were dead that night," John whispered at last.

"But I'm not dead, right?" She locked eyes with John. "I'm alive, right?" She took his hand, and he grasped hers tightly. He covered her hand in both his own, and she gave him a puzzled smile. "John?" she repeated nervously, and his jaw tightened. He looked on the point of speaking, when Charlie suddenly turned her head toward the window.

"What is it?" John said with alarm. Charlie put a finger to her lips and tilted her head to listen. *There's someone outside.* John watched her face intently, then his eyes widened as he registered the sound, too: the footsteps crunched one last time on gravel outside, then were silent.

Around back, he mouthed, and Charlie nodded, dropping his hands and steadying herself on the trunk behind her as she stood. John hastened to help her, but she waved him off.

"Come on," she whispered. "Back door?"

"I don't know." He started to make his way toward the hall, motioning her to follow. "Charlie, hurry." John had doubled back to her, and was pointing urgently to the door. She shoved the letter into her back pocket, and followed him, picking her way cautiously through the debris of the storage room.

In the hallway, the thick and musty air hit like a wave, and Charlie swallowed her revulsion, trying not to picture her aunt's body curled up in the next room. They crept down the hallway toward the front room, and the door, shuffling their feet so as to make no noise. At the end of the hall, John stopped, and Charlie waited, listening. There was only silence, then a wind chime rattled outside the front door, and they pulled back into the recess of the hall. John looked grim. "There." He nodded to the door opposite the storage room, which was slightly ajar. "Was that open before?"

"Yes," Charlie answered. "I mean, I think so." They made their way slowly toward the open door: Charlie breathed shallowly, trying to register the slightest noise over the pounding of her own heart. As they reached the doorway, she heard a rustling, like someone stepping on soft leaves. John and Charlie split up and stood on either side of the doorway, Charlie by the hinges and John by the knob, and slowly, he pushed the door the rest of the way open. Charlie saw the relief on his face before she saw what was in the room: a bed, a dresser, and absolutely nothing else, not even a closet. There was a window open, and John turned back toward Charlie. "I think we've got a way out," he said. She smiled back shakily. "Stay back while I check," he whispered, and before she could answer, he had pushed the door farther open into the room, and was moving stealthily toward the open window, keeping in a straight line through the center of the room. Charlie stayed in the hall, pressing the door open so she could see the entirety of the room.

Charlie watched nervously. *Hurry,* she urged him silently. Then as she thought it, she felt the door stop against her fingers as though something was blocking the way. *Is there something behind the door?* Slowly, noiselessly, she leaned to the side and put her eye to the crack in the door, along the hinges. Her heart stopped.

Another eye was looking back at her.

Charlie staggered back. The door wavered for a moment, then slammed shut. From inside the room something banged and crashed over and over against the wall. "John!" Charlie cried, and beat against the door. Suddenly, the house went still, and a few moments later the door drifted open and a figure glided out gracefully, stepping into the hall with care as though trying not to wake a sleeping baby. Charlie stared disbelievingly at her duplicate, her mind hazily registering all the tiny differences between them as she struggled for words.

"You're not me," Charlie managed to say, and her own face smiled cruelly back at her.

"I'm the only *you* that matters."

CHAPTER TWELVE

s it working?" Marla asked, nervously tapping the device in her ear. Carlton sped up the car.

"Mine worked," he said brusquely. He glanced at her; she was kneading her hands together, her knuckles going white. "I mean, you can't *really* tell if it's working until . . ."

"Until what?" Marla said.

"Well, until you're in danger, and . . ."

"And what?" Marla seemed impatient.

"And you don't die." Carlton nodded reassuringly.

"So how do we know if they're *not* working?" Marla's voice had lost its energy.

"Well, if it doesn't work, you won't have to worry about it for long." He smiled.

"Right." Marla stopped fidgeting with the device and put her hand in her lap.

"It will work. I rewired yours exactly like mine."

"I'm not usually in the thick of this stuff," Marla said. "I come in afterward with hugs and Band-Aids. If this were a movie, I'd be the lame babysitter, not the action hero." There was a hint of bitterness in her voice, and Carlton looked at her, surprised.

"Carlton, the road!"

He snapped his attention back to what he was doing and gave the wheel a controlled jerk.

"Marla, I've seen you in the thick of this stuff—remember Freddy's?"

She gave a halfhearted nod.

"And don't dismiss the power of hugs and Band-Aids," he added, slowing the car as the restaurant's sign came into view: CIRCUS BABY'S PIZZA blazed out over the night, casting half the block in garish red light. "Can't miss this," Carlton remarked as they pulled into the parking lot. As soon as they were past the neon sign, its brilliant, witchy light faded into the background: the lot was stark and bare.

"No one's here. Are you sure about this?" Marla said urgently.

"No, but I know what I saw." Carlton drove slowly toward the entrance, pointing toward the clown girl mascot leaning over the entryway sign. "And *that* is who attacked me."

They parked close to the building. Carlton stopped to rummage around in the trunk for a minute, coming up with two small flashlights. He flicked one on and off experimentally, then handed it to Marla.

"Thanks," she whispered.

They started around the side of the building and Carlton swept his light along the wall, illuminating a row of tall, rectangular windows. The window surfaces were tinted so dark they could not see in, and the frames were smooth black metal, with nowhere to force an opening. Carlton shook his head, and gestured toward the back of the building. Marla nodded, gripping her flashlight like a lifeline.

There was more parking behind the building, and the back wall was lined with trash cans, two Dumpsters sticking out on either side of a metal door. The only light came from a single, flickering orange bulb, set above the plain door like a decoration.

"Looks like this is our way in," Carlton whispered.

"Look." Marla shone her light down onto fresh prints in the mud, tracking close to the wall and leading up to the door. "Jessica?" Marla looked to Carlton.

"Maybe."

Marla grabbed the door handle and pulled hard, but it didn't budge.

"I don't think we'll find another way in," she whispered, and he grinned.

"You think I didn't come prepared?" Carlton said, slipping a flat leather case from his pocket. He held it out to her. "Hold this," he said, and selected several thin strips of metal as she balanced the case for him.

"Are those lockpicks?" Marla hissed.

"If there's one thing I've learned from watching my dad, it's that lockpicking can be used for good," Carlton said solemnly. He bent over the lock, trying to keep his head out of the way of the light, and slowly began to wriggle the lock picks into place.

"Oh, whatever. You can't pick a lock . . . can you? Is it even legal to own these?" Marla asked. He looked back at her; she was holding the kit away from her body as if trying to disassociate herself from it.

"It's legal as long as you don't pick any locks," he said. "Now be quiet so I can pick this lock." Marla looked around nervously, but didn't say anything. He turned his attention back to the door, listening for the telltale clicks of the tumblers falling into place as he carefully made his way through the mechanism.

"This is taking forever," Marla whined.

"I didn't say I was good at this," he said absently. "Got it!" He grinned, triumphant.

The door opened with a creak, revealing a wide hallway with a gentle upward slope. The hall itself was dark, but a few yards ahead, they could see the dim glow of florescent

lights. Marla pulled the door closed behind them, cushion-
ing it with her hand so that it wouldn't slam. The light was
coming from an open door on the left side of the hall: they
waited, but no sound came from its direction, and they started
to move, hugging the wall. As they got closer, Carlton sniffed
the air. "Shh," Marla hissed, and he jerked his head toward
the door.

"Pizza," he whispered. "Can't you smell it?" Marla nodded, and impatiently waved him forward.

"Of all the smells in this place, *that's* the one that catches
your attention?" The open door proved to be the kitchen,
and they glanced around briefly, then Carlton went to a
large refrigerator and pulled it open.

"Carlton, forget the pizza!" Marla said in dismay, but the
refrigerator held only racks of ingredients. Carlton closed
the door.

"You never know who could have been hiding in there,"
he said quietly as they exited the kitchen. At the end of the
hall was a swinging double door, with small windows just at
Carlton's eye height, and he surveyed what he could see of
the next room, then pushed the door open. Marla gasped.

"Creepy," Carlton said mildly. The dining room in front
of them was lit with the same dim, florescent light, giving
the brand-new place an odd dullness. There were tables and
chairs at the center, and arcade games and play areas along all
the walls, but their eyes were drawn immediately to the

small stage at the back corner. Its purple curtain was pulled open, and it was empty, except for a bright yellow rope strung across the front and a sign with a picture of a clock on it. NEXT SHOW: it read in neat, handwritten letters, but the clock had no hands. Marla shivered, and Carlton nudged her. "It's not the same," he whispered.

"It's exactly the same," she said. Carlton looked around at the rest of the room, his eyes lighting on a ball pit that stuck out from the front wall in a half circle, a round red plastic awning arcing over it, trimmed with white.

"Look at the monkey bars." She pointed. Across the room, three small children steadily climbed the tangled structure of red and yellow bars. Carlton, startled, looked at Marla with surprise, then ran to them.

"Are you okay? Where are your parents?" he asked breathlessly, then his mouth went dry. The children were not human, or alive. Their animatronic faces were painted like clowns, their features absurdly exaggerated: One had a round, red nose that covered half its face and a white wig of synthetic curls; another had a molded smile on its face and a painted red grimace. The third, a red-cheeked, smiling clown with a rainbow-colored wig, looked almost cute, except for the gigantic spring that replaced the middle of its torso, boinging up and down each time it moved. All of them had black eyes, with no iris or pupil, and they did not appear to see Carlton. He waved his hands, but they did not turn their heads, just kept grasping the bars with their pudgy hands, and pulling themselves along the structure with uncanny precision. All of them emitted a loud whirring sound, as if they were wind-up toys that had been set loose to climb. The child with the spring suddenly flung its top half over the top of the bars, the spring extending into a long, wavy wire, then it grabbed a bar, and its feet shot into the air wildly, and came snapping back into place on the other side.

"My mistake, you're not the kids we're looking for, carry on," Carlton whispered shakily, as the creatures continued, weaving over and under, back and forth through the structure. "They don't see us," Marla whispered, and it took him a moment to register her voice.

"What?" he said, his eyes still on the clown-children.

"They don't see us," she repeated. "These little things are working." She tapped her ear.

"Right, good," Carlton said, pulling himself away from the scene. Marla was smiling with relief. "We still have to be careful, though," he warned. "I can't guarantee it works on everything, and it definitely won't work on people."

Marla shivered, then nodded quickly. "There's a room past the stage," she said.

"Looks like an arcade," Carlton said grimly.

Marla slowed by the stage, her hand drifting toward the curtain as if she might try to look behind it. "No." Carlton grabbed Marla's hand. "The last thing we want to do is call any attention to ourselves." Marla nodded in agreement.

The arcade smelled overpoweringly of new plastic, the games gleaming and scarcely played. There were a dozen or so freestanding arcade cabinets, and two pinball machines, one—predictably, by now—clown-themed, and the other painted with cartoonish snake charmers. Carlton gave them a wide berth. Marla caught his sleeve and gestured to a closed door on the wall to their left, an EXIT sign glowing red above it, and he nodded. They headed for it, creeping past a "test your strength" game, governed by an adult-size clown with a face made of jagged metal plates who nodded continuously, its painted smile maniacal. As they passed Carlton watched it carefully, but its eyes did not seem to track their movements. When they reached the door, Carlton took a deep breath, then gently pushed on the bar. It gave way immediately, and Marla sighed with relief. Carlton pushed the door open, holding it out for her, then froze as the unmistakable clack of servos broke the silence behind them.

They both spun around; Carlton braced his arm in front of Marla's chest protectively, his heart racing, but nothing was moving. He scanned the room, then saw it: the clown standing over the game was staring at them, its head cocked to the side. Carlton glanced at Marla, and she nodded minutely: she had seen it, too. Slowly, she backed through the door, as Carlton watched the animatronic, but it showed no further signs of movement. When Marla was safely through the door, Carlton waved his arms, hoping desperately that it would not see him. The clown remained motionless, having apparently returned to stasis. Carlton slipped out of the room and closed the door carefully behind him. He turned, and almost fell over Marla, who was backed up almost to the wall. "Watch it," he whispered good-naturedly, catching her shoulder for balance.

Then he looked up, and swayed on his feet, disoriented by a dozen distorted, menacing figures. He took a breath, and the room fell into place: *mirrors*. Before them was an array of funhouse mirrors, each one distorting the images it reflected. Carlton's eyes flitted from one to the next—one showed him and Marla as tall as the ceiling; in the next they were blown up like balloons, crowding each other out of the frame; in the next their bodies looked normal, but their heads shrank to stalks an inch wide.

"Okay, then," he whispered. "How do we get out of here?"

As if in answer to his question, two mirrors slowly began to swivel, turning toward each other until they had made a narrow door in the wall of close-set panels. Beyond the small opening lay more mirrors, but Carlton could not tell how many there were, or which way they were directed, as one mirror caught another, doubling the reflections until it was impossible to see what was real and what was not. Marla stepped through the gap and beckoned: there was a gleam in her eye, but Carlton couldn't tell if it was excitement, or the strange, dim light. He followed her, and as soon as he was through the gap the panels began to pivot again, closing them inside. Carlton glanced around, growing nervous now that their exit had been blocked off. They seemed to be in a narrow corridor that branched off in two directions, the walls made of more floor-to-ceiling mirror panels.

"It's a maze," Marla whispered, and gave him a smile when she saw the look on his face. "Don't worry," she added. "I'm good at mazes."

"You're good at mazes?" Carlton said with irritation. "What is that supposed to mean? *I'm good at mazes.*"

"What's wrong with saying that? I've always been good with mazes." Marla shook her head.

"What, like the *hay maze*? When we were five? Is that what you're talking about?"

"I got through it before anyone else did."

"You climbed over the top of the bales. You're not supposed to do that."

"Oh, you're right." Marla's face flushed. "I'm not good at mazes."

"We will get through this together." Carlton took her hand, long enough to stop her from having a panic attack, then released it.

She looked in both directions, thoughtful, then pointed decisively. "Let's try that way," she said. They started down the path she had chosen, and Carlton followed, keeping his eyes on her feet in front of him. After only a few steps he heard her sharp intake of breath, and snapped his head up: they were at a dead end.

"Dead end already?" he said, surprised.

"No, the panel closed," she hissed.

"This way, *hay maze*," Carlton said with a hint of amusement. "Back this way."

They started back the way they had come, and this time Carlton saw the panels move: as they moved back to the spot where they had come in, a panel swung toward them, cutting off their path. A second later, another panel swung away, opening a new corridor. Marla hesitated, and Carlton stepped up beside her. "No choice, let's go," he said. She nodded, and they walked deeper into the maze.

As soon as they had crossed the new threshold, the panel swung shut. They looked around for the new opening, but there was none: they were enclosed on all sides by mirrors. Carlton walked the small perimeter quickly, beginning to panic.

"Carlton, just wait, another one will open," Marla whispered.

"*I kn-ow you're in h-ere.*" An unfamiliar voice rang out. It seemed to come from everywhere at once, echoing like it was bouncing from panel to panel. The sound was mechanical, glitching out midword. They exchanged a glance: Marla's face was pale with fear.

"There!" Carlton pointed. A panel had opened while they were distracted. He rushed for it, and walked into a mirror, smacking his head on the glass. "Ow."

"It's there," Marla hissed, pointing to the opposite side of the enclosure.

The panel began to swing shut, closing the room off again.

"I'll f-ind you . . ." The glitching voice had a strange, unsteady tone.

"Carlton!" Marla stood in the gap, holding out a hand, and he ran for her, both of them making it through just as the panel rotated back to its position.

"What were you going to do, stand there and let it crush you?" Carlton hissed.

"I hadn't considered we could get caught between the panels. This place is just asking for a lawsuit." Marla straightened herself. "It's been a lovely evening, but I think I'd like you to take me home now," she said calmly.

"Take you home? Take *me* home!" Carlton said before pausing to listen.

"I know j-ust where you a-re . . ."

They were in a hallway again, this one with two corners to choose from. They exchanged a grim look and turned to the left, moving slowly. Carlton kept his eyes on Marla's shoes ahead of him, trying not to look at the walls on either side, where ranks of their duplicates marched silently beside them, misshapen and warped in the mirrors, then, occasionally, appearing normal. When they reached the corner, something flashed in the corner of his eye, a reflection of a reflection of giant eyes, staring at them. Carlton grabbed Marla's shoulder.

"Over there!" She shuddered.

"I saw it, too."

"Come on, go, go, go," Marla whispered. "Just follow me. Stay calm; remember, nothing can see us."

"I'm getting clo-ser . . ." The mechanical voice echoed through the chamber.

"It's just a recording," Carlton whispered. "It's coming from everywhere, I don't think there is anything actually in here with us." Marla nodded, looking unconvinced. A few steps ahead of them, panels began to pivot again, closing off their path: Carlton glanced behind them—the other end of the hall had closed, too. Marla inched closer to him.

"I see you . . ."

"Shut up," Carlton whispered. He tried to slow his breathing so it made no sound, imagining the air going in and out, filling his lungs without touching the sides. The panel to their right began to swing open slowly, and they backed out of its way. Marla gasped, and Carlton grabbed her arm, seeing it: there was something behind the slowly opening mirror, though he couldn't make out what. They backed up farther, taking small, cautious steps. Carlton searched the mirrored panels for an exit, but saw only his own face, bulging and deformed.

"There you are . . ."

The panel opened, revealing a kaleidoscope of purple, white, and silver, glancing off every mirror disjointedly. Carlton blinked, trying to make sense of the reflections, then a figure at the center stepped into the makeshift room.

He was a bear, built like Freddy Fazbear, and yet entirely unlike him: his metal body was gleaming white, accented with vibrant purple. He held a microphone in his hand, the top sparkling like a disco ball, and on his chest, at the center of a purple metal shirtfront, was a small, round speaker. Only a few feet from them, the new Freddy turned his massive head from side to side, his eyes passing over them. Carlton glanced at Marla, who tapped her ear and nodded. He put his finger to his lips. Freddy took two steps forward, and they stepped back, pressing against the wall. Freddy looked from side to side again.

"I kn-ow just wh-ere you are . . ." The sound was earsplitting, rattling Carlton's teeth, but Freddy's mouth did not move—the voice was projecting from the speaker in his chest.

Carlton held his breath as the bear's eyes passed over him, reminding himself that he was masked, but the bear's eyes hesitated on him before moving away. Carlton could feel the sweat beading on his forehead.

The wall behind them repositioned, and Carlton shifted his weight just in time not to fall, Marla moving just behind him. The panel swung open slowly, and they edged away as Freddy walked slowly in their direction, heading for the new exit—where they were now standing. Marla touched Carlton's arm, guiding him to the side just as Freddy lumbered past them, his shiny surface almost brushing against Carlton's nose.

"I'm get-ing closer," Freddy stuttered menacingly as he disappeared around a corner. The panel began to swing shut, and Marla pointed urgently to the door Freddy had come in. They raced for it, making it through just before the mirrors closed.

Carlton and Marla stared at each other, gasping as if they'd run miles. "Was that Freddy?" she whispered. He shook his head.

"I don't know, but he was different," Carlton said.

"What? Different from what?"

"The other animatronics we've seen so far. He was . . . looking at me," Carlton said uncomfortably.

"They're all looking at us."

"No, he was looking *at* me."

"I can hear you; come on out!" Freddy called out as if on cue. His voice echoed through the maze of mirrors, as impossible

to locate as it had been before. Carlton took a deep, steadying breath.

"How are we supposed to get out of here?" he whispered, trying to sound calmer than he felt. "Where even are we?"

"There, that light." Marla pointed over their heads at the rafters above them, where a red stage light beamed down over the entirety of the maze.

"What?"

"I saw that light when we first came in, but it must have been at least twenty feet away, now it's right over our heads. We just have to keep moving away from it now," she said confidently. Carlton studied the ceiling for a moment, considering what she'd said.

"I told you; I'm good at mazes." She winked. "We just have to wait for the right panels to open." She pointed toward a specific panel.

"That could take ages," Carlton said despairingly.

"It will take longer if we don't keep track of what direction we're going in," Marla said. "Come on." She set off down the path she had indicated, and Carlton followed close behind.

"I'm getting clo-ser . . ." Freddy's voice resounded through the maze.

"That sounded like it was behind us again. He's coming around," Carlton whispered.

"Okay, okay. Then we go around, too."

"Just get us out," he said quietly. Marla nodded, and they walked cautiously onward, flanked by their various, distorted duplicates.

The pivoting panels forced them nearly in a circle before giving them a choice of direction, and Marla leaped on the chance, grabbing Carlton by the hand and almost running down the passage until they were stopped again, and made to turn.

"Shh," Carlton hissed frantically.

Marla pushed experimentally on the side of one of the panels, but it didn't budge; Carlton stepped up to help, throwing his full weight against the mirror, but even under their combined force, it would not turn. "I don't know why I thought that would work," Marla whispered.

"I've almost g-ot you . . ." Freddy intoned. Marla looked around uncertainly.

"I've got a really terrible idea," Carlton said slowly. Marla gave him a warning look. "Are you still keeping track of where we are? Or at least, the direction that we should go?"

"I think so," she said, scanning the rafters again, a look of comprehension dawning on her face.

"Close enough," he said.

"What are you going to do?" Marla asked, sounding like she already regretted it. Carlton took the flashlight out of his pocket and made a fist around it, wound up his arm, and smashed the butt of the light into the mirror in front of them. The glass shattered with a high, clear noise, and a dull pain reverberated up his arm.

"I can h-ear you in th-ere . . ." Freddy's voice sputtered from all around them.

"Does he just say that, or did he actually hear that?" Marla said.

The panel with the broken mirror swung open, but before they could move there was a rushing sound of heavy footsteps and crunching glass shards. Carlton held his breath, and nodded to Marla. Freddy stepped into the room with forceful steps, then immediately stopped in the center, his upper body slowly turning to scan the surroundings. Carlton and Marla crept around the glass shards, and snuck through the open panel behind the animatronic. In the corridor, Carlton looked questioningly at Marla, and she pointed. He nodded, strode to the farthest mirror, and smashed it.

In an instant, Freddy pivoted toward them. The wide-eyed face turned from side to side. After a moment, another panel began to open beyond the freshly broken mirror. Carlton and Marla ran for it, the glass breaking beneath their feet. "There!" Marla yelled.

Carlton looked up and could see an EXIT sign above a door, just a few yards from where they stood. Marla caught Carlton's eye and mouthed, *We're almost there.*

"Come back here!" said Freddy's maniacal voice, and then they all stepped out into the last passage: a jauntily painted

ticket booth was visible, and beyond that, an open wall. Marla and Carlton exchanged a glance, and cautiously sped up. *"Got you,"* Freddy said. The speaker was right behind Carlton's head, and Carlton startled, tripping over his own feet.

He righted himself with a palm on the mirror, then took off after Marla, and ran straight into his own reflection, hitting his face on the glass. "Marla, wait!" he screamed: he could see her reflected in three mirrors, but was still unsure of where she had actually gone. "Wait." He rubbed his forehead, and looked into the nearest mirror, trying to see if he was bleeding. He was not, but something was wrong. It took him a second to realize that his earpiece had been knocked loose. He looked around in panic, when suddenly Freddy loomed behind him in the mirror.

Carlton froze in place; the massive white-and-purple bear's head was staring at him from the mirror, looming over his shoulder. He looked down and saw the earpiece at his feet, in one swift motion he leaned down to grab it. His hands were shaking, and he struggled to get it back into his ear. When he looked up, Freddy was standing over him, and Carlton was lifted off his feet with a sudden, painful force. Carlton jerked and dropped back to the ground, the earpiece falling beside him.

Freddy drew back and stared at Carlton for a moment, his eyes clicking back and forth, and his mouth opened just enough to reveal two long rows of perfectly polished white teeth. Carlton leaped toward the earpiece on the ground just as Freddy's arm shot out and shattered another glass panel. Carlton hit the wall headfirst with a bang, and recoiled in pain.

Freddy turned his head, first from side to side, then all the way around to face backward, his eyes searching wildly. Carlton scanned the ground in a panic, and saw the earpiece again, but it was in three places, in three mirrors. The glass crunched again nearby, but Carlton kept his eyes on the earpieces, switching from one to another in a desperate attempt to see which one was real. Suddenly, a human hand reached down and grabbed the earpiece in each of the three panels.

"Carlton!" Marla called, and he turned toward the sound and saw her, not a reflection but the real Marla as she threw the earpiece to him. Carlton snatched the earpiece out of the air, and shoved it into his ear. Freddy stopped in place, his arms still outstretched. Carlton didn't dare move, though the microphone was inches from his face. In his peripheral vision he could see Marla inching toward a door with EXIT over it. Freddy turned his head from side to side again as he slowly straightened from his attacking posture.

"*I'll f-ind you . . .*" came the voice from his chest, and he lowered his arms. Marla turned the doorknob, and pushed the door slowly open, just enough to see that it was unlocked. Scarcely breathing, Carlton backed away from Freddy, keeping his eyes on the animatronic until he was beside Marla.

In one fluid motion, she eased open the door, they darted through it, then shoved it closed behind them. There was a deadbolt near the top, and Carlton flipped it, put his ear to the crack. There was nothing but silence from the other side, and he turned to Marla and heaved a sigh, light-headed with relief. They were in a dark hall, completely free of mirrors.

"Dark, scary hallway," Marla muttered.

"It's beautiful," Carlton said.

A scream ripped through the air from somewhere nearby, and they both froze.

"Not finished yet," Carlton said, and took off running toward the sound, Marla close at his heels.

CHAPTER THIRTEEN

E veryone, be very quiet," Jessica whispered. The children just stared at her, their eyes wide and solemn. They stood together in the back corner of the small, dank room, awaiting her instructions: Three-year-old Lisa was still huddled behind Ron, her chosen protector, and Alanna had taken hold of the little blond boy's hand, though he was wriggling in her grasp. Jessica swallowed. *Why do I have to be the leader? It's bad enough when I'm just in charge of myself.*

She bent down to the children's level, trying to summon some kind of leadership quality. *Should have listened to Mom. Should have played a team sport. But no, I had to be the quiet girl in the corner chewing the eraser off her pencil.*

Jessica studied the door again, then took a more serious tone. "Is there something out there?" Alanna and Ron exchanged a worried glance. "What's outside? You can tell me," Jessica pleaded.

"It comes in through the door," Alanna said, not meeting Jessica's eyes. "She . . ." The little girl broke off and covered her face, mumbling something unintelligible behind the mask of her hands.

"She? Who, the . . . woman who took you?" Jessica asked gently, trying to contain her impatience. Alanna shook her head vigorously, her face still hidden.

"We thought it was a toy. It wasn't scary like everything else." Ron searched for words, and Lisa tugged on his shirt and whispered something, too quietly for Jessica to make out. Ron nudged her. "Tell her." Lisa looked up at Jessica with a suspicious expression on her grubby toddler's face.

"She's all mangled up," the girl said, then turned away again, hiding her face in Ron's shirt. He gave Jessica a distressed look.

"Who? Who's all mangled up?" Jessica said slowly, searching her mind for what they might be talking about. "Was something broken? Did you break one of them?" she asked hopefully. The little kids all began to sniffle again, and she ground her teeth. "What is it?" Jessica nearly snapped, but none of them seemed to notice her tone.

"It's not broken," Ron said, his voice rising in panic, and then the floor shook with a resounding thud. Alanna grabbed Jessica around the waist, and Ron huddled closer, pulling

Lisa with him. The little blond boy stayed where he was, frozen in place with a look of terror. There was another thud, this time louder, then the pounding continued over and over, coming closer. Jessica could hear it moving in the hall, reverberating deep in her chest as whatever it was came thundering toward the door outside. She heard wood cracking, and clutched the children's shoulders as something struck the wall three times in quick succession, rocking them all back. There was a final, clattering noise that seemed to come from all around.

"What is that?" Jessica whispered, searching the walls and ceiling, unable to make sense of the noises. Then everything fell silent. They waited. Jessica listened, counting to ten, then twenty, and the sound did not come again. She counted to thirty, then sixty. *I have to do something.* She straightened, carefully extracting herself from Alanna's grasp. "Wait here," she whispered. She crept toward the door, stepping as softly as she could; as she moved she could feel their eyes on her. The door was ordinary-looking, a wooden door with a brass knob—the kind you'd see on a closet. Jessica took a quick, deep breath, then stretched out her arm to take the knob.

Before she could touch it, the knob turned, and the door began to slide open. Jessica held her breath, and took steady steps backward, desperately wanting to rejoin the group, even if they were just children. At first, Jessica saw only pink and white, the shapes indistinct, then her mind made sense of it: slowly, the enormous head of a garishly painted fox peered into the room.

Foxy? Jessica thought, hazily taking in pointed pink ears and yellow eyes. Its cheeks were painted with red circles, like the animatronic girl's had been. The creature looked at her for a long moment, and she stared back, unable to remember how to move her feet, and then the fox head retreated, and all the children screamed. Something new sprang violently into the room, a long and segmented metal limb like a spider's leg. It braced against the floor just as a second metal leg violently invaded the space, embedding itself in the nearest wall. The children screamed, and Jessica raced toward them, looking frantically for a way out. The room was filling with arms and legs, extended and contorted, some with hands, others without. Jessica searched for a place to run through the steadily thickening mass of legs. Her eyes met the yellow eyes of the fox head, now suspended in the air by rods and beams. But there was another set of eyes as well. *Does it have two heads?* The unskinned metal skull lowered itself; it was connected to the mass above by cables and cords, and seemed to move of its own will.

One high-pitched scream rose above the others, a blood-curdling wail. *"LISA!"* Ron cried, and Jessica saw that the thing had one hand on the little girl's arm and was pulling her toward it. The skinless metal head studied her, then swiveled and swung on its cables to the others, taking an aggressive stance toward them as the metal limbs entangled the little girl and pulled her toward the door.

"NO!" Jessica cried, climbing through the snares of metal coils and grabbing Lisa's tiny hand. A violent surge threw her back, but she held fast to whatever she had managed to grasp, letting go only as she hit the floor. She struggled for air as she got to her feet, but the creature had already retreated through the doorway and disappeared. Jessica whirled, looking frantically to the children, and her heart nearly burst with relief: Lisa was on the ground beside her, and Ron and Alanna were helping her up. Jessica rushed to them. "It's okay," she whispered, then the momentary relief vanished. The blond boy, the one who might have been Jacob, was gone.

"I couldn't hold on to him," Alanna wailed, as if reading Jessica's mind.

Jessica looked to the door in despair, but quickly steadied herself. "We'll get him back," Jessica said, because it was all she could think of to say. She glanced around helplessly, then froze as the doorknob slowly began to turn again. "Stay here," Jessica said in a low voice, and she moved quickly to the door. She stood to the side, bracing herself to jump on whatever came through. *This is your plan?*

The door opened, and Jessica screamed and lunged into the doorway, as though ready to karate-chop whatever was coming through.

Carlton and Marla jumped back with startled expressions, and Jessica stared for a moment, then seized Carlton in a hug, holding tight to his shoulders as if he could stop her from shaking.

"Jessica?" Marla said, spotting the children. Jessica pushed Carlton away.

"Something got one of the kids, a little boy," she said in a rush. "I didn't see where it went."

Marla was already beside the children, checking them for injury. "We have to get them out," she said.

"Oh, really, Marla? Is that what we should be doing? Here I was painting my nails," Jessica said crisply. Carlton reached for his ear and pulled something out.

"Here, take this," he said.

"What? Ew." Jessica made a face instinctively, then peered at the tiny device. "Is that a hearing aid?"

"Not exactly. It makes you invisible to the animatronics. You and Marla take these kids out, I'll find the other kid they took."

"How does it—?" Jessica took the device and studied it. "I have to put it in my ear?"

"Yes! You have to put it in your ear! I'll explain later."

"But, are your ears even clean?" She leaned in, peering suspiciously at Carlton's ear. Marla grabbed the earpiece out of her hand and shoved it into Jessica's ear.

"OW!" Jessica cried.

Marla turned back to the kids. "Shouldn't we give them to the children, instead?"

"There are only two earpieces, and you can both protect them better if you're invisible, right?" Carlton said irritably.

"What if Jess and I stay here with the kids, and you take one out at a time, wearing the earpieces?" Marla pressed. Jessica shook her head immediately.

"And what if that thing comes back and kills us all while we're waiting for Carlton to take his sweet time? We have to make a break for it, Marla, it's the only way."

They were all quiet for a moment. Carlton looked from Jessica to Marla and back.

"Right? Now, give me thirty seconds to get away from here, that way if something chases me, I can draw them away from you. Anything I should know?" Carlton paused at the door.

"Afton's still alive," Jessica said, and he nodded.

"This ends today," he said quietly. "One way or another. Not one more child dies because of that psychopath. I owe that much to Michael."

Jessica bit her lip. "We all do," she said.

He forced a smile. "Good luck."

"Good luck," she echoed.

"Right." Carlton clenched his jaw, then squared his shoulders and held the door open, poised to exit. "This was my idea?" he muttered, then closed the door behind him.

"Marla, do you know the way out?" Jessica asked, surprised to hear her own voice come out clear and steady. Marla nodded, standing up.

"We came in the back way. But I think if we go back down that hall, we can get out into the main dining room; should be easy to get out from there, right?"

"You'd think so," Jessica muttered with an edge.

Marla gave her a level look. "You got something better?"

"No. I don't." Jessica turned to the three remaining children, who were watching them with wide eyes. "We don't have to get far," she said, searching for scraps of hope to offer them. "I need you to stay together, and stay with me and Marla. If you can do that, we'll all be okay." They looked at her like they knew she was lying, but no one said a word.

Jessica opened the door again carefully. The hallway outside the little room was dark, but Marla led them onward as if she really did know where they were headed. She held a large, battered flashlight out in front of her. She looked poised to turn it on but refrained from doing so, seemingly afraid of attracting more unwanted attention. Jessica's eyes adjusted to the dim light as she took up the rear, alert to the slightest sign of danger.

They came to a T in the hall, and Marla turned without hesitation. A few yards ahead there was light: strings of small, bare bulbs lit the way at intervals, and the next fork in the hall was visible. *We're getting closer*, Jessica thought, as they moved cautiously onward.

A soft popping noise caught Jessica's attention overhead, and she froze. "Marla," she hissed, and Marla and the children ahead stopped and turned around. Marla pointed up with a worried expression, and Jessica looked up to see that some of the bulbs over her head had gone out, their glass made opaque with a sooty film. "Just old lights," Jessica breathed.

A light above Marla burst and died, and all of them jumped. Alanna clapped both hands over her mouth, and Ron put a hand on Lisa's shoulder. "Can we go faster?" Lisa whispered. All at once, the rest of the light bulbs flickered and clattered. Jessica held her breath: they stayed on, preserving the little light, but overhead something hollow and metallic rattled in the ceiling.

Marla's face went pale. "Keep moving," she said tightly. Jessica gave a sharp nod. The rattling noise kept pace, sometimes seeming to come from above them, and sometimes from the dark corners just out of view, scraping and clattering in a vent or crawl space. Lisa whimpered; the older children's faces were stony, but Jessica could see the glimmer of tears on their cheeks. Suddenly, Marla stopped short, and Jessica almost bumped into Ron. "What?" she hissed, then saw: a thin curtain of dust was falling from above. Jessica looked up, and saw the open duct directly above them.

A multisegmented metal arm covered with springs and wires dropped down through the open duct, anchoring itself to the floor right next to Jessica's foot. Everyone screamed. The arm retracted, then two more of the creature's contorted limbs smashed down to the ground, raining down plaster and dust. "*RUN!*" Marla screamed. They took off down the hallway as the creature lowered its full form into the space, its shiny white fox head turning and smiling in their direction as they fled. Jessica glanced back, and the unskinned head dropped, too, grinning upside down, a red bow tie joining their necks ridiculously. Jessica fled; behind her came an enormous thud. *Run faster!* she wanted to scream, but the others were gasping for breath, already running at their full capacity.

The children were pounding along as fast as they could, but Lisa, the smallest, began to fall behind. The creature shot past Jessica, reaching out for the little girl again, and Jessica grabbed her, yanking her up and out of reach just in time. It reared back to strike again, and Jessica clutched Lisa to her chest and ran on. They rounded a corner, and with a flare of hope Jessica saw that the hall was short, ending in a heavy set of double doors. Marla sped up, and Alanna and Ron did the same; Jessica kept her pace, staying at the back as Lisa clung to her with startling strength.

Marla reached the end of the hall and slammed herself against the emergency bar, and the doors split open. They raced through, and Marla flung the door shut, grabbing a nearby sign post and jamming it through the door handles.

"Keep running," Jessica said with a fresh pump of adrenaline. She looked around: they were up against the wall, behind a popcorn popper and a cotton candy machine. She glanced back briefly at the sign Marla had barred the door with: LET'S EAT! it read in big, round letters. Ron leaned to the side, about to peek between the machines. "Hold on," she hissed, putting a hand on his shoulder. He drew back as if something had burned him.

"It'll be okay," Marla said, and Jessica marveled briefly that she sounded like she believed what she was saying. Behind them, something crashed against the door again, rattling the doorframe. Jessica waited, her eyes on the makeshift barricade, but nothing came.

"We have to move slowly and quietly," she whispered, and the three children nodded in unison. "Stay back," Jessica told them, and stepped out past the popcorn machine, alert to danger. She took a second to get her bearings: The walls of the dining room were lined with arcade games and children's play areas, and on the far side of the room, blissfully, were the wide glass doors of the entrance. She motioned the others forward; the children, huddled together, followed her into the open room with Marla close behind.

"Hurry," she urged, and Marla nodded, taking Lisa's hand as Alanna and Ron followed behind her, their faces pinched with exhaustion. Suddenly, Alanna screamed, and Jessica jumped. "What? What is it?" The girl was pointing at a jungle gym a few feet away, where two toddlers, too small to climb the bars, were nonetheless doing so.

"It's okay, they're just toys," Marla said, looking back at Jessica with a frazzled expression. "We saw them on the way in."

Alanna screamed again, and ran to Jessica, grabbing on to her waist. "It bit me!"

"What?" Jessica looked down: Alanna's ankle was bleeding, though not badly, and a few feet away was another crawling, robotic child.

"Jessica!" Marla screamed, touching the device in her ear nervously. "It can't see us, but it can see them." As she spoke, the two other robotic children on the monkey bars lowered themselves unsteadily to the ground and began to crawl straight toward Lisa and Ron; they backed away, and a fourth appeared, boxing them in. Marla scooped up Lisa and Alanna and tried to hold them away from harm. "Jessica!" Marla screamed. "Help!"

"It bit me," Alanna repeated, panic in her voice, and the children clung together as the crawlers came closer, a slow march of determined toddlers with the black eyes of insects. "They can't see us," Jessica said with determination, darting forward and grabbing the nearest robot baby. It was heavier than it looked. Jessica held it out from her body. It was facing away from her, and she held on tight as it continued its crawling movements in the air, steadily putting its hands and feet into position, one after the other. She glanced around, then spotted the ball pit: at least four or five feet deep. Jessica threw the crawler down into the colorful balls as hard as she could, and it landed, half-buried, on its side, still repeating its motions, and slowly sank out of sight.

"Marla, come on!" she shouted. Marla set down Lisa and Alanna beside Ron, then turned her attention to the baby crawling toward them. Her hands were shaking, like she was preparing to pick up a giant cockroach. "Marla!" Jessica shrieked. Marla screamed and shook her hands in the air, and the baby suddenly charged forward, clawing at the ground and biting at the children's feet. Lisa cried and fell to the ground, and the heavy creature grabbed at her legs as it crawled up on top of her. Marla bolted forward with a blood-curdling scream and yanked the metal crawler off the little girl. Marla cried out again as she spun and threw the creature through the air. It missed Jessica's head by an inch, slammed into the net canopy above the ball pit, and dropped down into it, sinking out of sight.

"You almost hit me!" Jessica had barely spoken the words when the third and final robot baby flew through the air and landed at her feet with a resounding bang. Marla let herself fall to the ground, breathing heavily, her eyes wide with panicked fury. Jessica stared down at the creature as it locked its sights on the children again. "Oh, no you don't." Jessica picked it up just as it started to crawl. She held it over the pit and it turned its head around completely to face her with its ant-like eyes. Its little rosebud mouth opened, flashing two rows of pointy predator's teeth, then snapped shut, chomping the air. Jessica shuddered and dropped it, watching with grim fascination as it churned its arms and legs, digging itself deeper into the pit.

"Jessica!" Marla cried, and she spun around. Lights had come on behind them, illuminating a large show stage with a bright purple curtain as its backdrop. On the stage, and in the spotlight, was a glossy and white Foxy animatronic, its mouth open and arms wide, ready to perform for a cheering crowd. The Fox looked down at them with delight.

"Was that there a second ago?" Jessica whispered.

Suddenly, the fox's body began cracking apart: metal plates split away from the center of its torso, from its arms and legs, lifting out, splitting again and folding back, leaving only its canine head untouched, grinning maniacally as its body was horribly transformed. Jessica ran to the children as all at once, tentacle-like metal limbs erupted from what had been Foxy, and the mutilated skeleton creature stretched out into its new, semi-arachnid form.

"Get them out!" Jessica cried. Alanna and Ron were frozen to the spot, staring, and Marla slapped their cheeks lightly. Ron snatched up Lisa's hand, and together they all ran for the front door.

"Jessica!" Marla cried as they reached the door. "We can't let it get out!" The creature was on top of the monkey bars now, elongating itself to terrifying proportions as if showing off its tangled metal spines.

"Get them out!" Jessica shouted again, pushing away from them, then turning her attention back to the mangled pink-and-white fox. The thing began to slowly dismount the monkey bars, its limbs slipping over and around one another, changing its shape with every step it took. Its foxlike face, and its vaguely human one, were both intent on the children, the heads angled slightly toward each other so that each of its eyes could focus. Jessica took a deep breath, then pulled the earpiece out of her ear, struggling to steady her hands long enough to slip it into her pocket. "Over here!" she screamed as loudly as she could, her throat going raw, and the canine head ducked under the other neck, its eye rolling around to fix on her. "Yeah, over here!" Jessica cried, her voice hoarse, and the thing came down from the monkey bars with menacing grace and began to slink toward her. She glanced around. *Should have thought this through.* At the door, she could see Marla bracing it open and shooing the children through, one at a time, then looking back to Jessica.

Jessica nodded her head and waved Marla away. She grabbed a folding chair from a nearby table and hefted it over her head, then flung it at the creature. It landed with a clatter on the floor, missing the thing entirely. The fox head cocked to the side, its mouth hanging open to show all of its teeth, then it lurched forward, its metal appendages banging against the ground. Jessica turned and ran.

She looked around wildly for an escape as she darted through the mass of tables at the center of the room; she shoved over a table behind her, but the thing just climbed over it like it was flat ground. Jessica sped up. The creature was right behind her, the fox head snapping its jaws as the unskinned skull grinned ghoulishly from its swing. She raced back the way they had come, ducking between the cotton candy machine and the popcorn cart. The sign block-ing the doors was still in place, and she flung it away and yanked the door handle. It rattled in place, but still wouldn't open.

Something crashed behind her, and Jessica spun around to see the popcorn cart knocked over, popcorn strewn across the black-and-white floor tiles. The creature stretched out a limb and pushed the cotton candy machine experimentally; it rocked but did not fall, then another limb shot out. It hit Jessica's leg with a smack, and she stumbled back against the door, an involuntary shout of pain blurting from her mouth. The fox and the unskinned head looked at each other, the head bouncing on its cables, then in unison they turned their eyes on her as the creature undulated its limbs, displaying their full extension. Jessica felt in her pocket for the earpiece, but couldn't find it. It must have fallen out while she was running: she darted her eyes from side to side, afraid to move even her head. She was cornered, caught between the wall and a children's climbing set: there was no way past the thing.

All at once the creature seized the cotton candy machine with three of its limbs, crushing it; shattering glass sprayed in all directions as it carelessly flung the machine aside. Jessica shielded her face, turning away, and as the machine cracked the floor tiles behind her, she saw it: the red-and-yellow bars of the playset nearby led high above the room below, where a colorful pipe maze began, bolted tight to the ceiling, and disappearing into a circular hole in the wall and into the next room. *That's my way out.*

Jessica set her foot on the bottom rung of the playset and started to climb as fast as she could. Below her came a wrenching noise, and she glanced down to see the creature tearing up the playset, the unskinned head swinging and bobbing gleefully. It reached up and tore out the rung below her, and she climbed faster, hurling her upper body into the tube just as one of the creature's hands grasped the last piece of the playset. Jessica scrabbled for a handhold, at last managing to pull her full body inside the tube. She crawled as fast as she could, the pipe shaking with every movement, then stopped to look down. Although some of the plastic tunnel was bolted to the ceiling, there were large portions that were not. *This was made for kids, not me.* Jessica rocked herself carefully, and the section of plastic below her rocked as well, the plastic segments creaking at the seams. Jessica shivered. *Slow and steady.* She checked her hands and knees, making sure they were safely in place, then started forward again.

She was in a narrow, unadorned tube, hovering above an empty hallway, lit by a single, exposed florescent light that hummed as it flickered. The hum of the florescent light seemed to grow louder as she made her way cautiously along the fragile plastic flooring, filling her ears almost painfully, as if she had gone deep underground. She worked her jaw open and shut, trying to clear the sensation, but the noise persisted. When she reached the segment of tubing that went into the wall above the door, she hesitated, trying to see inside, but there was only darkness. Jessica took a deep breath, and carefully crossed into the next room.

Silence fell: the humming noise was blissfully gone. The only light was behind her, and bizarrely it did not penetrate into the room, as if it were somehow being filtered out. She looked back and saw the circle of light where she had come, but everything else was in darkness. Jessica blinked, waiting for her eyes to adjust, but all she saw was black. *Okay, then.* She shuffled slowly forward, feeling carefully and sliding her knees along the support beams that ran along sections of the tunnel. After a few minutes, she came to a turn, bumping her head gently on the plastic, and she felt her way around it with a vague sense of accomplishment.

A point of orange light appeared below her, and she startled, her hand slipping off the support beam and rattling the plastic. She caught her balance, her heart racing, and a pair of green lights appeared, a few feet away from the first one. They vanished, then reappeared, and another pair, purple, sprang out of the darkness beside them, and this time Jessica saw the dark pinpoint at the center of each circle. Jessica tensed with an awful recognition, as more and more sets of colored lights appeared: *Eyes. They're eyes.* The room below was slowly filling with sets of eyes, until it seemed impossible that so many creatures could fit into the space; they all stared upward, unblinking at Jessica. She moved slowly forward, her hands shaking as they found their way along the beams, and the eyes followed her as she went. *Don't look down.*

Jessica set her gaze on the darkness in front of her and shuffled on and on for what felt like ages; each time she glanced down there were more pairs and pairs of watchful eyes, all of them rapt on her progress. Jessica shivered. She moved faster, still feeling carefully before she slid her hands and knees along, then the tube curved slightly, and a circle of dim light came into view. Jessica crawled for it as fast as she dared, the tube swaying precariously as she moved. She crawled through the hole and turned back: the room was in darkness again; all the eyes had vanished.

Jessica shuddered, revolted, then looked down at the room she now hovered above. The light was dim and unsteady, flashing strange colors at intervals, but she could see clearly. Peering down, Jessica saw that it was coming from the carnival games that filled the room, some flickering noiselessly and others giving steady light in every hue. She took a deep breath and looked ahead, trying to see where the tube led. *I really hope there's another way out*, she thought, and started crawling again. The plastic tubing rattled as she went, the only noise in the dark room. Jessica swallowed; as the adrenaline waned, she was beginning to remember how much she hated enclosed spaces. *Just keep moving.* She reached a split in the tubing: one way snaked around the perimeter of the room, the other through another wall, into the pipe maze bolted to the ceiling of the next room. She scanned the room, then made her choice. She took the turn, taking the tunnel that fed through the neatly cut hole in the wall, and found herself back in the main dining room.

She paused and listened. There was no sound of movement in the dining room, and she craned her neck to look down through one of the large plastic panes, searching the area: the creature was nowhere to be seen. She had not noticed the play pipes that covered the ceiling before climbing up into them, but now she saw the extent of them, with no end in sight, and no way down. The playset she had climbed to enter the tunnels was utterly destroyed. *How am I going to get out?* She cast her eyes helplessly over the maze, tracing the paths she could take, and suddenly she saw it: the ball pit where she had thrown the baby crawlers was across the room, and it had a canopy made of climbing rope that stretched fifteen or twenty feet above the floor. The tube went directly over it. Jessica took a deep breath and crawled farther out into the room, bracing herself. She made it to the first turning point, and suddenly the pipe shook. She paused, but the structure shook again, and again. The light was being obscured from below her, and Jessica looked down.

The unskinned skull grinned up at her with yellow eyes, suspended below as if out of nowhere. The head swiveled sideways and elevated up and over the plastic tunnel. Jessica looked up in dread, and saw the body of the creature right above her, its limbs wrapped around the tube like a monstrous squid seizing a ship. She stifled a scream, and her heart skipped as she fought not to hyperventilate. The fox head lowered to eye level and snapped beside her, and she screamed and shied away; her hand hit the plastic floor between the support beams and the segment fell straight down. Jessica clamored back before falling with it, and quickly took a corner, heading off to a new direction. The fox head swooped upward in a blur and vanished.

Jessica crawled in a straight line, keeping her eyes fixed ahead. The structure continued to shake, and she could hear plastic breaking behind her, as well as large segments of the pipe maze crashing to the ground. Soon she reached the ball pit, and she stared down at the canopy of ropes through the bottom of the tube, hesitating. *Now what?* The structure shook again, but this time it was different. This time it trembled as though someone, or something, were in the maze with her. The entirety of the structure swayed and rocked on the bolts it hung from. Jessica kicked out the plastic below her, bracing herself on the sides of the tube as she looked down. Something moved in the pit below: three of the crawlers' heads were above the surface, staring up at her disembodied with blank eyes. In unison, they snapped their little jaws, and she startled, hitting her head on the top of the plastic tube. "Stupid babies," she muttered. When she looked down again, they were back in motion, swimming through the balls and snapping, apparently at random. Jessica shivered and froze, suddenly paralyzed at the next step of her plan. For a moment, she prayed that it wasn't too late to just stay silent, and wait for danger to pass.

The structure trembled again, this time over and over in rapid succession. A spiral of shimmering metal flew through the tunnel, then she saw its gleaming fox's head, its mouth open in an impossible smile. Jessica screamed and fell sideways through the hole, landing heavily on the rope canopy. It sank inward, giving her a split second before she began to slip downward.

She grabbed wildly at the net, the ropes burning her hands and entangling her feet, then she got her footing, and scrambled back up the slope to the top, wrapping her hands around the metal support bar. She watched the hole in the bottom of the pipe that she had fallen through, expecting something to come out, but nothing did. There was motion in the pipes, barely visible through the thick foggy plastic. Jessica searched in panic, trying to locate the creature, but there was movement everywhere: every pipe seemed to be crawling with life. Then she realized, all of the movement was flowing in the same direction. Jessica followed the flow with her eyes, through pipe after pipe, all the way up to a plastic end cap just above her. With a crash, the end cap burst out of place, and bolts rained down from the sky, hitting Jessica on the head. The fox head beamed down at her. More of its body pushed its way through, more and more limbs emerging as it balanced itself delicately on the edge of the pipe like a cat preparing to pounce on a mouse.

Something fell out of Jessica's pocket with a *ding*. It was the earpiece, which must have been wedged into her other pocket. Jessica held steady, violently fumbling to retrieve the earpiece. The fox head craned sideways as the last piece of the monster exited the pipe and joined the rest of the metal mass, perched like a vulture on the rickety infrastructure of the pipes.

Finally, the fox lunged.

Jessica crammed the earpiece into her ear and jumped, and the creature slammed into the netting where she had been, its limbs shooting through the spaces in the net. Jessica landed on her back on the top of an arcade cabinet, then fell to the floor below with a thud, the wind knocked out of her, and she wheezed. The creature struggled to free itself from the net. The limbs writhed, then the whole body sank down with the net, tearing it off the frame as it went. The creature was stuck, its limbs tangled in the mesh. It thrashed and flailed, and its long, snakelike appendages lashed through the air. The net rocked back and forth, straining in its bonds, then gave way in an instant. The thing dropped straight down into the pit, sending colorful plastic balls splashing over the sides of the pit. It twisted frantically, still tangled in the torn netting, then suddenly it began to twitch. Jessica watched, wide-eyed, as the bound creature slowly sank into the ball pit with a sound like metal grinding metal; after a moment it vanished entirely, though the balls boiled up frenziedly as the gnashing sound continued. Briefly, she caught a glimpse of a black-eyed crawler, chewing contentedly. She drew in a shaky breath, then ran for the front entrance. Jessica burst out through the double door and into the cool night air, and swayed on her feet.

"Are you all right?" Marla asked with alarm.

"I'm fine." Jessica looked at each of the children, confirming that they were all there, all safe. *Except one. Carlton, do you have him?* She forced herself to smile. "So, who wants to visit a police station?"

Carlton crept quickly down the hall, scanning the walls and floor for signs of struggle—of anything that would indicate something had passed through. There was another door a little way down the hall, and he paused outside it, carefully turning the knob while staying outside the frame. Bracing himself, he pushed the door in, and waited. Nothing came out and he cautiously peered inside: the room was completely empty. "Calm before the storm?" he whispered to himself, and shut the door.

When he reached the T in the hall he paused. *Where are you, kid?* He closed his eyes, listening. There was nothing, and then, a muffled scraping came from the wall behind him, back the way he and Marla had come. Carlton went toward it, and put his ear to the wall. The rustling continued. It was an odd sound he could not quite pinpoint, but it sounded like someone moving. He stepped back, examining the wall: It was plain, painted beige, with a large, silver air vent near the baseboard, about three feet high and almost as wide. *That's strange* . . . Carlton knelt down in front of the vent and turned on his flashlight—which worked, somewhat impressively, after its extended use as a blunt instrument. He turned the beam on the vent, and squinted, trying to see inside, but the slats were too close together to make out anything.

A faint sound came from somewhere deep inside; it was indistinct, but it was unmistakably a voice. Carlton tugged at the grate with his fingernails, and it moved easily; he pulled the whole thing out, revealing a dark tunnel about four feet high. He shone his flashlight inside: The walls were concrete, painted red on one side and blue on the other in faded colors. Incomprehensible words were scribbled on them in crayon, and the yellow linoleum floor was scuffed with black sneaker marks, scratched, and turning up at the edges. "This place *is* brand-new, right?" Carlton muttered as he crouched down and crawled inside, keeping the light ahead of him. It was unsettling to think of someone carefully laying down a new floor, then marking it with deliberate signs of wear; adult hands mimicking children's painstaking handwriting and simple drawings. He cast the light around:

on the red wall there was a drawing of a house and stick figures; underneath someone had written *My House* with the *e* drawn backward. The sound of the voice came again, echoing faintly through the tunnel ahead, and Carlton crawled forward awkwardly with the flashlight in one hand.

The wall color changed every few feet, cycling through the rainbow at random, with childlike graffiti spaced unevenly all along the way. He came to what he thought was an opening to a new tunnel, but when he turned the light toward it, he saw that it was only a cubbyhole, small enough for a child to squeeze into. In the corner of it was a little blue sneaker, the laces untied, and Carlton swallowed. *What is this place?*

His flashlight lit on a silently screaming face, and Carlton jumped back, dropping the light. He snatched it up again, his heart thumping, and shone it on the figure: it was a jack-in-the-box stuck in its "surprise" position: a white-faced clown, its mouth gaping in perpetual laughter. "This isn't a vent," Carlton whispered, letting the light leave the painted face and continue down the colorful hall littered with hiding spaces and scuff marks. "This is part of the play area."

The light fixed on a rainbow stretching above one of the hiding spaces. HIDE-AND-SEEK HALLWAY, it read. "This can't be good." Carlton winced. The child's voice echoed again, this time a little louder, and he shook off the eerie sensation. *I'm coming, kid*, he promised silently.

He rounded a corner, but stopped short: there was an animatronic baby in a cubbyhole, motionless, laying on its back. Carlton's elbows and knees trembled. *Please don't move.*

Black, insect-like eyes stared blankly at him from a sweet, plastic face; the crawler did not move, apparently deactivated. He backed away cautiously, and turned his light on the path ahead; he was approaching a turn, but there was still no sign of an exit. He crawled on, passing stick figures and houses that were beginning to look suspiciously repetitive.

"I s-ee you . . ."

Carlton whirled around. There was nothing in sight but a closed door. It was the size of the other cubbyholes, child-height, with a small, heart-shaped window near the top. As he passed his light over the little door, something glinted through the heart-shaped window. Carlton stiffened, but before he could think to move, the door broke off its hinges as Freddy crawled forcefully out, a maniacal grin on his shiny purple-and-white face as he unfolded from the cramped space he had stuffed himself into. Carlton crawled backward frantically, and Freddy matched his motions, keeping a distance of inches between them. Carlton glanced around, then turned and crawled as fast as he could down the tunnel, his knees and hands slamming into the floor painfully as he raced to get away. He glanced back: Freddy was crawling behind him, his mechanical arms and legs thundering faster than Carlton could hope to escape. He rounded a corner, and Freddy caught his foot, the iron fingers digging into his heel. Carlton kicked with his other foot, wresting himself free, and got to his feet and started to run, hunched down to half his height and scraping the ceiling with his back. From behind, he could hear the sound of Freddy bearing down on him, his hands and knees pounding the floor with vibrating force.

Carlton turned another corner, and relief surged through him: there was a vent along the tunnel, an *actual* vent that led to a large room. Carlton kicked it out without hesitation and scurried through to the room on the other side.

The room was enormous, seemingly designed to house a single, giant carnival ride: it was a ring of seats set on an angle, held together by huge metal arms on a spiral, a terrifying variation on the merry-go-round that would whip around at high speed while tilting nauseatingly up and down. On the far side of it was a door marked EXIT. Before Carlton could run for the door, Freddy burst out of the tunnel, climbing to his feet, his eyes sickeningly reflective in the dark.

"I see you so clearly now," said the speaker in Freddy's chest.

Carlton turned to run, then smacked into the carnival ride, biting his lip and drawing blood.

He turned back just in time to see Freddy lunge at him, and Carlton ducked under the ride, the blow just missing him and hitting the metal side of the tilted merry-go-round.

The sound rang out in the vast, empty room, and he shuddered, then leaped back as another blow hit the ride above him, reverberating so hard it rattled his teeth. Carlton looked up: the metal had bowed out above his head, caving to Freddy's strength.

"You can't escape . . ."

Carlton scrambled away, tripping over the heavy steel beams that undergirded the ride, bolting it to the ground. Freddy's shiny purple-and-white calves stalked him calmly, keeping pace with him along the perimeter of the ride as Carlton ducked under heavy cables and mysterious, frightening-looking gears.

"I've alm-ost got you . . ." Freddy announced.

"Not yet," Carlton muttered as he carefully untangled his foot from the heavy wire that had ensnared him. He craned his neck, trying to see the room around him: There was no way he could get past Freddy, and even if he did, he would pursue him relentlessly. Carlton was backed up against the tilted end of the ride, and up against the control platform. As he craned his head upward he could see a large on/off lever, which was almost in reach.

"Nowhere else to run . . ."

Carlton waited for Freddy to make his way deeper under the ride, pressing and contorting his body to get at Carlton between the beams. Carlton squeezed out from under the ride and hoisted himself just high enough to pull the lever and activate the ride, then dropped to the ground and covered his head. Freddy reached for him, but the ride tilted abruptly.

Carlton saw Freddy jerk about, wrenched by the moving parts, until the ride jolted hard. Carlton clutched his head as his ears rang with the impact, a growing shriek of tearing metal and grating gears as the ride slowed, wobbling unsteadily on its axis. Carlton didn't move: from where he had landed he could see the apparatus in motion, shredding through the body of what had been Freddy as the machine ground on inexorably through its routine. Scraps of purple appeared and vanished, then fell to the floor, spat out by the machine. A yellow eyeball appeared in a space above two gears, and Carlton watched with shocked fascination as the rest of the precariously balanced body was pulverized by the alternating beams, then dropped to the ground in several distinct masses.

The machine screeched ear-splittingly, then slowed and sputtered to a dead stop. Carlton didn't move for a moment. He got to his feet and cautiously moved away from the apparatus, carefully avoiding the littered scraps of metal and plastic on the ground. He didn't dare climb under the thing again, but he prodded it gently with his toe, then yanked his foot back as something dropped out.

Half of Freddy's head, one-eyed and still grinning insanely, fell out of the machine near Carlton, spun partially on the ground, then stopped moving, and its single eye flickered on, then sputtered and died. The speaker in the now-smashed chest piece, laying armless and legless nearby, crackled with static, then spoke, *"Thanks for playing; come again soon!"* The voice trailed away and went silent.

In the distance, the child's scream came again, and Carlton was startled back to himself.

"Hang on, kid," he whispered, and headed grimly for the door.

CHAPTER FOURTEEN

harlie's duplicate stared back at her, looking stunned for an instant, then Charlie watched her own face curve into a bright, cruel smile. The other Charlie didn't move, and Charlie's fear receded as she watched this strange imitation of herself, astonished. *That's my face.* Charlie reached up and touched her own cheek, and the other girl imitated her; Charlie tilted her head to the side, and the girl mirrored her movement—Charlie could not tell if she was being mocked, or if the other girl was simply as entranced as she was. The duplicate was a little taller than Charlie, and Charlie flicked her eyes to the girl's feet: her black combat boots had heels. She was wearing a red V-neck shirt and a short black skirt, and her hair was long and hung in shiny waves—a look Charlie had given up even attempting halfway through ninth grade. She looked polished; confident in her stance. She looked the way Charlie wished she could be: some version of herself that had figured out curling irons, and sophistication, and taking up space in the world without apology.

"What are you?" Charlie whispered, mesmerized.

"Come on," the other Charlie said, holding out her hand, and Charlie started to reach out to her, then stopped herself, yanking her hand away. She shrank away, stumbling back across the hall and her duplicate closed the distance between them, leaning in so close Charlie should have felt her breathing. A long moment passed, but the other Charlie did not draw breath. "You need to come with me," she said. "Father wants us to come home." Charlie startled at the phrase.

"My father is dead," she said. She pressed back against the wall, as far from the girl's face as she could get.

"Well, would you like to have a live one?" the other Charlie asked, with a mocking edge.

"There is nothing that you can give me, and certainly not that," Charlie said shakily, inching backward into the storage room; the duplicate followed her step for step. Charlie glanced past the duplicate and into the open bedroom door; John emerged into the hallway, leaning heavily on the doorframe and gripping his side.

"Are you okay, Charlie?" he asked in a low, steady voice.

"Oh, I'm just fine, John!" Charlie's duplicate said cheerfully.

"Charlie?" John repeated, ignoring her. Charlie nodded, not daring to take her eyes off the imposter.

"She says *Father wants us to come home*," Charlie said.

John stepped up behind the other Charlie.

"Father? Would that be William Afton?" John demanded. He took a few sprinted steps and grabbed a lamp by its base, raising it for attack. The other Charlie smiled again, then swiftly raised her arm and backhanded John across the face. He dropped the lamp and staggered backward, catching himself against the wall, and the duplicate grabbed for Charlie's hand. Charlie ducked away, running for the hallway with the girl on her heels.

"Hey! That was just round one!" John shouted, beckoning his assailant to come back. He grabbed the duplicate girl's arm, yanking her back toward him and away from where Charlie had run. The duplicate allowed John to hold her close, not resisting. John was washed with fear as he stood eye-to-eye with the imposter. *Now what do I do?*

"Just like by the old oak tree when we were little, John," the duplicate whispered. She pulled him close and pressed her lips against his. His eyes widened, and he tried to push her away, but he could not move. When she finally released him and pulled back, she was Charlie, *his* Charlie, and there was a high, painful ringing in his ears. He covered his ears, but the ringing increased exponentially, and for the few brief seconds before he collapsed to the ground, he saw her face morph into a thousand things. The room spun, and his head hit the ground with a crack.

The girl smiled and glanced at Charlie, then drew back her foot and kicked John in the ribs, knocking him onto his side and against a heavy wooden trunk. Charlie ran toward him, but before she could reach him, the girl grabbed her hair, bringing tears to her eyes. The imposter pulled upward, lifting Charlie several inches off the ground, and then flung her aside. Charlie tried to regain her footing but tripped backward over a cardboard box and slammed hard into the opposite wall, knocking the wind out of her as John got warily to his feet. Charlie climbed to her knees. She dragged in heavy, grinding breaths, watching helplessly as the other Charlie strode toward John.

He straightened, and without a pause, she punched him in the stomach. He doubled over, and before he could stand, she hit the back of his head with her fist, like it was a hammer and he was a nail.

John fell forward, catching himself on his hands and knees, and scrambled up. He lunged again at the girl, catching her shoulder with his fist, but the blow glanced off her, and he yelped in pain, clutching his hand like it had hit something harder than flesh and bone. The imposter took him by the shoulders, lifting him off the ground, and carried him across the room, then pressed him against the wall. She released him and let him stand, turning to look at Charlie momentarily, then she placed her open palm against John's chest.

Suddenly, John began to gasp for breath, his face turning red. The imposter's face remained unchanged, her open hand slowly pressing harder against his chest. "I can't—" John gasped for air. "Can't breathe." He clutched at her arm with both hands, but it was no use as she continued to steadily press into him. John slowly began to slide up the wall, inch by inch, the pressure forcing his entire body upward.

"Stop!" Charlie cried, but the other Charlie didn't flinch. *"Please!"* Charlie scrambled to her feet and ran to John's side, but the other Charlie snapped out her other arm and caught her by the neck without moving her hand from John's chest. Her fingers closed on Charlie's throat, closing off her windpipe as she lifted her up onto her toes. Charlie choked, kicking and gasping. The imposter held her there, looking expressionlessly from Charlie to John as she kept them both immobilized and struggling to breathe.

"Okay," Charlie wheezed. "I want to talk. Please," she begged hoarsely. The imposter dropped them both. John fell motionless to the floor. "You've hurt him, let me help him." Charlie coughed, pulling herself up.

"You're so attached to something so . . . easily broken," she said with amusement. Charlie strained to see past her, anxiously watching John's chest as it rose and fell. *He's alive.* Charlie took a breath, then turned to face the girl who had her face.

"What do you want to talk about?" she asked tightly.

Carlton let the heavy door slam shut behind him and ran on without looking back: there was another door up ahead, and dim light filtered through a small window near the top. The child's cry echoed again, and Carlton froze, unable to pin-point its direction. The high-pitched sound pierced the air again, and he grimaced at the sound: it was raw and thin, the scream of a kid who had been screaming for a long time. Carlton peered through the window in the door—it looked deserted, and he opened the door cautiously, then stopped dead. Everything looked the same: every hall, every room. Lights flickered, speakers hummed. One light seemed to be about to burn out, making a high-pitched screech that echoed through the chamber.

"Kid," he whispered, but there was no answer, and Carlton was suddenly aware that he may have been chasing echoes and lights for the last ten minutes. He suddenly felt the weight of how alone he was, and it became a physical thing; the air itself seemed to grow heavier around him. His breath slowed, and he dropped to his knees, then fell back to sit. He stared down the empty hallway despairingly, and finally scooted to the side, maneuvering his back against the wall so he could at least see his assailant before he died—whoever— or whatever—his assailant might turn out to be.

I've failed. I'm not going to find him. Tears sprang to his eyes unexpectedly. *Michael, I'm so sorry.* In the days after Michael disappeared, his father had asked him so many questions, going over that one afternoon like he believed together they could re-create it and solve the puzzle. *I searched for the missing piece, I promise, I searched.* He had gone over every moment of the little party in his mind, desperately trying to find the clue his father needed, the detail that would make everything clear.

There were so many things he could have done to stop what had happened, if he had known then what he knew now.

But now I know it all, and there's still nothing I can do.

"I failed you, Michael." Carlton put his hand on his chest, trying to calm himself and not hyperventilate. *I failed you, again.*

"So, what do you want to talk about?" Charlie repeated. The other Charlie narrowed her eyes.

"That's better, a lot better." The girl smiled, and Charlie leaned back as far away from her as she could. It was unnerving to see her own face glaring back at her, accusatory and petulant.

"I'll listen to anything you want to say, just don't hurt him more," Charlie pleaded, her hands raised in surrender, her heart fluttering. Charlie's duplicate flushed with anger.

"This is why," she hissed, shaking her finger accusingly.

"What? *This is why?* I don't understand," Charlie cried.

Charlie's imposter paced the floor, her anger seeming to have drained as quickly as it came. Charlie took the opportunity to look to John again, who had rolled partially onto his back, holding his side as though in immense pain, his face still red. *He needs help.*

"What are you?" Charlie growled, her anger rising at the sight of John.

"The question isn't what am I. It's what are *you?* And what makes you so special, over and over again?" Charlie's duplicate approached her with renewed anger, grabbing Charlie by the throat once more and lifting her off the ground. She pinned her to the wall, baring all her teeth.

The ruse of Charlie's imposter faded, revealing a painted clown face, somehow looking angrier than the human facade. The white plates of the face opened like a flower, revealing yet another face, made of coils and wires, with bare black eyes and jagged prongs for teeth. *Her real face,* Charlie thought.

"Ask again," she growled.

"What?" Charlie choked.

"I said ask me again," the metal monster snarled.

"What are you?" Charlie whimpered.

"I told you, that's not the right question." The metal girl held Charlie out at a distance and looked her up and down. "Where did he hide it?" She held Charlie's throat with one hand and put her other hand on Charlie's chest, then ran a finger down the length of her breastbone. Then her eyes shot to Charlie's face, and she grabbed her chin and turned her head forcefully to the side. She seemed lost in thought for only a moment then snapped back. "Ask again."

Charlie locked eyes with the metal face. The face plates closed over the tangle of twisted metal, reassembling the face of the clown, with her rosy cheeks and glossy lips. Soon the illusion returned, and Charlie was staring into her own eyes again. Charlie felt herself growing uncannily calm as she began to realize what the right question was.

"What am I?"

The imposter loosened her grip, and lowered Charlie so that her feet touched the ground. "You are *nothing*, Charlie," the imposter said. "You look at me and you see a soulless monster; how ironic. How twisted. How backward." She let go of Charlie's throat and took a step back, her red lips losing their savor for the moment. "How unfair."

Charlie was on her knees again, struggling to regain her strength. The imposter approached her and knelt with her, placing her hand over Charlie's. "I'm not sure how this will work, but let's give it a try," she whispered, running her fingers through Charlie's hair and firmly grasping the back of her neck.

She was a little girl, holding a piece of paper in her hand, excited and full of joy. A bright gold foil star shimmered on the page, above the glowing words of her kindergarten teacher. Someone gently touched her back, encouraging her to run forward into the room, into the dark. She eagerly ran inside, and there he was, standing by the work desk.

"How long did I stand there before he shooed me away?" Charlie searched her mind, but the answers didn't come.

"He didn't *shoo* me away," Charlie's other voice answered.

Her eagerness didn't fade, she remained patient and joyful. After the first push, she came back to try again. It was only after the second push that she hesitated to go back, but she carefully returned anyway, this time holding the paper into the air. Maybe he didn't see it.

"He saw it," Charlie's other voice spoke down to her.

This time it hurt; the ground was cold, and her arm ached where she had fallen on it. She looked for the paper: it was on the floor in front of her, her gold star still shone bright, but he was standing on the page now. She looked up to see if he noticed, tears in her eyes. She knew she should leave it, but she couldn't. She reached forward to tug at the corner, but it was too far away. She finally crawled to it on her knees, her dress dirty now, and tried to pull the page from under his shoe. It wouldn't come loose.

"That's when he hit me."

It was difficult to make out anything in the room after that. The room was a smear of tears and pain and her head was still spinning. But she made out one thing, a shiny metal clown doll. Her father had turned his attention back to it, lovingly polishing her. Suddenly, her pain faded to the background, replaced with fascination, obsession.

"What is all of this?" Charlie cried.

Now she was looking at herself in the mirror, holding a stick of lipstick that she'd stolen from her teacher's purse. But she wasn't painting her lips with it, she was drawing bright red circles on her cheeks. The lips came next.

"Are you listening to me?" the doppelganger whispered.

Night had swept over everything. The rooms were dark, the halls were silent, the lab was still. Her feet made soft pats against the smooth white tiles. A tiny camera in the corner had a red blinking light on it, but it didn't matter what it saw, it was too late to stop her.

She pulled the sheet away from the beautiful clown girl, beckoning her to speak. Where was the button, the one he always pressed?

The eyes lit up first, and then other lights from within. It didn't take long for the painted face to search the room and find her, greeting her with a sweet smile and soft voice.

"Then there was screaming." The illusion was broken, and Charlie pushed herself away. "Then there was scream-ing," the imposter repeated. "It was coming from me, but . . ." She paused and pointed to her own head with a look of curiosity. "But I remember seeing her scream." She looked thoughtful for a second, and suddenly the illusion dissipated, and she appeared again as the painted clown. "It's strange to remember the same moment from two pairs of eyes, but then we were one."

"I don't believe that story," Charlie growled. "I don't believe that story at all. You aren't possessed! If you think I will believe for one second that I'm talking to the spirit of a sweet and innocent little girl, then you're crazy."

"I want you to call me Elizabeth," the girl said softly.

"Elizabeth?" Charlie answered. "If you were this little girl, Elizabeth, I can't bring myself to believe that that little girl would be capable of all of this."

"The anger isn't from her," Elizabeth said, her painted face shifting: she looked like a wounded animal, vulnerable but still poised to attack.

"Then what?" Charlie cried.

"My anger is from a different father." Elizabeth strode to Charlie again, grabbing her neck again and jostling her into a white light and pain, where suddenly all was calm.

A hand was stroking her hair. The sun was going down over a field of grain. A cluster of birds were fluttering overhead, their calls echoing out over the landscape. "I'm so happy to be here with you," a kind voice said. She looked up and nestled against him.

"No, this is mine," Charlie protested.

"No," Elizabeth intruded. "That doesn't belong to you. Let me show you what *does* belong to you."

Agony erupted, flooding the room with its sound. The walls went black and streams of water poured down from behind the window curtains. A man lay curled on the floor, something cradled tightly in his arms, and when his mouth opened, the room shook with the sound of his anguish.

"Who is that?" Charlie said anxiously. "What is he holding?"

"You don't recognize her?" Elizabeth said. "That's Ella, of course. It's all your father had left after you were taken."

"What, no, that's not Ella." Charlie shook her head.

"He cried over that cheap store-bought rag doll for two months," Elizabeth snarled with disbelief. "He cried into it, he bled into it, he poured his grief over it. Very unhealthy. He began to treat it as though he still had a daughter."

"That was my memory, me sitting with my dad, watching the sun go down. We were waiting for the stars to come out. That's my memory," Charlie said angrily.

"Look again," Elizabeth instructed, forcing the image upon her once more.

There was a hand stroking her hair. The sun was going down over a field of grain. A cluster of birds were fluttering overhead, their calls echoing out over the landscape. "I'm so happy to be here with you," a kind voice said. He gripped the doll tightly, and smiled despite the tears streaming from his face.

"Of course, he wasn't content with that, you had to grow up. So, he made more."

Her arms hung off the side of the workbench. The joints were stiff enough to carry something lightweight, and her eyes were more realistic than he had ever made them before. He propped her up and extended her arms straight in front of her, carefully balancing a small tray on them, then setting a teacup on the tray. He furrowed his brow with frustration for a moment, turning a brass knob over and over until the room quivered and flashed, then everything stood still, and the little girl looked at him and smiled.

"That's MY memory!" Charlie screamed.

"No, that's *his* memory," Elizabeth corrected.

"Jen, I swear she is more than another animatronic doll. You should see. She walks, and she talks."

"Of course she walks and talks, Henry." Jen's voice was angry. *"She walks because everything you build can walk, and she talks because everything you build can talk. But the reason why this one seems so real is because you're destroying your mind with these frequencies and codes."* Jen threw her arms in the air.

"She remembers, Jen. She remembers me. She remembers our family."

"No, Henry. You remember. Zap your head with enough of those rays and I bet you can get the teakettle to tell you about your lost family."

"My lost family," Henry repeated.

Jen took pause, looking regretful. "It doesn't have to be that way, but you need to let go of this. Your wife; your son, they can still be a part of your life, but you have to let go of this."

"She is in this doll." He gestured to Ella, who was standing upright with her teacup perched on the tray. A little rag doll sat in a wooden chair in the corner, its head draped over the armrest, its eyes staring out over the room.

"It took him a while to figure out that it was the rag doll, the little store-bought rag doll. Maybe he never *sensed* you when it wasn't around, I don't know. But over time, he started putting it inside *his* Charlie, whatever new Charlie he built."

Charlie sat speechless, remembering all the times with her father, questioning each of them. *Sitting on the floor of his workshop, building a block tower out of scraps of wood as he bent over his work. He turned back to her and smiled, and she smiled back, beloved. Her father went back to his work, and the jumbled creature in the far, dark corner twitched. Charlie startled, knocking her blocks to the ground, but her father did not seem to hear. She began to rebuild the tower, but the creature kept drawing her gaze: the twisted metal skeleton with its burning, silver eyes. It twitched again, and she wanted to ask, but could not make herself speak the words.*

"Does it hurt?" Charlie whispered, the image so clear that she could almost smell the hot, metallic scent of the workshop. Elizabeth froze, then all at once the illusion vanished and the metal plates of her clown-painted face stripped back, baring the coils and wires, and jagged teeth. Charlie shrank back, and Elizabeth moved with her, maintaining the distance between them.

"Yes," she whispered, and her eyes blazed silver. "Yes. It hurt."

The plates of her face folded back in, but her eyes still glowed. Charlie blinked and looked away; the light blinded her, poking pinpoint holes in her vision. Elizabeth stared bitterly. "So, you remember me, then?"

"Yes." Charlie rubbed her eyes as her vision began to clear. "In the corner. I didn't want to look. I thought it was . . . I thought you were . . . someone else," she said, her voice sounding thin and childish to her own ears.

Elizabeth laughed. "Did any of those other *things* really look like me? I'm unique. Look at me."

"It hurts my eyes," Charlie said faintly, and Elizabeth grabbed her by the chin and pulled her close. Charlie shied away, closing her eyes against the light, and Elizabeth slapped her cheek with painful force.

"Look at me."

Charlie took a shaky breath and obeyed. Elizabeth's face looked like Charlie's again, but the silver light poured out coldly from the place where her eyes should be. Charlie let it flood her vision, blotting out everything else.

"Do you know why my eyes were always glowing?" Elizabeth asked softly. "Do you know why I twitched and shuddered in the dark?" Charlie shook her head slightly, and Elizabeth let go of her chin. "It was because your father left me turned on all the time. Every moment, every day, I was aware, and unfinished. Watching him as the hours passed, and he created toys for the little Charlie, unicorns and bunnies that moved and talked as I hung in the dark, waiting. Abandoned." The glare from her eyes faded a little, and Charlie blinked, trying not to show her relief.

"Why am I even talking to you about this. You weren't even there yet." Elizabeth turned her face, almost in disgust.

"I was," Charlie answered. "I was there. I remember."

"You *remember*," Elizabeth mocked. "Are you *sure* you were there for all of those memories?" Charlie searched her thoughts for anything that could confirm the memories she clung to.

"Look down," Elizabeth whispered.

"What?" Charlie whimpered.

"Your memory. I'm sure it's crystal clear, since you were there and all." Elizabeth smiled. "Look down."

Charlie returned to her memory, standing in front of her father's workbench. She was immobile; she didn't have a voice. "Look down," Elizabeth whispered again. Charlie looked to her feet, but didn't see feet at all, only three legs of a camera tripod anchored to the ground.

"He was making memories for you; making a life for his little rag doll, making her a real girl.

"I'm sure many of those memories have been elaborated upon, edited, and embellished, but make no mistake, Charlie wasn't there." Elizabeth leaned closer to Charlie.

"He made us one, two, three." Elizabeth touched Charlie's shoulder lightly, then brought her hand back to her own chest. "Four." Her eyes flickered, and the silver glow faded until her eyes looked nearly human.

"Charlie would be a baby, then a little girl, and then a sulky teenager." She looked Charlie up and down with a pointed sneer, then her expression cleared as she continued. "Then at last she would be a woman. She would be finished. Perfect. Me." Elizabeth's face tightened. "But something changed, as Henry labored, racked with grief, over his little girl.

"The littlest Charlotte was made with a broken heart. She cried all the time, day and night. The second Charlotte he made when he was at the depth of madness, almost believing the lies he told himself; she was as hopelessly desperate for her father's love as he was for hers. The third Charlotte he made when he began to realize he'd gone mad, when he questioned every thought he had, and begged his sister Jen to remind him what was real. The third Charlotte was strange." Elizabeth gave Charlie a contemptuous look, but Charlie scarcely saw it. *The third Charlotte was strange*, she repeated silently. She ducked her head and rubbed the flannel of her father's shirt with her thumb, then looked back up. Elizabeth's face was stiff with rage; she was nearly trembling.

"What about the fourth?" Charlie asked hesitantly.

"There was no fourth," she snapped. "When Henry began to make the fourth, his despair turned to rage. He seethed as he soldered her skeleton together, pouring his anger into the forge where he shaped her very bones. I was not Charlotte-drenched-in-grief. I was made alive with Henry's fury." Her eyes flared again with silver light, and Charlie stayed herself, forcing herself not to blink. Elizabeth leaned in closer, her face inches from Charlie's. "Do you know the first words your father ever spoke to me?" she hissed. Charlie shook her head minutely. "He said to me, *'You are wrong.'*

"He tried to fix the flaw he saw in me, at first, but what was wrong, as Henry saw it, was the very thing that made me alive."

"Rage," Charlie said softly.

"Rage." Elizabeth drew herself up and shook her head. "My father abandoned me." Her face twitched. "*Henry* abandoned me," she corrected herself. "Of course, I could not comprehend those memories until I had received a soul of my own—once I took it for myself." She smiled. "Once I had endowed myself with a soul, I experienced those memories anew: not as an uncomprehending toy, twitching and seizing with an all-consuming rage I could not fathom, but as a person. As a daughter. It's rather a cruel irony that I would escape the life of one neglected daughter only to embody another."

Charlie was silent, and for a moment her father's face returned to her, his smile that was always so sad. Elizabeth laughed abruptly, shaking her out of her memories.

"You're not Charlie, either, you know. You're not even the *soul* of Charlie," Elizabeth mocked. "You aren't even a person. You're a ghost of a man's regret, you're what's left of a man who lost everything, you're the sad little tears that fell unceremoniously into a doll that *used* to belong to Charlie." Elizabeth suddenly glared at her as if looking through her. "And if I had to take a guess . . ." She grabbed Charlie under her chin and pulled her upright, studying her torso for a moment. She made a quick motion with her other hand and Charlie gasped; the room was spinning again. Elizabeth's hand had disappeared, but it soon reemerged, and she was holding something.

"Look before you lose consciousness," Elizabeth whispered. There, before Charlie's eyes, was a rag doll, and recognition flared.

"Ella," she tried to whisper.

"This is you."

The room went dark.

What was that? Carlton lifted his head, holding his breath as he waited to hear it again. After a moment he did: someone was whimpering, and the sound was coming from nearby. Carlton took in a renewed gulp of air, instantly filled with new purpose. After hours of flickering bulbs and distant echoes, this was right beside him. Carlton leaped to his feet: across the hall a door was ajar, with an orange light glowing unsteadily from inside. *How did I not notice that?* Carlton made his way across the hall, sliding his feet along the floor so as not to make a sound. When he reached the door, he peered in cautiously through the crack: The orange light was from an open furnace set into the wall, its mouth large enough to fit a small car. The furnace was the only light in the dark room, but he could make out a long table, with something dark lying on it.

The whimpering came again, and this time Carlton's eyes lit on its source: a small, blond-haired boy was huddled in the darkest corner of the room, opposite the furnace. Carlton ran into the room and knelt beside the boy, who looked up at him numbly. He was bleeding from shallow cuts on his arm and one corner of his mouth, but Carlton saw no other visible injuries.

"Hey," he whispered nervously. "Are you okay?" The boy didn't respond, and Carlton took hold of his arms, readying to pick him up. When he touched the child, he could feel the tremors throughout his body. *He's terrified.* "Come on, we're getting out of here," Carlton said. The little boy pointed to the creature on the table.

"Save him, too," the boy whispered tearfully. "He hurts so bad." He squeezed his eyes shut. Carlton glanced at the large, motionless figure on the table by the furnace: he hadn't considered that it might be a person. He scanned the room to make sure nothing else was moving, then patted the boy on the shoulder and got to his feet.

He approached the table cautiously, keeping to the wall instead of walking across the center of the room. As he got closer, the burning smell of metal and oil rushed up against him, and he covered his face with his sleeve, trying not to gag as he examined the prone figure.

It's not a person. On the table, illuminated by the flickering orange light, was a mass of metal: a melted, clumpy skeleton of metal bulges and blobs, barely resembling anything at all. Carlton studied the thing for a long moment, then looked back at the little boy, uncertain what to say.

"Heat," a voice snarled, and Carlton spun around to face a twisted man, creeping out from the shadows. "Heat is the key to all of this," the man went on as he haltingly approached the table. "If you keep all this at just the right temperature, it's malleable, it's moldable, and it's highly, highly effective; or maybe *contagious* is the word. I suspect you could put it in anything, but it's best to put it into something that you can control—at least to a certain extent." William Afton lurched into the light, and Carlton stepped back reflexively, though the table was between them. "It's an interesting alchemy," William continued. "You can make something that you control completely, but that has no will of its own, like a gun, I suppose." He ran his withered hand over the silver arm of the creature. "Or you can take a drop of . . . pixie dust." He smiled. "And you can create a monster that you . . . *mostly* control, one with unlimited potential."

Carlton. He stepped back with a shout of surprise: the voice was so clear in his head that he recognized it instantly. "Michael?" The single word was enough. Carlton turned to the table with a new, terrible clarity. He knew exactly what he was looking at: the endoskeletons of the original Freddy's animatronics, welded and melted together, immobile and featureless. And still inhabited by the spirits of the children who had been murdered inside of them so many years ago. Still filled with life, and motion, and thought—all trapped; all in terrible pain. Carlton forced himself to look William Afton in the eye.

"How could you do this to them?" he asked, nearly trembling with rage.

"They do everything willingly," William said plainly. "The process only truly works if they freely release a portion of themselves." The flames rose without warning, and heat radiated in painful waves from the gaping furnace. Carlton shielded his eyes, and the creature on the table convulsed.

William smiled. "Scared of fire. But they still trust me. They don't see me as I am now; they only remember me as I was, you see."

Carlton broke his eyes away, feeling like he was waking from hypnosis. He darted his eyes desperately around the room, looking for something, anything, to attack with. The chamber was strewn with scrap metal and parts, and Carlton grabbed a metal pipe that lay by his feet and hefted it like a baseball bat. Afton was gazing down at the creature on the table, apparently insensible to anything else around him, and Carlton hesitated, considering the man for a moment. *He looks like he could fall apart all on his own*, he thought, taking in Afton's fragile, hunched body and the thin skin of his head, seeming to scarcely cover the skull beneath. Then he looked back to the creature on the table. *I think I've got the moral high ground here*, he decided grimly, and raised the pipe over his head as he stalked around the table toward Afton.

Suddenly, his arms were jerked above his head, the pipe dropping from his hands and hitting the ground with a bang. Carlton struggled with the cables that gripped his wrists, but he could not wrestle free. Slowly, he was lifted off his feet, his arms stretched painfully out to his sides by two cables that extended from opposite sides of the room, seeming to attach to nothing.

"I've never tried this on a human being before," William muttered, pressing some kind of mechanical syringe into the chest of the molten creature on the table. He wrenched the tool sideways, extracting something with great difficulty. The syringe was opaque, and Carlton could not see what filled it, but his heart raced as he began to suspect he knew where this was going. He tugged harder at the cables that bound him, but each time he pulled, he only wrenched his shoulders from side to side. Afton pulled the syringe out of the creature and gave a satisfied nod, then turned to Carlton.

"Usually this goes into something mechanical; something I made. I've never attempted it on something . . . sentient." William gave Carlton a measured stare. "This will be an interesting experiment." William lifted the mechanical syringe, carefully placing it over Carlton's heart. Carlton gasped, but before he could try to move, William plunged the long needle into his chest. Carlton screamed, then realized distantly it was really the blond boy in the corner screaming: Carlton wheezed and gasped, but could make no sound as his chest burned with a blinding agony. Blood soaked his shirt, and it clung to his skin as he convulsed in his bonds.

"For your sake, you'd better hope my little experiment does *something*; because I doubt you will survive otherwise," William said mildly. He nodded toward the cables and Carlton dropped to the ground; the pain in his chest was unthinkable, he felt like he'd been hit full-on with a shotgun. Blood sputtered from his mouth, dripping onto the floor, and Carlton curled around himself, squeezing his eyes shut as the pain intensified. *Please make it stop*, he thought, then, *Please don't let me die.*

"Maybe the heart was too direct," William lamented. "Well, that's the point of this, to learn, trial and error." He turned his gaze toward the blond-haired child, who still huddled weeping in the corner.

CHAPTER FIFTEEN

Steps echoed endlessly in the dark, pacing back and forth across the enclosed space.

"Are you still listening to me?" a voice rang out.

Charlie was lost in the dark, spinning silently and trying to get to the surface of whatever void she was in.

"Unlike you," the other Charlie uttered, unseen, "I was real. I was an actual little girl, one who deserved the kind of attention showered over you. You were nothing."

Charlie opened her eyes, the room still spinning. She tried to breathe but all her breaths stopped short of going in or out. There was a doll laying on the floor a few feet in front of her. She reached for it convulsively, like gasping for air.

"Do you want to know where my hate comes from? It's

not from this machine that I reside in, and it's not from my *past life*, if that's what you want to call it."

Charlie clawed at the floor with her fingers, unable to move the rest of her body. She gripped the doll with her fingertips and pulled it closer.

"I hate because, even now, I'm still not enough," Elizabeth whispered. She held out her sleek metallic fingers in front of her face. "Even after this; embodying the one thing Father did love, I'm not enough. Because he can't duplicate this, he can't make himself like me." Her voice began to grow angry again. "He can't duplicate what happened to me, or maybe he's too scared to try it on himself. I broke free of my prison, I emerged from the flames and the wreckage of Henry's last great failure, and I went to my father. I gave myself to him, to study, to use, to learn the secrets of my creation. And still it is *you* he wants."

Charlie clambered up onto her hands and knees and dragged herself toward the hallway. Elizabeth didn't seem concerned, taking slow steps behind her, not trying to catch her, only to keep her in sight.

"You, maybe he can re-create. Henry somehow got a piece of himself into you, and that's something we haven't seen before. That's . . . unique."

Charlie kept crawling steadily: She was beginning to feel stronger, but she kept her movements slow and clumsy, getting as much distance as she could between herself and Elizabeth. Charlie looked up and down the hall, searching for something—anything—that might give her an advantage. The door to the next room was open, and she could see a desk: sitting on it was a round stone paperweight. Without picking up her pace, Charlie crawled across the room, dragging her legs as if they pained her, while Elizabeth's slow, patient steps followed a pace behind.

"Can you get the green for me?" a voice called. Carlton blinked. He was sitting upright but felt only half-present, as if he had been daydreaming. "The green," the tiny voice repeated. "Please?" Carlton cast his eyes around for something green; the floor was black and white, and they were sitting somewhere a little dark. A little boy was hunched over a piece of paper, drawing. Carlton looked up. *We're under a table. Under the table at Freddy's.* There were drawings scattered in front of him on the floor, and a box of crayons spilled out across the tiles. Carlton spotted a green crayon that had rolled up against the wall, and he grabbed it and handed it to the little boy, who took it without looking up.

"Michael," Carlton said, recognition dawning. Michael continued to draw. "Where . . . ?" Carlton looked around, but what he saw didn't make sense to him. The pizzeria was brightly lit, yet Carlton couldn't see more than five feet away, as though there was a blurry cloud masking everything beyond. He ducked his head out cautiously from under the table, but the bright lights hurt his eyes, and he shielded them with his hand, crawling back under. Michael had not moved; he was drawing steadily, his brow furrowed in concentration. Carlton studied the pictures on the ground with a vague sense that something was wrong. *I don't belong here*, he thought, yet part of him felt completely at home.

"What are you doing?" he whispered to Michael, who looked up from his drawing at last.

"I have to put them back together," Michael explained. "See?" He pointed out from the table, at the pizzeria around them. Carlton squinted into the blurry horizon, seeing nothing at first, then they began to appear: he saw pages and pages of colorful drawings, some on the walls, others blowing through the air. "They're all in pieces," Michael said. He shuffled the pages in front of him and found two that showed the same child, then he placed one on top of the other, and began to trace the lines. "These go together," Michael said, holding up the picture: the two drawings had become one, the separate pages somehow bonded together; the lines were clearer and the colors more vibrant.

"What are you putting back together?" Carlton asked.

"My friends." Michael pointed to a single picture propped up against the wall. It showed five children: three boys and two girls, standing together in a cheerful pose, with a yellow rabbit standing behind them.

"I know this picture," Carlton said slowly. His mind was

still foggy, and as he tried to grasp at the answer, it only slipped further away. "Who is that?" Carlton whispered, pointing to the rabbit.

"He's our friend." Michael smiled, not looking up from his work. "Can you go get more for me?" Carlton looked out into the pizzeria: the space he could see had expanded a little more, and now he could make out the blurs of other children who seemed to be grasping at pages as they flew by, trying to grab the drawings. Carlton got out from under the table and stood up, walking through the midst of the mirage and colors. A boy in a black-and-white-striped shirt came running up, chasing a piece of paper.

"What are you doing?" Carlton asked as the boy grabbed empty air, and the page flew away into the blurry distance.

"My papers blew away," the boy cried, and hurried off. Carlton turned and saw another boy in the same outfit on the opposite side of the room, chasing other pages. A little girl with long blonde hair ran past him, and he whirled around, recognizing her far away: there were duplicates of each child, all of them chasing different pages.

A single figure stood still amongst the chaos, out of phase with the surroundings. At first it seemed to be a man bent over a table, but as Carlton's head throbbed with waves of confusion, the man became a yellow rabbit, not standing over a table, but over five children, tied together as one. The second image washed away, and the rabbit became a man again, standing in the dark. The children ran past the man as if they could not see him; as Carlton watched, several children ran straight through him without seeming to notice. Carlton approached the man, and as he got closer, the yellow rabbit appeared again, turning to look at him momentarily before blowing away like smoke, leaving the man underneath.

"This isn't real," Carlton gasped, trying to parse the two overlapping realities that seemed to be swirling around him. Three figures seemed to hold fast, while the rest of his surroundings flickered in and out of existence: the man standing at the table, a blond boy in the corner—the only child not running, and not repeated—and a body lying on the floor, curled in a puddle of blood. *Is that me? Am I dead?*

"No, silly!" a child called. "You're with us!"

The syringe mechanism recoiled with a loud snap: the man in shadow had taken something from the metal body on the table. Suddenly, another drawing flew into the air, and another ghostly child appeared to chase it.

The little girl with blonde locks of hair and a red ribbon bouncing on her shoulders ran past as well.

"Stop!" Carlton called, and she obeyed, her eyes still locked on the drawings she had been pursuing. "Who is that?" Carlton directed her attention to the yellow rabbit flickering in and out of existence.

"That's our friend. He helped me find my puppy!" she exclaimed before running off again.

"They don't know," Carlton whispered, releasing her as she disappeared into the blur surrounding him. Carlton searched the air as drawings blew by, snatching at the ones with images that seemed familiar.

"What are you doing?" the little boy in the striped shirt asked.

"I'm going to help you put these together," Carlton said, reaching for another picture as it blew past.

When she had finally crawled her way to the desk, Charlie reached up and grabbed for the top of it, then pulled herself up, feigning a struggle. She winced as she put weight on her feet, continuing to act weaker than she actually was: in reality she was nearly back to her full strength. She leaned heavily on the desk as if for support, putting one hand directly on the heavy stone paperweight.

"We both know he won't be able to re-create you, either." Elizabeth was near. "And the real question would be, would we really want him to? Besides . . ." Elizabeth approached Charlie from behind, moving faster. "I think I hate you more than I love him." She raised her hand in attack and Charlie spun around, swinging the rock in a single motion. There was a thunderous crack as it slammed into Elizabeth's face, and Charlie fell back with the shock, dropping the paperweight. She hit the ground hard, cradling her hand.

Elizabeth staggered backward, holding her hand over her face, but she could not conceal the damage without her illusion. One entire side of her gleaming white jaw had been knocked off her face, revealing the wires beneath. She cocked her head to the side for a moment, as if running a system check; Charlie didn't wait for the result. She leaped to her feet, pushing past Elizabeth as she ran back the way she'd come. Charlie heard Elizabeth moving, and dove for the hall closet, pulling it shut tight behind her.

"I know it may sound very childish of me," Elizabeth cried; her voice sounded like she was still at the end of the hall. "But if he doesn't want me; then he won't get you, either."

The footsteps drew closer, and Charlie looked one way and another, hoping desperately for a place to hide in the small closet. Then suddenly, as she turned completely around, she saw a familiar thing. *You.* The faceless robot wielding its knife, the mannequin, the construct that her father had built for one purpose, to end his life.

"Your dad thought you were so special, your memory was just too precious to let go of."

The blank face was almost peaceful in the dark. It had been built for one thing; it had completed its duty, and had remained in silence ever since, standing as a memorial to pain, and to loss.

The closet door moved slightly as Elizabeth gripped the knob; Charlie could see her shadow under the door. She grabbed at the clothing hanging behind her, old coats and dresses, and pulled them forward, concealing the construct as best she could. "You can't overpower me," Elizabeth whispered. "You aren't like me," she added with relish. Charlie waited in front of the blank-faced creature, not hiding. Gently, Elizabeth pulled the door open.

"I shouldn't be here," Charlie whispered to Elizabeth.

Charlie heard John cough from the room behind them, and relief rushed through her. *He's going to be okay. He's alive.* Elizabeth glanced back as though considering him, then trained her eyes on Charlie and took two deliberate steps forward.

"Charlie!" John called from outside.

"It's okay, John," Elizabeth answered, her voice indistinguishable from Charlie's. "I'll be right out." Instantaneously, she looked like Charlie again, not the grown-up Charlie she had been masquerading as, but Charlie as she was really, a mirror reflection. She shifted awkwardly, her eyes darting back toward John for just a moment, then gave Charlie a cruel smile. "How far do you think I could get with him before he noticed?" she whispered.

"You're right, Elizabeth," Charlie said. Elizabeth's smile faded. "I was never supposed to be here."

"No?" Elizabeth took the last step, closing the distance between them. She gripped Charlie by the neck, pressing up against her.

"Neither of us were." Charlie gripped the rag doll close to her chest. Elizabeth frowned in confusion, then peered over Charlie's shoulder, seeing the robot standing directly behind her. Charlie flinched her other hand, which was behind her back, doing something unseen with a quick motion. A metal pulley screamed.

Charlie closed her eyes, hugging the doll, and when the knife went through them, it did not hurt.

Elizabeth gasped as the blade plunged through her, too, sounding almost human. Charlie saw Elizabeth's face, rigid with shock, then it was gone, replaced by the smooth metal plates of her robotic form. Sparks burst in the air above her as Charlie's vision began to fade, and the smell of hot plastic came to her from very far away.

"It's not fair." Elizabeth's voice sputtered with static. "I never had a life."

Charlie struggled to take in a breath, still clutching the rag doll to her chest. She reached for Elizabeth's dangling hand clumsily and caught it; Elizabeth looked at her confusedly, and Charlie strained to pull her hand up to the rag doll. Fumbling, she closed Elizabeth's fingers around the doll, then, still holding her hand, Charlie pushed with the last of her strength, sliding the doll across the four-inch stretch of blade between them until it rested against Elizabeth's chest. Charlie tried to smile, but everything was dark; she had forgotten how to see. Charlie felt her head fall forward, and could not pull it up again. Elizabeth twitched for a moment longer, rattling the blade that pierced them both, then her head slumped forward, too, resting against Charlie's forehead.

Charlie! John was screaming her name. *CHARLIE!*

I love you, too. The words didn't come, and then there was nothing at all.

"Here, right here!" Carlton called. The little boy in the striped shirt helped align two more pictures, and Michael traced over them, connecting them into a single drawing. A second boy in a striped shirt appeared from the blurry surroundings and sat down on top of the one already sitting with them, merging into him seamlessly. Only Carlton seemed to notice the merging of the two children, not even the boy in the striped shirt himself seemed aware.

Beside them was the little girl with blonde curls: they had found all her drawings and put them together, and now she looked solid and real, no longer ghostly like the others. She was able to speak in full sentences, her cognitive abilities having steadily grown stronger as her drawings were united. Carlton struggled to find matching images for the others: he was keeping track of the three stable figures, the man, the boy in the corner, and the body, and it was clear he was running out of time. The man was making preparations to harm the boy in the corner.

"You said he saved your dog?" Carlton asked the blonde girl, grasping for answers.

"Mommy said that he went to heaven, but I heard Daddy say he was hit by a car. But I knew it wasn't true, Bonnie told me it wasn't true; he said that he had found my puppy." She brushed a lock of hair from her shoulder with her hand.

"And did he take you to your puppy?"

"He took me, but I don't remember . . ."

"But it was *him* who helped you?" Carlton pointed to the yellow bunny in the drawing that showed all five kids.

"Yes! That's him." She smiled. "My name is Susie," she added. "And that's Cassidy." A girl with long black hair approached, carrying more pictures in her arms. "And you?"

Carlton looked briefly at a little boy with freckles. "I . . ." He struggled to speak, and Carlton glanced nervously at the man in the room as he matched two more drawings together.

"There!" Michael exclaimed proudly. Another ghostly image of the freckled boy climbed under the table, and merged with the one who was already there: he instantly became less ghostly, and more whole. "I'm Fritz." He smiled, suddenly filled with more life.

William Afton clenched his fists, studying his own hands for a moment then looking toward the medical monitors in the corner. "I feel that my time is running short." He looked toward Carlton thoughtfully, but Carlton was still lying on the floor, motionless. "That's unfortunate," he growled. "I hoped to learn something. But maybe that's not the problem." He looked toward the metal table. "Maybe we just need some new life in this mass of metal." He smiled at the little blond boy, who recoiled and tried to scoot away, though he was already as close to the wall as he could get. "You'll have to forgive me, though, as I'm not sure how to do that, either." William took steps toward him. "I can think of a few things to try. At the very least, it will be fun; like old times." His lips peeled back, revealing two full rows of stained yellow teeth.

The door creaked as it opened, and William's eyes darted toward it as a tangled metal mess lurched toward him, scraping across the floor. "What are you doing back here?" William asked. The white painted fox head was turned at an alarming angle, clearly not functioning properly. Its limbs were all turned and pivoted, some of them broken and dragging, all inching the remains of the creature into the room. The fox head's eye spun wildly, searching the ceiling. William pointed to a corner. "You're no use to me anymore; get out of the way," he said dismissively, then drew back, surprised: following the fox was another motorcade of broken parts, their wires reaching for one another like vines, pulling each other along and holding themselves together. Mounted on the back of the entanglement was the white-and-purple face of a bear. *"I'm heeeere!"* a voice came from a speaker somewhere within the mess, cracking and popping with static.

William made a face, unnerved by the wrecked, comingled creatures. "Get back," he uttered, giving the Freddy face a kick. The mass of parts slid away without resistance, sounding almost disappointed as they came to a stop a few feet away. "What a waste," he hissed. He turned his attention to the fox again, apparently the most intact. "Bring that boy to me," he instructed, and the fox turned its eye to the corner.

"I have to go do something for him," Susie said cheerfully, getting to her feet.

"Something for who?" Carlton asked with alarm, and took hold of her arm.

"Bonnie." She smiled, gesturing toward the cheerful yellow rabbit wavering in and out of existence beside the table. "He asked me to do something for him just now. He wants to bring a new friend for us and he needs my help."

"Bonnie isn't your friend," Carlton said, still holding her arm. He gasped at the imminent danger that the little blond boy faced, as the girl struggled to break away.

"He *is* my friend! He found my *puppy!*" she cried, and yanked her arm free.

"No, don't go to him!" Carlton pleaded.

John.

"Get back!" John screamed and jolted awake, swinging his arms up to block an attack and jerking back. His head cracked against the cabinet behind him. "Ow." He groaned, regaining awareness of where he was. He rolled over, holding his side gingerly, then held perfectly still, tilting his head to listen. Silence reverberated through the space, weighing down the room with emptiness. "Charlie," he whispered, everything that had happened rushing back all at once. *The hallway.* John pulled himself to his feet with a sick dread, bracing himself against the cabinet door. His right foot gave way as soon as he put weight on it, pain shooting up through his ankle, and he put a hand against the wall for balance, then hopped on his left foot to reach the door.

He crashed hard against the doorframe, wincing as his ribs flared with pain, then squinted, trying to see in the dark. "Charlie!" he called. The closet door was open, and he could see figures inside, but he couldn't make out anything distinct. He made his way to the closet, leaning on the wall and trying to ignore his throbbing ankle. It was difficult to see through the hanging coats; and he began to shove them aside, then stopped abruptly, scarcely avoiding the blade of a massive knife—almost a sword—pointed directly at him. He blinked as his eyes adjusted: the blade was connected to an extended metal arm—the figure he had first thought was holding the knife had instead been run through with it, and behind that was something else—something familiar. He backed away, bending to look at the inhuman face of the creature impaled on the knife.

He stared for a moment, his face growing hot, then suddenly he turned away and doubled over, overcome with a wave of nausea. He dropped to his knees and retched, his ribs screaming protest as he heaved, but there was nothing in his stomach to throw up. He gasped, trying make it stop, but his stomach clenched and spasmed until he felt like he would be turned inside out.

When at last it began to abate, John rested his forehead against the wall, his eyes watering. Light-headed, he got to his feet, feeling as if years had passed. He did not look into the closet again.

John limped toward the door, grinding his teeth with every step, but he did not stop moving until he was outside the house, and he did not look back.

"There!" Michael cheered, momentarily distracting Susie from trying to leave. The last phantom of the girl with long black hair came and sat with them. When she had merged with the others like her, she blinked, then looked up and took in a long, calm breath. "We're all together now,"

Michael said with a smile. The drawings on the ground had disappeared, and five real-seeming children sat with Carlton under the table, no longer ghostly images.

"The rabbit isn't your friend," Carlton repeated. Susie gave him a puzzled look, and pointed to the only drawing left, the large one that showed all five children with the smiling yellow rabbit.

"I said bring him to the table," William said angrily, drawing Carlton's attention across the shadows. The painted fox cocked its head to the side, but before William could scold it again, more noises came from the hall. The door opened, pushed like something was bumping against it, and a variety of mechanical things made their way into the room, crawling and clawing their way across the floor in various states of disrepair. There were the climbing babies, and the gangly clown that had sat atop a carnival game in the dining room; others filed in that Carlton did not recognize: waddling dolls painted with clowns' faces, disjointed circus animals, and other things he could not even name.

"Get back," William hissed at the macabre processional, and brushed a crawler aside with his foot, struggling to keep his balance. The little blond boy had stopped crying; he was staring stunned at the creatures, shrinking away with his hand half blocking his face.

"Afraid of *them*, now?" William turned on the boy. "Don't fear them. Fear me," he snarled with renewed strength, and he clenched his jaw, taking stiff but deliberate steps toward the boy. "I'm the only thing in this room that you should be afraid of," he said, and the boy turned to him again, his face still full of fear. "I'm just as dangerous as I've always been," William growled. He grabbed the boy by the arm and dragged him to the table.

"No, no, no!" Carlton shouted as he watched the shadowy figure hoist the boy onto the table. He glanced helplessly at the children, but they looked at him blankly. "Can't you see? He's hurting that boy!" The children just shook their heads confusedly. "He's in danger, I have to help him. Let me out." Carlton struggled to get up, but his legs were weighted down, and anchored to the illusion.

"That's just Bonnie." Susie smiled.

"Bonnie is not your friend! He's the one that hurt you, don't you remember?" Carlton cried with mounting frustration. He grabbed the final drawing from the wall, the one with the five children standing with the yellow rabbit, and laid it flat on the floor, then took up a red crayon. He bent over the drawing and began to make thick marks on it, pressing the crayon deep into the paper. The children strained closer to see what he was drawing.

"Here we go," William Afton said from the shadows. Carlton glanced up to see the little boy squirming on top of the mass of metal, where William was holding him in place. The table was heating up, the orange glow beginning to flare from within it. "I'm running out of ideas," William said, failing to hide his anxiety. "But if I'm not going to survive this, then you certainly aren't, either." William pressed down on the boy's chest, and the boy struggled to free himself.

"Ouch!" the boy cried as his elbow touched the table below, where the orange glow was spreading. He jerked his arm up and cradled it, sobbing, then shrieked as his foot pressed onto the table and began to hiss. He yanked it back, howling.

"We will see where this takes us," William said.

"Look!" Carlton yelled, tapping the drawing hard with his crayon. The children huddled close. The yellow rabbit's eyes were now dark red, and blood dripped from its mouth. The children looked confusedly at Carlton, but there was a spark of recognition in their faces. "I'm sorry," Carlton said desperately. "This—is the bad man. *This. This* is the bad man." Carlton pointed from the drawing to William Afton and back again. "*He* is the bad man who hurt you, and right now he's about to hurt someone else," Carlton pleaded.

A hand gripped William's pant leg, and he shook it off. "Get away from me," he growled, but the hand persisted. The tangle of parts connected to the purple Freddy head was gathering around William's ankles, pieces plucking at him. "I said get off me!" he said again. His legs shook beneath him, and he let go of the boy, teetering as he struggled to regain his balance. He grasped for something steady, and his hands instinctively found the table. He recoiled, gasping in pain, and fell backward onto the floor, watching helplessly as the little blond boy rolled off the table and ran to the back wall.

Afton struggled to right himself as the wires and mechanisms scattered about the room all marched toward him to collect into a central mass, crawling up onto his body and threatening to engulf him. He pulled the pieces off and threw them aside to break apart on the concrete floor of the basement, then got unsteadily to his feet. William set his eyes on the boy once more: nothing else mattered. He took three laborious steps forward, machines still wrapped around his legs. The head of the white fox snapped at him from his ankle, where it had wound its limbs around his leg, and the purple bear had sunk its jaw into his calf, and was biting down. One of the crawling babies had climbed up onto William's back, where it thrashed its weight back and forth, setting his frail body swaying. Another crawler held fast to his ankle, chewing at his flesh. Blood dripped onto the floor with each step he took, but William's eyes remained fixed on the terrified boy, his fury only growing. Finally, in a burst of anger he flung the robotic baby from his back and stomped down on the metal bear's head, breaking its jaw and dislodging its teeth from his leg.

At last, William reached the child. The blond boy

screamed as William brushed his bony fingers over the boy's face, then suddenly William felt something blazing hot wrap around his waist, and yank him back. He twisted wildly and saw: the creature from the table was standing, and its two melted metal arms were now gripping William from behind, pulling him away from the boy. Its skin contorted and moved like molten metal, its motions jerky and unnatural. Its joints popped and snapped as it moved, as though each movement should have been impossible.

"No!" William cried, hearing the crackle of flame as his hospital gown caught fire, pressed against the burning creature.

Carlton opened his eyes and took a breath, a *real* one; he clutched his chest and tried to remain motionless, lifting only his eyes to watch as the amalgamation of metal and cords pulled William Afton backward into the massive furnace. Smoke and fire erupted from the thing with a roar, and then the room was still. The creatures and parts that had been wriggling on the floor stopped at once, and did not move again.

Carlton felt the searing pain in his chest surge, and he slipped into darkness.

Carlton. Carlton opened his eyes; Michael was sitting patiently beside him, apparently waiting for him to wake up.

"Is he okay now?" Michael gave Carlton an anxious smile. Carlton looked up to see four small figures disappearing into a flood of light. Only Michael remained under the table. "Is he okay?" Michael repeated, waiting for confirmation.

"Yeah," Carlton whispered. "He's okay. Go be with your friends." He smiled, but Michael didn't get up. He was looking at Carlton's chest, where someone had placed a drawing over his wound. "This is a part of you," Carlton said, grasping at the picture.

"You'll die without it," Michael whispered.

"I can't keep this." Carlton shook his head as Michael pushed it back. "You can give it to me next time you see me."

Michael smiled, and the drawing began to fade, hovering where Michael had placed it for a last moment before the ghostly image vanished, seeming to sink into Carlton's chest.

Thank you. Carlton heard the echo of Michael's voice, but Michael was gone, and there was nothing but the light.

"Carlton!" John.
  "Carlton, hang on!"
  "We're going to get you out of here!"
  Marla. Jessica.
  "Carlton!"

CHAPTER SIXTEEN

"So, what happened then?" Marla had scooted so close to Carlton's hospital bed that she was practically in the bed with him.

"Ouch, Marla! The nurse said I need to sleep, and I shouldn't be exposed to a lot of stress right now." He reached for a juice box nearby, but Marla pushed it out of reach.

"Oh please, I practically am a nurse, and besides, I want to know what happened." Marla lifted a series of tubes and pulled them out of her way so she could get closer.

"Marla! Those are attached to *me*! Those are keeping *me* alive!" He searched frantically around his bedside table. "Where's my panic button?"

Marla felt around the edges of the bed until she found the small device with a red button on it, then set it neatly in her lap, clearly under her protection. "No juice; no nurse; tell me what happened."

"Where's Dad—Clay?" He lifted his eyes, searching the room until he found his father, who was standing by the window, his face tight with worry.

"I'm right here," he said, and shook his head. "You gave us a scare, and it wasn't a practical joke this time."

Carlton grinned, but it was short-lived as he glanced around the small room in distress.

"Are the kids all right?" he asked, not sure he wanted to hear the answer.

"They're safe. All of them," Jessica said quickly.

"*All* of them?" Carlton said in joyful disbelief.

"Yes. You saved him, the last one." Jessica smiled.

"And he's okay?" Carlton said again for confirmation, and Jessica nodded.

"And Charlie?" he said softly. Jessica and Marla looked at each other, unsure.

"We don't know," Clay said, stepping forward. "I've been out to look for her, and I'm going to keep looking for her, but so far . . ." He broke off, then cleared his throat. "I'm going to keep looking," he repeated.

Carlton looked down thoughtfully, then looked up once more. "And what about *hot* Charlie?"

Marla slapped Carlton's shoulder and he recoiled. "Marla! Ouch! I almost died; this is blood on my bed!"

"That's Kool-Aid. You spilled it all over yourself about an hour ago." Marla rolled her eyes.

"John?" Carlton suddenly spotted him in the doorway, hanging back so far he was almost in the hall. John waved, smiling slightly.

"Looks like they have you patched up pretty good," he said, nodding toward Carlton's bandages.

"Yeah." *Something's wrong.* Carlton considered John for a moment, but before he could formulate a question, a nurse stepped briskly into the room.

"Visiting time's over for now," she said apologetically. "We need to run some tests."

Clay stepped up to the bed, displacing Marla briefly. "Get some rest, huh?" he said, and patted the top of Carlton's head.

"*Dad*," he groaned. "I'm not five." Clay smiled and headed for the door; John stopped him.

"You're going to keep looking for Charlie?" he asked.

"Of course," Clay said reassuringly, but gave him a confused look before leaving the room.

"You're not going to find her," John said softly. The rest of them watched, discomfited, as John slipped out the door without another word, not waiting for anyone else.

"Hey, we found this next to you. I wasn't sure if it was important," Jessica said, pulling Carlton's attention back, and handed him a folded piece of paper, heavy with crayon marks within. He unfolded it, revealing a grassy hill with five children running over it, the sun overhead.

"Yours?" Jessica asked.

"Yeah." Carlton smiled. "Mine."

"Okay." Jessica gave him a suspicious look, then returned the smile, leaving the room. Carlton held the drawing close and gazed out the window.

He had come into the room cautiously, afraid to wake her up. The room was dark except for the light filtering in through the small dirty window, and she peered at him for a moment as if she could not see him.

"John?" she whispered at last.

"Yeah, did I wake you up?"

She was so quiet for a time that he thought she was asleep, then she murmured, "You said you loved me."

The memory turned bitter here, and it had been nagging at him ever since—since everything ended. *You said you loved me*, she said, and he had babbled nonsense in response.

He stood in the gravel parking lot for a moment, feeling woefully unprepared. He tapped his hand nervously on the metal fence post, then took a deep breath and went through the gate. Slowly, he followed the path he had once watched

Charlie take, hindered a little by the brace on his ankle. Most of the cemetery was as green and well kept as any park, but this corner was all scrubby grass and dirt. Two small, plain tombstones sat together just beside the fence, a telephone pole rising behind them like a sheltering tree.

John took a step toward them, then stopped with the sudden feeling that he was being watched. He turned in a slow circle, and then he saw her. She was standing beneath a tree just a few yards away, where the grass grew lush and green.

She smiled, and extended a hand, beckoning him to her. He stood where he was. For a moment the world seemed blunted, his mind had gone numb. He could feel that his face had no expression, but he could not remember how to move it. He looked back at the stones with a sharp stab of longing, then swallowed and took steady breaths until he could move again. He turned to the woman under the tree, her arm still extended, and went to her.

A warm gust of wind rolled over the cemetery as they walked away together. The trees rustled, and a rush of leaves blew across the stones, sticking to some. Beneath the telephone pole, the grass rolled with waves, brushing against the two stones that sat together in the setting sun. The first was Henry's. The other read:

BELOVED DAUGHTER

CHARLOTTE EMILY

1980–1983

From the telephone pole above, a crow cawed twice, then launched itself into the sky with a flurry of wings.